FOREVER YOUNG

A Danny Boyland novel

HENRY HACK

Copyright© 2017 Henry Hack

All rights reserved. No parts of the contents of this book may be reproduced or transmitted in any form, by any means, without permission of the author.

ISBN-13: 9781548652746
ISBN-10: 1548652741

"You're never too old to become younger" — *Mae West*

This novel is a work of fiction. Names, characters, places, organizations and events are the product of the author's imagination or are used fictitiously, and any resemblance to actual persons bearing the same name or names, living or dead, is entirely coincidental.

Also by Henry Hack

Harry Cassidy Novels

Cassidy's Corner
The Last Crusade
The Romen Society
Election Day

Danny Boyland Novels

Danny Boy
Cases Closed
Mommy, Mommy

Collection

Portraits in Blue

www.henryhack.com

Chapter 1

Every workday morning the traffic slowed to a crawl through this half-mile stretch of the westbound Southern State Parkway as it wound its way through Nassau County. Sometimes, for no explicable reason, the cars came to a complete stop for several seconds, then once again began the slow, stop-and-go, jerky, aggravating trek toward their destinations, like three frustrated, multi-colored columns of warrior ants temporarily blocked by a river. This stoppage happened most frequently as the traffic approached to within a mile from the exit for the Meadowbrook Parkway where many vehicles turned off to head north toward Mineola, the county seat, and this warm May morning was no exception.

Jonathan Holmgren was not at all upset at the slowdown as many of the drivers around him appeared to be – some scowling, one or two pounding the top of their car's steering wheel, others shaking their heads. Jonathan, although not yet forty years old, had been through a helluva lot more travails and troubles than morning traffic conditions, that was for sure. He pressed the buttons to completely roll down both his and the passenger's side windows and enjoyed the cross breeze on this cloud-free, warm morning. The scent of new-mown grass from the strip between his lane and the tree line reminded him of the mornings of his youth growing up on the Pacific coast. Long Island was not as livable as his previous life had been, but he'd take it. Not that he had a choice.

In retrospect, he had done extremely well since moving here seven years ago. A well-paying job at a prestigious accounting firm in Uniondale – he was excellent with figures – a loving wife, two young, fairly-well behaved children, and a modest ranch house in Massapequa. And if someday his past caught up to him and things turned sour, he had over a million dollars stashed away in a safe-deposit box, money from his previous life he managed to squirrel away, and who no one, not even his wife, knew about.

Jonathan reacted to the sound of the horn behind him, not a prolonged blast, but a short beep. He realized he had allowed a space of almost two car lengths to open up ahead of him. *Horrors, a mortal sin in New York.* He took his foot off the brake allowing his Prius to slowly close the gap. As he re-applied the brake, the bullet passed through the open passenger window, entered his right temple above the frame of his eyeglasses and blew out a substantial portion of the left side of his face and head onto the closed passenger side window of the vehicle next to his in the center lane. The woman driver shrieked in horror as the bloody mass stuck to the glass and registered its grisly presence on her brain. The traffic moved a bit in front of Jonathan and the driver in back of him, totally unaware of what had happened, honked his horn once again.

* * *

I was sitting at my desk in Nassau Homicide writing up a report when Sergeant Francis Finn ambled out of his office and shouted, "Who's catching?"

Finn knew damn well that I was the primary squeal man today, and my now steady partner, Virgil "Spider" Webb, was my back-up. But Father Finn, as we in the squad affectionately referred to him, had been doing this for so long – over twenty years – that he was not now going to modify his behavior. To irk him a bit I said, "You know it's me Father, so why are you yelling?"

"Get your dumb Irish ass in here, Danny Boy – and bring the Spider with you."

As we crossed the twenty or so feet to Finn's office, I wondered if we were going to get a Big One, or another easy ground-ball case that had been our lot for well over a year. I was bored with the routine stuff – you know, poppa shoots momma and the kids, then turns the gun on himself; robberies gone bad where we grabbed the perp the next day; or hit-and-runs solved in a few days. I needed a challenge, and I knew Spider did, too. Maybe this was it, but our hopes were crushed when Finn said, "We got a guy shot dead about fifteen minutes ago on the Southern State Parkway…"

"That's not our jurisdiction, Sarge."

"I know Danny, but the Troop L commander called me to request our assistance on this one. They have all their investigators either in court or tied up on two major accidents, with several dead, out on the east end of the Island. The only one left is brand new. Name's Tom Ferguson. Meet him at the scene and give him the benefit of your vast investigative experience."

"Be glad to," I said. "Anything to get out of the office, but I was hoping for something a bit more interesting."

"Me, too," Spider said.

"You never know how things will turn out, do you?" Finn said with a devious grin playing across his wrinkled face. "You two hot shots oughta know that by now."

We both caught the jab at our past disastrous experiences. "Point taken, Father Finn. We're on our way," I said, smiling back at him.

* * *

A State Police vehicle, red and blue strobe lights flashing methodically, blocked the Newbridge Road entrance to the westbound lanes of the Southern State parkway. We slid up to it and rolled down our windows, displaying our shields to identify ourselves and Spider said, "Heard you State boys are having a busy day all over the Island."

The trooper grinned and said, "Understatement of the year, Detective. We got our hands completely full. Ferguson will appreciate the help."

He motioned us to go around him and we pulled up on the grassy shoulder of the parkway a few minutes later. Ferguson was easy to spot inside the yellow crime scene tape surrounding the vehicle with the victim's body in it. He had a cell phone to his ear and he was waving at a couple of uniformed troopers to keep the few on-lookers away from the car. Spider and I hung our gold shields from our jacket handkerchief pockets and pushed under the tape, approaching the lanky investigator, whose tie was askew, and whose troubled face was wet with sweat. He finished his conversation on the phone and extended his hand. "Tom Ferguson. Thanks for coming by."

"Danny Boyland and Spider Webb," I said. "What have you done so far?"

"Notified the medical examiner's office and the district attorney's office. They're on the way, but my crime scene guys are still tied up out east."

"Do you want us to call for ours?" Spider asked.

"If it's okay, I sure would appreciate it."

"Hey, we're here to help however we can," I said. "Can we see the body?"

Spider called Crime Scene on his police radio as we walked over to the car and peered inside. The body was slumped on its left side, the entrance wound clearly visible above the right temple, slightly into the hairline. "Could be a .30 caliber," I said as I picked up his head causing his eyeglasses to fall to the floor.

Ferguson sucked in his breath as we all gazed at the massive exit wound. "And a powerful one, too," Spider said.

"I have a witness parked over there on the grass," Ferguson said. "She was in the center lane, and matter from the victim's head splattered all over her passenger's side window. She's pretty shook up."

"And an extremely lucky lady the bullet didn't continue through *her* head," Spider said.

"Yeah, I wonder where it did end up."

"Could still be in the roof," I said looking up above the victim's head of dark curly hair. "I see a hole in this bent metal trim here, but no exit hole apparent on the outside of the car. If Crime Scene can't locate it, I'll have them tow it in to our headquarters after we get the body out of here."

"By the way, Tom," Spider said, "what's the vic's name?"

"Er... I don't know yet."

"Did he have a wallet in his pocket, or ID in the glove compartment?" I asked.

"Uh...I didn't look. I didn't want to disturb..."

"No sweat, we won't screw anything up. You check the glove compartment, I'll check his clothing."

I fished a wallet out of the guy's left rear pants pocket and Ferguson retrieved the auto's registration and insurance documents from the glove box. We spread everything out on the fender of the car and discovered the vic's name and address and observed a few photos of him with what we assumed was his family – wife and two children. I said, "Tom, are there other witnesses to speak with besides that woman?"

"No. According to her – name's Marie Candela – she was the only one who pulled over because of the splattering. Oh, she didn't hear a shot, and she seems to think the driver of the other cars in the vicinity had no idea what had occurred."

"She could be right," Spider said, "but after we close the scene up you should get hold of your press officer and have him contact the media requesting help and information from the public."

"I sure will, Detective. Thanks."

"Hey Tom, call me Spider. Everyone else does."

"How'd you get that name?"

"I'll tell you after we wrap up here when we all go for a nice cold beer."

* * *

The Crime Scene Search Unit arrived followed by the deputy medical examiner and assistant district attorney from the Homicide Bureau. After sufficient photos to everyone's liking were snapped, a crime scene tech went to work on the bullet hole. Working carefully, so as not to put any tool marks on it, he extracted the copper-jacketed slug in about six minutes, placed it in a plastic bag, initialed the outside and held it up. "Who gets it?" he asked.

"I guess I do," Investigator Ferguson said taking the bag from the tech.

"Put your initials and the time and date on it," I whispered.

Tom did as I suggested and said, "I'll send this up to our Crime Lab in Albany."

"Let me make another suggestion," I said. "We'll have one of our lab guys in ballistics give it a look to see if he can tell us anything about it to aid your investigation before you send it 150 miles away."

"Thanks. Uh, how should we proceed now?"

"Let's all put our heads together with the ME and ADA and we'll go from there."

Doctor William Maguire matter-of-factly said, "One shot to the right temple is all I can see. Pronouncement made, internal temperature recorded, time of death about an hour ago. Ship him over, and I'll post him this afternoon."

"What do we have so far?" asked ADA Judy Greenblatt.

I nodded at Tom who told her what we had, which wasn't much, in the way of witnesses or immediate solvability factors.

"Is this intentional or maybe just a horrible accident?"

"That's what we three super detectives are going to find out as soon as you and the doctor leave and we get this vehicle towed out of here," I said.

"Super detectives, my ass," grunted Maguire, lighting up a big cigar.

"Thought you quit," Spider said as the strong tobacco smoke wafted into his nostrils.

Maguire grunted again and walked away saying, "I'll call you at the squad when I'm done."

Judy said, "He's grouchy today, isn't he?"

"As long as I outlive him, I don't care," I said. "Wise bastard always tells me he can't wait to get me on one of his tables and open me up."

They all laughed and Judy said, "I'm outta here; please keep me in the loop."

"As we always do, counselor," Spider said.

* * *

The tow truck arrived, the witness left, now calmed down enough to drive away, and the state troopers re-opened all three lanes of the parkway to westbound traffic. In a few minutes, except for our two sedans parked on the grassy shoulder, everything seemed normal and routine. However, there was now one less innocent human being alive on Long Island. "Okay," I said, "let's see if we can find out where the shot came from."

We walked directly back from where the victim's car had been when he was shot, with me in the middle, and Tom and Spider flanking me a few feet on either side. As we approached the tree line Tom said, "Shouldn't we notify his wife soon?"

"That's next on our list," Spider said, "as soon as we finish up here."

"You know," I said, "Tom has a point. I don't trust the goddamn press. They were gawking all over the scene."

"But we didn't release his identity," Spider said.

"Yeah, but I wouldn't put it past those bastards to find his name and address from his license plate number and descend upon that poor woman and her kids. Tell you what Tom, you and Spider take your car and get out to Massapequa and make the notification. Spider's excellent at this, I assure you."

"Thanks, I wasn't looking forward to bringing this news to her."

"And of course, you'll do your best under these circumstances to get as much information as you can about the late Jonathan Holmgren, most importantly any enemies. Spider knows what to ask if you get stuck."

"Thanks again, guys. This is my first big case involving a death like this. The rest were auto crashes."

"You're doing fine so far, and while you guys are out there I'll check out the scene. We'll keep in touch by cell phone and decide where to hook up later."

* * *

After Tom and Spider drove off, I proceeded into the tree line and began looking around for anything, a spent .30 caliber cartridge would be nice wouldn't it? But then we might be definitely looking at an intentional act instead of an accident, wouldn't we?

There was plenty of sunshine coming through the trees and little undergrowth, but I turned up no cartridge cases or anything else that could be construed as evidence of a recent rifle discharge. I worked my way through the trees trying to walk on a straight line back from the shooting site, and after fifty yards or so, was stopped by a four-foot high chain link fence. The fence formed the border of a rear yard, and continued in both directions for as far as

I could see, enclosing similar size backyards. All the yards appeared to be sixty to eighty feet wide and at least a hundred feet deep before reaching the backs of the homes on the property.

I was going to hop over the fence until I spotted a large dog walking unchained near the back of the house. When I first reached the fence I thought what an easy target these homes would be for a burglar. Park his car where mine was on the shoulder, enter the woods, jump the fence and knock off a couple of houses, and make a quick getaway back to Queens or Brooklyn. Maybe that's why the dog, and maybe that's why the rear-facing spotlights I noticed on all the homes in my view.

Walking back to my car while again keeping my eyes glued to the ground for any evidence, a question formed in my mind. The trees, now in full leaf and fragrance, were closely spaced, and I wondered if a bullet fired from one of the houses could possibly have made it through them all to hit poor Jonathan Holmgren right in the head. I knew who to call for that answer, but first I had to knock on a few doors.

A bright flash of red startled me as a cardinal flew past my head and landed on a nearby branch. An idyllic spring setting to be sure, but one spoiled by the fact it may have recently sheltered a stone cold killer.

Chapter 2

I retrieved my car and got off the next parkway exit, and worked my way back along Parkway Drive North, until I arrived at the light-yellow painted, two-story home with the spruce-green shutters I had recently observed from its rear view. The home was well-maintained with a neatly-clipped front lawn. I walked up the four cement steps and rang the bell. Within a minute an attractive brown-haired woman in her mid-thirties opened the door and said, "Yes?"

I showed her my shield with accompanying ID and said, "Detective Danny Boyland, perhaps you can help me?"

"If I can," she replied, with a puzzled look on her face.

"Did you hear a gunshot earlier in the day? Maybe two hours ago?"

She shook her head. "I don't recall any loud noises at all, but please come in. I'm Betty Kernan."

I followed her inside and she called out, "Kevin, where are you?"

A faraway voice responded, "In the basement."

"Come up, please. There's someone here."

A few seconds later a man came up the stairs and into the living room where I stood with Betty. "Kevin, this is Detective Boyland."

The color drained from Kevin Kernan's face as we shook hands. He said, "I guess someone called about the gunshot."

I suppressed my emotions at this sudden admission and said, "Can you tell me what that was about?"

I observed Kevin closely as he took a moment to answer. He seemed to be in his mid-thirties like his wife, and had a full head of brown hair with a ruddy, clean-shaven face. He said, "It was the damn squirrels."

"Pardon me?"

"They go after our bird feeders all the time, spilling the seeds and gobbling them down. Betty and I have several in our backyard trees. I used to shoot at them with a .22 rifle until my neighbors complained I shouldn't be shooting any kind of firearm in a residential neighborhood. I'm from Colorado where we shoot outdoors all the time. So I switched to a BB rifle, but today I grabbed the wrong one."

"What do you mean, Kevin?"

"When I saw the buggers – there were four of them there this morning – I ran down to the basement and grabbed what I thought was the BB rifle and ran back upstairs and out to the backyard. As I brought the gun up to fire it I realized I had one of my .30 caliber hunting rifles in my hands. And then I did a stupid thing. This one squirrel was sitting not thirty yards away on one of the feeders staring at me, defying me, daring me to shoot his rodent ass. I squeezed the trigger in haste because I was so angry, and of course I missed him by a mile. The report was extremely loud, and I figured a dozen people heard it and would call the police. But that was a couple hours ago and the cops never came."

"Until I arrived, but that's not the real reason I'm here. Uh, can we all sit down for a few minutes?"

"Oh, sure," Betty said. "Would you like coffee or something else to drink?"

"No, thank you. Kevin, earlier this morning a man was shot and killed with a single .30 caliber bullet. He was in his car on the Southern State Parkway directly opposite your home."

"Oh, my God," he said burying his face in his hands.

"Are you saying Kevin's shot went all the way through those trees and killed that poor man?" Betty asked.

"It seems that way. We have had no other reports of gunshots in the area. In fact, no one called in your gunshot either."

"This must only be a horrible accident."

"Well, let's first see if the bullet that killed our victim came from Kevin's gun. I'd like to see it, please."

"Sure, it's back in its rack in the basement."

He started to rise from where he was sitting on the sofa and I stopped him. I said, "Let me read you your Miranda rights first."

"I guess you're going to arrest me?"

"Most likely, so be quiet and listen carefully."

I took out two business-size cards that had all the necessary warnings printed on them. I had Kevin follow along as I slowly read each sentence. When I was done, he and I signed and dated both cards, and I gave one to him to retain. I said, "Do you want to call a lawyer now?"

"No, and I'm willing to talk to you without one. If I did this I deserve to be punished."

We went down to the basement together and Kevin pointed to the rifle which stood in a nicely-crafted, varnished, dark-oak gun rack screwed to the wall. It was near the middle of a group of eight. Kevin unlocked the rack and I took the rifle out and said, "You fired one round?"

"Yes."

"Is the cartridge case still in the chamber?" I asked, noting it was a single-shot, bolt action model.

"Yes, it should be. I don't remember pulling the bolt back after the shot."

We went back upstairs and I smelled the aroma of brewing coffee. Betty said, "I think we all may need some caffeine now."

"I could use something stronger," Kevin said. "What a dummy I am. How the hell could I have been so stupid? That poor guy. Jeez, was he married with a family?"

"We're looking into that now. If you're still comfortable speaking with me I'd like to get your full statement on paper now."

"Sure. Uh, what am I facing, uh, I mean will I go to jail for a long time?"

"I doubt it, Kevin. You didn't murder anyone..."

"But..."

"What I mean is you did not *intentionally* kill that man – his name is Jonathan Holmgren, by the way – you caused his death accidentally. You will most likely be charged with criminally negligent homicide which is the least of the crimes in the homicide statutes, and the case will have to go to the Grand Jury.

"How serious is that?"

"It's a class E felony punishable by a maximum of four years in prison. First time offenders with a clean record usually get sentenced to one and a half to three years, and are out in about a year."

"I guess we can survive a year if I go back to work," Betty said.

"Where do you work, Kevin?" I asked.

"I'm still looking. We're new to the area. Came here about six months ago after I got laid off at my job in Seattle. I still have a year of unemployment checks to go."

"Okay," I said taking a sip of coffee. "Write out your statement while I make a couple of calls."

* * *

The first call I made was to my favorite expert firearms examiner in the police lab, Detective Walter Gennaro. When he answered I said, "Danny Boy, Walt. Want to get out of that stuffy place and into some fresh air?"

"Love to, what's cookin'?"

I explained the situation and told him I would keep Kernan here until he arrived. I called Spider who told me he and Tom Ferguson had finished up with Holmgren's wife. He said, "This was a tough one, Danny. She's still crying hard. We got a neighbor to come over to stay with her until the kids come home from school. What's happening on your end?"

"As Inspector Clouseau used to say in those old Pink Panther movies – 'the case is sol-ved.'"

"Wha-a-a-t?"

"Got a guy who admits letting a round go in his backyard off the parkway at the time Holmgren got hit. I have Gennaro on the way over."

"He gave you an admission?"

"Writing up his statement now. Why don't you and Tom get over here – 1721 Parkway Drive North – and we'll wrap this up."

"Great job, partner. Ferguson should be real happy this one went down so easy."

When Spider had mentioned Holmgren's kids I thought to ask the Kernan's if they had any children. Betty said they had two – both boys – ages eight and ten. I said, "We'll have Kevin out of here before they get home from school."

"How long will he be in jail?" she asked as Kevin sat mute once again with his head in his hands.

"Just overnight assuming he can make bail in the morning."

"How much…?"

"Betty," I interrupted her, "you have to get a lawyer – now. He'll handle it. You can't take on the legal system alone."

"We're new here, I don't know…"

"Got a phone book? The Yellow Pages?"

She went over to a closet and retrieved it from a shelf and I opened it to *Attorneys*. "I can't make a recommendation, but look for those who specialize in criminal law. They should all be capable of representation for Kevin."

"Thank you, Detective. I'll call one as soon as you take Kevin away."

I figured she should call one this minute, but I just nodded as I heard the front doorbell ring. Walt Gennaro came in with his equipment kit and I roused Kevin and made the introductions. "Detective Gennaro will go over the details of the shooting with you – where you were positioned, where you were aiming, that kind of stuff. And he will take your rifle with him when he leaves."

"Okay," Kevin said wiping his eyes and arising from the sofa.

As they prepared to go out the back door I said, "I think there's a loose dog out there, Walt."

"Oh, that's Teddy." Betty said. "He's harmless, but I'll go tie him up."

I had another cup of coffee with Betty and by the time Walt and Kevin re-entered the house, Spider and Ferguson were pulling up to the curb. I had come to some conclusions, but kept them to myself. Let everyone else develop their own thoughts and we'd kick them around later. I introduced Tom Ferguson as the lead investigator from the state police and Tom said, "I'll read you your rights…"

"That's okay," Kevin said, "Detective Boyland already did that."

"I know, but as the arresting officer I'd like to do it again. Please bear with me."

This was a good move on Tom's part in case Kevin was to utter some additional incriminating words when I wasn't around. When Tom finished he brought Kevin's arms behind his back and snapped the handcuffs – not too tightly – on his wrists. "Betty," I said, "tell your lawyer we'll be taking Kevin to Mineola after we process him at Troop L headquarters in Farmingdale. We'll keep you informed when he arrives there if his lawyer wants to talk to him before tomorrow's court appearance. We won't be able to make arraignment today."

"Thank you so much, Detectives," Betty said as I handed her my card. "I'll call the lawyer as soon as you leave."

As we went out the door with her husband in handcuffs I said, "Betty, if Kevin fired that rifle in the backyard as he told us, why didn't you hear the report?"

"I don't know. Maybe I was in the basement, or the bathroom."

And, since there were no calls, obviously no one else heard it either.

* * *

We left the house trying to keep Kevin's handcuffed wrists shielded from any neighbor's prying eyes. Walt headed for his car with the rifle and said, "Come to my office after you dump Kevin. We gotta talk."

"We'll all be there," I said wondering what was on the ballistic expert's mind.

I got in the back seat of Ferguson's car with Kevin and Spider took our car and followed us to Farmingdale, a twenty minute drive. After placing Kevin in an interview room we were met by the troop's deputy commander who also was the head of investigations. Captain Wesley Hinchman, who Spider and I had met on several previous occasions, had a big smile on his normally serious face and said, "Guys, great job! Tom called me after you told him you solved it, Danny. Terrific!"

"Glad to be of service, Captain. We understand you've been very busy."

"That's an understatement. The last thing I needed was to have Tom get involved with a lengthy whodunit. Let's get some coffee and you can give me all the particulars."

When we were all seated with our coffee cups in the captain's office, I gave him the facts and circumstances of the case. After I finished he congratulated me once again and said, "I'll be sure to tell the chief of detectives what a great help you two have been. The state budget crisis has stretched us so damn thin. Tom, as soon as you remand Kernan in Mineola I need you back here right away. I have two cases waiting that need your immediate attention. As I said before, thank God this was an easy one."

"Not so fast, Captain."

Everyone in the room turned their eyes to me as Hinchman said, "Oh?"

"This may not be as easy as it appears. Why didn't any neighbors hear that gunshot and call 911?"

"Maybe they weren't home," Ferguson said.

"Maybe a team of state police investigators should knock on their doors and check that out."

"What's the significance of that, Danny?" Hinchman asked, and I could see he was a bit perturbed, his lips tightening and his eyes narrowing.

"The ballistics expert who I called to the scene wants to talk to us after we get Kernan over to detention. I have a feeling what he might say. I am not a firearms expert myself, but I've been in Homicide for many years and know more than the average detective. What I'm saying is a guy fires a gun in his backyard in broad daylight and no one hears it, not even his wife? He aims at a squirrel on a bird feeder maybe five feet off the ground, and the bullet travels through a forest of close-spaced trees, and descends to a perfectly straight path three feet high, perfectly parallel to the ground, and accurately enters a car window killing the driver? What I'm saying is, *Bullshit* with a capital B."

"So what do you think *really* happened, Detective Boyland," Captain Hinchman said, fixing me with a steely-eyed glare.

I picked up on the change from *Danny* to *Detective* and knew Hinchman didn't want to hear this at all. He didn't want the gift-wrapped present we had given him to unravel the least bit. I said, "No one heard the shot because the shot took place near the end of the woods, maybe ten feet in. Kernan was in a prone position hidden by the weeds and trees and he popped Holmgren, deliberately and intentionally."

"Can you prove it?"

"Possibly, but this is not my case."

"How would you go about it?" Ferguson asked.

"An in depth investigation of both the suspect and victim. Who is Kevin Kernan, and where did he come from? The same for Jonathan Holmgren. What relationship exists between them? What motives exist? Was it revenge or jealousy? Was it a contract murder? Yes, it can be solved, but a lot of hard work is involved."

"If your *opinion* is correct," the captain said, "Why don't we wait to see what your expert has to say before we go running off half-cocked here?"

Hinchman was downright hostile now, and I didn't want to rile him up further, so I said, "Great idea, Captain. You know me, the intense homicide guy always looking to complicate things. Maybe it's the way Kernan says it was – a terrible, unfortunate accident."

The captain seemed relieved, "Yes, to that. Call me after you speak to Gennaro."

I would have liked to go at Kernan in that interview room right now. Spider and I might have only this one chance to crack him wide open and get the real reason he killed Jonathan Holmgren, but I couldn't suggest it. It was not my case, and on second thought, I doubted Kernan would change his story the slightest bit. There was a reason he seemed so willing to do a year or more in jail. He was afraid of something – something more than any fear I could instill in him. So we took him out without a word and Tom did the necessary paperwork, and we drove him over to Mineola for printing and photographing and put him in a cell in Nassau Boro Headquarters.

When the jailer slammed the door on Kevin Kernan with a loud clang, he looked at us through the bars and said, "I appreciate the way you treated me through all this."

"And we appreciate the way you cooperated," Ferguson said. "We'll call Betty and let her know you're safely waiting for your dinner in this five-star restaurant. I hope she's retained a lawyer already."

We drove over to Westbury where the lab – technically the Forensic Evidence Bureau – was located. It was a little after four o'clock and we found Walt Gennaro in the coffee room puffing away on what was probably his fortieth

Marlboro of the day. He said, "Come back to my office and I'll give you my take on this."

Gennaro had the rifle on a table and the recovered slug in a small plastic envelope beside it. "The bullet came from the rifle – I got a perfect match with the test slugs despite the degree of deformity. Now take a good look at that bullet because it's not often you witness a miracle."

"A miracle?" Ferguson said.

"Yes, like the bullet in the Kennedy assassination back in 1963. You see, this bullet started out at an upward angle, then miraculously turned downward, then miraculously assumed a parallel path to the ground and miraculously entered the temple of poor Mr. Holmgren whose head happened to be at the correct height for a kill shot."

Noting Gennaro had described the shooting the same way I had with Hinchman, I turned to Spider and Ferguson, and raised my arms out to an, "I told you so gesture."

"So, Danny Boy," Gennaro said, "you figured it out, too. I'm glad some of my vast knowledge rubbed off on you over the course of our long collaborations."

"Exactly what do you think happened?" Ferguson asked.

Walt picked up the rifle and pointed to the grooves on top of the stock. He said, "This rifle has had a scope attached to it at various times. I think that son-of-a bitch assumed a kneeling or prone position in the woods and expertly popped Holmgren. That's what I think."

"We better call Captain Hinchman, and I don't think he's gonna be happy to hear this."

After Hinchman digested the news he said, "Gennaro, is it possible the bullet hit a limb, or limbs, on its way from the backyard to the car?"

We saw Walt roll his eyes and he said, "Anything is possible, Captain."

"And was there any physical evidence found in the woods by you or Crime Scene to indicate someone lied in wait and intentionally shot Mr. Holmgren?"

"No, sir."

"I see. Tom, come back to the office now. This case is a wrap."

Chapter 3

"So Captain Hinchman slammed the door on the investigation hard and tight?" asked my lovely wife, Tara.

"Afraid so, dear. Now, as a former ace homicide investigator yourself, do you agree with Walt's and my assessment of the case?"

"One hundred percent, but let me give you some thoughts, okay?"

"Go right ahead."

"If Holmgren was intentionally shot, Kernan would have to know the traffic always came to a complete halt right there opposite his backyard. And he'd have to know Kernan took the same route at the same time every weekday, right?"

"Right."

"So what did he do, buy that house as part of the plan, so he could observe the traffic and lie in wait for Holmgren?"

"Or maybe the guys who hired Kernan to do the hit knew he lived there."

"You mean they just knocked on his door and said, 'Hey, buddy, you got a rifle? We want somebody killed. How about ten grand for the job?'"

"Well, whatever happened was well-planned out, and who knows what the motive may have been."

"And since it's not your case, I guess we'll never find out."

"Too bad, I'd love to work this one. It has the makings of a juicy mystery, a real sink-your-teeth-in whodunit."

"Oh, when is the wake for Holmgren?" Tara asked, a smirky little grin dancing across her face.

"I don't know yet," I said, knowing where she was going.

"Aren't you going to show up? You know, to catch the *real* mysterious killer when he comes to pay his respects? Don't they *always* show up at the wake, usually after they re-visit the crime scene? And speaking of the crime scene, don't you have a video camera set up in the woods to catch that visit?"

I had to laugh out loud at what my dear wife was doing. "Stop breaking my balls," I said, but I couldn't help continuing to chuckle.

"How many perps have you caught based on crime scene re-visits and wake attendances? I believe the answer is zero."

"Yeah, yeah, yeah. It seemed like a good idea at the time."

"Stop reading all those crime novels, Danny Boy. Those authors aren't real detectives, you know."

"I know, but those authors have two valuable traits more of us *real* detectives could use – imagination and insight. In fact, Michael Connolly or Dennis Lehane could take the facts in this shooting and write a whale of a story with a lot of twists and turns, and make it believable when they take the *real* killer down."

"Wow, you really do want to pursue this case."

"Oh, yeah, but it ain't happening."

"So let's have another cocktail and make dinner."

* * *

I met my second wife on the first day I was assigned to the Nassau Homicide Squad over eight years ago. She was Tara Brown then, divorced, and sour on men in general. A couple of years older than me she was, in my opinion, a dead ringer for the movie actress Halle Berry. And when I told her that she said, "Are you hittin' on me, white boy?"

I'm sure I blushed and stammered when I responded, "Oh, no, no. I'm married. I'm a straight arrow. You know, work, church and home."

She laughed out loud and said, "Bullshit. All you guys will stick it anywhere you can if given the right opportunity and you must have had plenty with those young Sean Connery looks and dark bedroom eyes."

"Not me," I insisted.

"Yeah, even you, Danny Boy."

And it turned out Tara was absolutely right.

When I caught my first big case – a real whodunit – I made the tragic mistake of falling head-over-heels in love with one of the main suspects, a gorgeous brunette by the name of Niki Wells. To make a long story short, I ruined my marriage and my career in short order. My wife Jean divorced me and left New York with our two kids. Niki ingeniously framed me for the murder and I served twenty months in jail and, of course, was terminated by the New York City Metropolitan Police Department. But thanks to the dogged determination of my lawyer and a retired detective, named Willy Edwards, I was cleared and reinstated by police commissioner, Harry Cassidy.

Tara had been my assigned partner on the case and stuck with me, believing in my innocence, throughout the entire ordeal. We became great friends as well as co-workers, and gradually developed romantic feelings for each other. Niki Wells had beaten all the murder charges against her, including the attempt on me, and unbelievably began to stalk me seeking to re-kindle our affair. Tara and I were now living together, and when Niki burst into our apartment, gun-in-hand, Tara shot her dead, saving my life.

After I was re-instated on the Force, Tara decided she had had enough of violence, blood and murders and got a transfer to the Nassau DA's squad where she now investigates white-collar crimes and whatever is left of organized crime. We recently bought a small cape-cod home in Carle Place, not too far from our offices in Mineola, and hoped to lead a normal, happy life together. Tara assured me we will, unless I fall for some other crazy *Dragon Lady*. And I assured her that will never, ever happen again.

* * *

Two days later Walt Gennaro called me with the analysis of the swabs taken from Kevin Kernan's hands. Both were positive for gunshot residue in varying amounts. I thanked Walt and told him I'd let Tom Ferguson know. Tom sounded abrupt when he answered the phone, but relaxed when I identified myself. "Still busy?" I asked.

"Yeah, it never lets up. What's new?"

I told him of the GSR results and he said Betty had retained an Ernest Gottlieb to represent Kevin. He said, "Gottlieb spoke to Judy Greenblatt at the DA's office and she said she had to put the case to the Grand Jury, but didn't expect they would indict for a charge higher than what Kevin was arrested for."

"So Gottlieb plans to plead him guilty to the negligent homicide charge?"

"Looks that way, and he I'm sure he got some promise of a light sentence."

"Anything new from Maguire at the ME's office?"

"Nope. Routine, he says. One shot to the head, toxicology negative. Case closed as far as his office goes."

"Well Tom, I guess that's it. I'll let you get back to work."

"Thanks, Danny. Thanks for all your help. And please thank Spider for me, too. By the way, I never did find out how he got his nickname."

"I'll thank him, Tom, and he got that nickname from Detective Manny Perez who gave all of us in the squad our nicknames. Manny had said, 'We don't need no goddamn Virgils in this squad. You are now *Spider*. Spider Webb, ready to catch the bad guys as you weave your web tighter and tighter around their punk asses.'"

"Funny, but it sure fits him well."

I did convey Tom's thanks to my partner and we both went in to inform our bosses, Sergeant Finn and the CO, Lieutenant Pete Veltri, of the wrap-up.

When we finished Pete said, "More holes in this story than a block of Swiss cheese, but it's out of our hands. Write it up as an assist FOA, and try to put it out of your minds."

"Boss," Spider said. "Danny and I agree this is no accidental shooting. The ballistic evidence is too strong, and this Kernan admitted to firing the gun too easily. This case demands immediate follow up now and…"

"And it's not our case," Finn said. "Period. Whether Pete and I agree with you is immaterial. Now go write the damn FOA report up."

FOA means *For Other Authorities* and basically the report accounts for your time spent working on a case where it's not an actual homicide occurring in your home jurisdiction. I typed out a few sheets on our involvement, assigned it a local investigation case number, and dropped it in Sergeant Finn's in box. He would review it, send it on to the boss for his signature and then it would be filed away never to see the light of day again, as I was supposed to file it away in the dark recesses of my mind and never think about it again. I would attempt to, but I made a copy of my report, stapled my hand-written notes to it, and took it home with me that night convinced somehow Kevin Kernan had gotten away with murder.

* * *

A few weeks went by and the Grand Jury indicted Kernan for Criminally Negligent Homicide to which he quickly pled guilty and was as quickly sentenced to one-and-a half to three years in prison as I had predicted. With good behavior he would walk out of the medium-security prison in upstate Wallkill in fourteen months, substantially shorter than the twenty months I spent there not long ago for a crime I did not commit at all. Ah! Justice!

My bitter reverie was broken by a piece of paper being slapped on my desk by the huge paw of Detective Bernie Gallagher, his voice booming out, "There, read that!"

Bernie pronounced that short sentence as if it were an order, but when I looked up at the big man, aptly nicknamed Doctor Death, he had a smug, self-satisfied grin on his jowly face. I picked up the sheet and read the neatly-typed sentence. *The revolving door of the criminal justice system spun crazily on its axis and spit Jimmy "the Nose" Harrington out onto the filthy sidewalk, like a huge wad of sticky brown phlegm.*

"Well, Danny Boy, how about that for an opening sentence?"

I figured something like this was coming based on all the questions Bernie had been pestering me with over the past few weeks. For some reason he had gotten the idea he wanted to write a crime novel and this must be his first attempt at putting some words on paper. I said, "Very descriptive, Bernie, but a bit on the crude side."

Bernie's face lit up and he said, "Right on, Danny! You gotta smack 'em right between the eyes with your opening sentence, right? You told me that, right? All those mysteries and thrillers you read start off with a bang, right?"

"How many chapters have you completed so far?"

"Hey, I'm just starting out here, you know."

"You mean this is it? One lousy sentence?"

"It ain't lousy," he said frowning and getting that mean, psycho look in his eyes.

Not wishing to anger the 280 pound volatile hulk I said, "No, the sentence is good. I meant I'd like to read a lot more of your work after that terrific opening."

"Oh," he said relaxing. "I'm working on it. Give me some time."

"Good for you, but tell me again why you have this burning desire to write a crime novel?"

"Who better than me to write a blockbuster? Over fifteen years in the Homicide Squad and I seen it all – and I should tell it all. Only you gotta help me."

"Why me?"

"Uh, well, you know, when you were involved with that crazy bitch – uh, the Dragon Lady – a few years back…"

"More than a few years, Bernie."

"Yeah, yeah, whatever. But you kept a journal of what was going on. I remember reading some excerpts and it coulda been a pretty good mystery story. And like I said, you read a lot of this stuff, too."

"That journal was a record of events. Dull, factual and boring. A self-serving justification of my stupid behavior. Something to do to pass time in the slammer."

"So you won't help me?"

"I didn't say that. Give me three chapters – say about 5,000 words – and I'll give you my opinion and suggestions, okay?"

Bernie's big face broke out into a huge smile and he patted me on the shoulder with his ham-like hand. "Thanks, Danny, I'll get right to work on it tonight. Yessiree, a best-seller is on the way."

I chuckled to myself shaking my head as Doctor Death shambled away dragging the odors of tobacco smoke, cheap after-shave lotion, and the Russian hockey team's locker room sweat with him. Bernie Gallagher a crime novelist?

A book written by a guy whose reports were sloppy, loaded with misspellings, typos and incoherent sentences? I had experienced and witnessed a lot of bizarre, unpredictable and astounding events in my time on the Job, so why not? Bernie Gallagher – New York Times best-selling author. Why the hell not?

* * *

Another four months had gone by and Spider and I had not caught an exciting case or any we could sink our teeth into and get our adrenaline surging. It was so bad we got to re-hashing our old cases with each other to relive some of their thrills and dangers. Then Spider surprised me when he said, "You know, I still think of Tiffany once-in-a-while. Goddamn shame what happened to that beautiful woman."

Shocked would have been a better word than surprised. I had promised Spider I would never mention her to him, or *anyone,* ever again. And here he was bringing her up himself. Tiffany Adams-Kim, lead investigative reporter for the *New York Chronicle*, was a tall, slim, bronze-skinned, multi-ethnic mix of raw beauty and steaming sensuality. One day while she was walking through the squad room, Bernie Gallagher drooled in open-mouthed astonishment as she sashayed by his desk. When he regained his composure he whispered, "Was that Beyonce?"

And when Tiffany Adams-Kim laid eyes on my handsome partner it was game on. Spider is a six-foot tall, well-built, medium brown-skinned man with a Denzel Washington smile and an engaging personality. As I had told Tara I was, Spider was also a straight arrow – work, church and home – and he did not at first take warmly to me based on my previous dalliance with Niki Wells. But when he became smitten with Tiffany, he said to me one day, "Now I understand why you did what you did with Niki."

Despite knowing what I did with Niki, and all the grief and heartache it had caused a lot of people, and despite repeated warnings and begging, Spider fell hard. Even after I explained to him she was using him to get the story of the murder case we were working on to further her career, he couldn't stop longing for her. He said, "I know all that Danny, and I don't care. All that matters is Tiffany."

I had slapped my hand against my forehead and shouted, "Look at me you dumb nigger! Don't do to yourself what I did. Please."

I don't use the N word, and I couldn't believe it came out of my mouth, harsh and stinging, and I immediately wished to reach out my hand and bring it back and stuff it down my throat. But to my amazement, Spider smiled and came over to me and hugged me. He said, "I know why you said that, Danny. To shock my dumb black ass back into reality. And on an intellectual plane, I know you are one hundred percent correct. But I just can't give her up."

I patted him on the back and said, "I know. I won't bug you about it again." I could see his marriage going down the drain as mine had done. His lovely wife Marla, his two decent children, Mark and Shari, thrown to the wind as I had discarded Jean, Patrick and Kelly. What was wrong with us? What was wrong with the male animal that made us violate our marriage vows of fidelity?

"Yeah, Spider, it was a rotten shame killing her the way they did. They were sick bastards, but we got them all."

"Yes, we did partner. But that didn't bring Tiffany back to life, did it?"

"No, it didn't." And I didn't say, but surely wanted to say – *But her death saved you, your marriage and your family, and that was a good thing – a damn good thing.*

Chapter 4

Less than a week later, still bored out of our minds, I heard Detective Manny Perez shout out, "Line one for you, Danny Boy!"

"Who is it, Manny?"

"None other than Superman. Remember him?"

"Sure do," I said, reaching for the phone.

I punched the blinking button and picked up the phone saying, "Danny Boyland here, Special Agent Havlek. To what do I owe this unexpected phone call?"

"Remember a case you were involved in several months back? The guy shot on the parkway?"

My pulse quickened, and I'm sure my heart skipped a beat as I said, "Sure do, Superman. Why are you interested?"

"I just left Troop L Headquarters after speaking with Investigator Tom Ferguson and Captain Hinchman. Are you available to chat with me? I can be there in fifteen minutes."

"Sure, Mike. I'll be here. What's up?"

"You never believed that shooting was accidental, did you?"

"Never."

"Neither do I. Put on a fresh pot of coffee."

I called over to Spider and said, "That was Mike Havlek, and he wants to talk about the Holmgren case."

"And why is Superman interested in the *accidental* death of Jonathan Holmgren?"

"We'll find out soon, he's on his way over."

The name Superman had been affixed to Agent Havlek by our resident nickname specialist, Detective Emmanuel Perez – and he was spot-on with this one, as he was with all of them, although we would never admit that to his face. When Agent Havlek had first walked into our squad room over a year ago looking to take over a case I was working on, Manny said, "Superman's here to see you."

I looked up to see a nice-looking, tall, dark-haired man dressed in a navy blue suit and sporting black-rimmed glasses. And with the cleft in his chin he sure was a ringer for Clark Kent as portrayed in the Superman movies. But whether he had a blue and red outfit emblazoned with a big gold S under that suit, was doubtful.

Havlek and I had gotten off to a rocky start when he tried to grab the Frankie Chandler case from me claiming it was now a multi-state serial murder case and therefore in his bailiwick. He was no doubt correct, but his attitude pissed me off, so I called in a favor. I had worked on a joint terrorist task force with the Feds and got close to a guy, Walter Kobak, who was now the FBI Director. Walt had a few words with Havlek on the phone, and that did the trick. We ended up working well together, and took down Chandler with minimal further loss of life.

Mike Havlek got off to a rockier start with Long Island's largest newspaper's top investigative reporter, Allison Hayes. Previously dubbed Lois Lane by Manny several years back, he told her she would be a perfect match for Superman. However, they locked horns over her involvement in the case, and I had to broker a peace between them for the sake of my investigation. Allison went on to win the Pulitzer Prize for her reporting excellence on Frankie Chandler and, to dismiss that old saying about first impressions, Mike Havlek and I are now good friends and Allison Hayes is now Mrs. Mike Havlek, with a super baby on the way.

Now Mike would be here shortly, and as I prepared the coffee, a hundred questions went through my mind. I hoped he had some answers for me and Spider.

* * *

When Mike arrived, and after we all shook hands he said, "Let me go say hello to the boss and Sergeant Finn."

A few minutes later Mike, Pete Veltri and Father Finn came out and we all went into the coffee room. I figured I knew what Mike was up to – keep the bosses in the loop, get them interested in the case, and then hit them with the request for our assistance. And he did just that, saying right up front, "I may need Danny and Spider's help, and I hope you agree when you hear my story."

Lieutenant Pete Veltri said, "We're a bit tight on manpower, but I'll give you their help if I can. Now convince me."

"I'll get right to the point. Jonathan Holmgren is an alias for Jerome 'Jerry' Harrison. Note the initials, which are the same, a condition suggested by Witsec."

"Witsec?"

"The Witness Security Program, the correct name for what is commonly known as the Witness Protection Program. Jerry was in it for several years."

"Why was he in hiding?" I asked. "He didn't appear to be a Mafia hit man."

"He was a white-collar criminal embezzling funds, manipulating his client's accounts, that type of thing. But he was a bit player compared to the firm's higher-ups, and when the shit hit the fan he was the first one to 'fess up. His testimony sent a lot of big-wigs, including the CEO of his firm, away for a long time. We picked up on rumors a contract would be put out on him, so into the program he went."

"And they finally found him, meaning his death was no accident, and meaning Kevin Kernan was a hired hit man."

"Maybe. That's what we have to find out, among other things, and that's why I need help."

"Be more specific," Veltri said.

"I want to first conduct this investigation the way it *should* have been conducted, the way Danny wanted to do it all those months ago."

"Your trail will be ice cold by now," Father Finn said.

"Yeah, but we still have to do it."

"Did Holmgren's wife know he was in the program?" Spider asked.

"I don't know, but you and Investigator Ferguson spoke to her after he got killed. You would be the guy to follow up with her."

"What about Ferguson? It's his case after all."

"Not anymore. I officially took it over much to the dismay of Ferguson and the relief of Captain Hinchman."

"Wait a minute, Mike," I said, "what am I missing here? What's the Federal connection, and aren't you a serial killer expert?"

"That I am, Danny Boy. Jonathan Holmgren is not the only victim who was in the program; in fact he's not the first. He is the *fourth* victim we are aware of. There could be more."

"Holy crap!" Veltri exclaimed. "How come this isn't all over the media?"

"Because we don't want it out there, Pete. And for reasons not yet known to us, neither do the killers."

"Do all your victims have anything in common?" I asked.

"You mean other than being all dead?"

"A feeble attempt at humor from the humorless Feds," I said, shaking my head. "Yes Mike, other than being fucking dead."

"All were made to appear accidental in one way or the other, specifically a drowning, a house fire, and an auto accident."

"How do you know they weren't accidents?" Father Finn asked.

"We don't, but if they weren't accidents they were expertly staged. But we all know there are no coincidences. All the victims were white-collar crime guys like Holmgren, and all were responsible for putting a lot of big-shot bankers and brokers in jail for many years."

"But our case is a bit different," I said. "Our *accident* has a perpetrator, and I can't wait to visit him in jail."

"Correct," Mike said. "This case has the most promise of all to provide some answers. Can I have Spider and Danny do this for me, Pete?"

"For you, or *with* you?"

"Basically *for* me. I trust both of them to investigate this completely without me around. I can't stay here. I'm spread too thin, and the other jurisdictions need my help a helluva lot more than you do here. I don't mean to disparage the other locals involved, but they don't have your savvy and ability."

Pete nodded his head and said, "You got them, Mike. You roped us in you crafty, flattering Fed. I'm real interested now."

"Mike," Father Finn said, "isn't Witsec the responsibility of the US Marshal's Service?"

"That it is, Francis, and they will be my first stop when I get back to D.C. As you can expect, they are bent out of shape over this, and that's why they reached out to us. You know, since the program started in 1970 they have not lost one witness yet?"

"Uh, are you forgetting the four dead ones you mentioned?" Spider asked.

"Technically, yes. The Marshal's have not lost one protected witness who followed all the rules and procedures. Those who left the program on their own, or who went back to their old neighborhoods, or who contacted friends and relatives, and in so doing got whacked, don't count. Accidents don't count either, so until we prove one of these four was an intentional hit, their record is still intact."

"And our case may be the one," I said. "I see why the Marshal's service must be in somewhat of a dither over this."

"That's putting it mildly," Mike said. "They are evaluating their internal security, their office staff, their computer systems and the whole Witsec process. If they have been compromised, we have a disaster in the making."

"Let's say they were compromised," Pete Veltri said. "I would think the killers would somehow leak the facts to the media as a warning you're not safe even if you are in the program."

"Which, since they haven't," Finn said, "leads me to believe the deaths were accidents after all."

"Or they are not finished killing yet," Mike said. "And when they knock off everyone on their target list, *then* they'll go public."

"How many people are in the program?" Spider asked. "A few hundred?"

"How about 8,500? And close to 10,000 family members."

We all looked at Mike Havlek in disbelief. Lieutenant Veltri broke the silence by asking, "And how many men does the US Marshal's service have to do this?"

"There are ninety-four US Marshals, one for each Federal court district, and a few thousand deputy marshals and staff."

"And they run the Fugitive Recovery Program too, right?" asked Sergeant Finn.

"Yeah," Spider said, "headed up by old Tommy Lee Jones chasing down poor bedraggled, innocent Harrison Ford."

We all chuckled, happy for the break in the tension caused by the seriousness of the situation at hand. Mike said, "I guess that's it. I'm back on a plane in a couple of hours. Please keep me informed as you go along. Your squad is our best hope to crack this thing wide open."

"Unless, as I said before, the death of Holmgren and the others were indeed accidents," Father Finn said with a twinkle in his eye.

"I think we all know better," Mike said getting up to leave.

I got up to accompany Mike out the door. I said, "Say hello to Allison for us."

"I sure will. She's due in about five months, and I'd like to wrap this case up by then. With your help, of course."

"That's a bit optimistic, isn't it?"

"Not with you and Spider on the job. So stop dawdling and get the fuck to work."

"And good-bye to you, too, you pompous Fed," I said, but I was smiling and pushed Mike out the door with a big pat on his back. I turned to Spider and said, "What do you say we grab some lunch and then go to work?"

"Where first?"

"Holmgren's widow."

"And then?"

"Betty Kernan and all her neighbors."

"And then we take a ride up to Wallkill to visit our accidental shooter?"

"Yes, indeed Spider. Yes, indeed."

* * *

When Jonathan Holmgren gave up his birth name and entered the Witness Security Program, he decided to turn his life around and follow all the rules to the letter. Witsec relocated him to an apartment in Brooklyn, and with his new credentials in hand, the twenty-six year old accountant by profession had no trouble landing a decent job at an investment bank. Gone for good were his

Wolf of Wall Street days. Gone was the Rolex watch, the $3,000 suits, the $500 shoes, the booze, the drugs, the high-maintenance women. Jerry Harrison had reformed. He knew he had been given a second chance and he took it, vowing to live a decent, clean honest life from then on. His conscience was troubled, but only a little, by the extra million dollars he embezzled from his firm before the whole world collapsed around him.

Jonathan Holmgren remained true to his vows. He met a sweet girl, a secretary at the first firm he worked for, and their romance blossomed into marriage, a family, and a comfortable home on Long Island. Each time he changed jobs it was for a big step up, and now he was the chief financial officer for a large insurance firm in Uniondale with the bonus of not having to ride the rails to Penn Station every day.

One day, while still working in Manhattan, after five years married to Evelyn, Jonathan took a noon lunch hour excursion to the Williamsburg Bank in Brooklyn and added Evelyn's name as a co-renter of the safe-deposit box wherein lay $1,100,000 in neat stacks of hundred dollar bills — one hundred of them in each rubber-banded bundle. Soon after he landed the position in Uniondale he rented another safe-deposit box, again with his wife as co-renter, at a local bank on Sunrise Highway in Massapequa. He placed within it a sealed envelope containing the key to the box in Brooklyn. On the envelope he had written the words, "For Evelyn #2."

Four more years had gone by and Jonathan still hadn't mentioned the existence of either safe-deposit box, or the money, to his wife. It wasn't he didn't trust her; in fact he was totally loyal to her and their children, and still very much in love. And Jonathan did not want to spoil everything by unnecessarily bringing up his past life, which he figured would be the end of all he had worked so hard to turn around. But then things changed.

Jonathan had always been cautious, and more than a bit paranoid, about being discovered even though he was safely ensconced with a new identity 3,000 miles away from the scene of his crime. Alert to strangers, doubling back occasionally while strolling the streets of Brooklyn and Manhattan, triple protecting his computers at home and in the office, he felt he had all the bases covered.

Over the years, when nothing remotely suspicious had occurred, he gradually let his guard down. So he failed to notice the well-dressed man who followed him from the parking garage in his office building right up to his office door and continued on by. He failed to notice the same well-dressed man in a gray sedan follow him from the parking garage to his home a few days later. But when they received a hang-up call at dinner time, and Evelyn remarked she had gotten a strange call during the day, Jonathan's interior alarms clanged loudly. He said, "Was that a hang-up also?"

"No, a male voice asked me if Jerry was home. I said there was no Jerry here and he must have a wrong number. He apologized and hung up. Should we be concerned?"

"I don't think so, honey," he said as a cold shiver ran down his spine. "If the calls continue, we'll report it to the local police and the phone company."

The next morning, all his senses now on high alert, and panic beginning to set in, Jonathan Holmgren *did* notice a gray sedan pull out from the curb a block behind him and follow him onto the parkway. However, when Jonathan turned off to the northbound Meadowbrook Parkway, the sedan continued westbound on the Southern State. This similar tailing occurred two more times, but not with the same car. The second time was a dark-blue sedan, and the third time a yellow sports car. Then it was back to the gray sedan. Why didn't they follow him to work? Unless they already knew where that was. Or unless he was delusional, and not being followed at all.

But the guy on the telephone had asked for *Jerry*.

The tails stopped completely two weeks later, and no further strange phone calls had occurred since he and Evelyn had spoken about them. He breathed a little easier, but decided he had to bring Evelyn into the loop – a little bit. One night after dinner when their two children were safely asleep in their upstairs bedrooms, Jonathan poured a little extra wine into their dinner glasses and said, "Let's go relax in the living room."

They snuggled up on the sofa and he reached for the remote, turning the TV's volume down. "You know Evelyn, I'm going to be forty years old soon, and I'm a little concerned."

"About what?" she asked sitting up straighter and turning to face him.

"My health. My heart. Remember I told you my dad and his only brother died of heart attacks in their mid-forties?"

"Yes," she said, now giving him her full attention. "Do you have chest pains, or other symptoms?"

"No, nothing at all. I didn't mean to alarm you. I wanted to talk about finances, you know, in case something did happen to me."

"Oh, you had me worried there."

"I am sorry, but I want to let you know you will be well taken care of if I die. My company insures my life for triple my salary, so you'll get about $450,000."

"I think you mentioned that once, but I don't like this conversation."

"I know honey, but there's something else. Come with me."

He took Evelyn out through the kitchen door into the attached garage and switched on the light. He fumbled around in the bottom of his metal tool box and came up with a small brown envelope. He said, "Inside is a safe-deposit box key. The box is in our local bank and the box number is here on the envelope. You are a co-renter on the box, so you will have no trouble getting the contents out. It's some extra financial protection for you and the kids."

"Another insurance policy?"

"Something like that. Let's hope it will be fifty years before you have to open it."

"I'll drink to that. Don't scare me like this again."

"I am sorry, but it had to be said. I love you so much."

"And I love you too, Jon. Let's get back to our wine and have a toast to your continued good health."

Nine months later Jonathan Holmgren, a/k/a Jerry Harrison, was dead.

Chapter 5

The morning after Jonathan's death, still in shock but with the assistance of two neighbor housewives, Evelyn Holmgren began making the funeral arrangements, which would not be elaborate. A one-day wake with a brief religious service by their Methodist minister, and cremation the following morning. After she hung up with the local undertaker, the phone rang and the president of Jonathan's firm expressed his deepest condolences, and said he would expedite a check for the life insurance proceeds to provide financial comfort during this stressful time. The tax-free amount would be approximately $460,000.

Thankful for this amount of money, she asked her neighbors if they would accompany her to the funeral home to help her choose a casket and finalize the arrangements. When they left in the neighbor's car, none of the three women noticed they were followed the two miles to the funeral home and the two miles back home. The wake would be held two days from today giving enough time for Evelyn's parents and one sister to fly in from Ohio. Jonathan had no known living relatives. He had told his wife his mother died when he was a child, and with his father and only uncle and all grandparents deceased, he assumed he was alone in the world.

The wake was fairly well attended, with a fair representation made by their neighbors and Jonathan's co-workers at Allied Insurance. At the night session after the minister spoke, a somber man in a dark suit and tie, looking to be in his mid-forties, came over to Evelyn and introduced himself as Stan Brady, a co-worker of Jonathan's. After expressing his regrets he said, "What a terrible tragedy, Mrs. Holmgren. Hard to believe an accident like that could happen."

"What do you mean?"

"It was so….so bizarre. I mean didn't the police seem interested in pursuing this further?"

Somewhere deep inside Evelyn's brain a slight alarm dinged on. Why was this Brady asking these questions? "I'm not sure I follow you, Mr. Brady. The man who shot Jonathan admitted it right away and is awaiting a hearing."

"Yes, I guess you're right. And the police never pestered you about this being something other than an accident?"

Now Evelyn's alarm level rose higher and she said, "No, not at all. What happened was an accident. Oh, what division do you work in at Allied, Mr. Brady? In the actuarial department as Jon did?"

"Uh, no, I'm in claims processing. Well, let me go and say a final prayer for Jonathan and I'll be on my way. I see there are others waiting to speak with you."

Had Detective Daniel Boyland attended Jonathan's wake as was his custom, he would have surely noticed this conversation between Brady and the grieving widow and followed up on it. But this was not his case, it was Investigator Ferguson's case, and he was not in attendance either. And, irony of ironies, it was the first case in Danny's long career where the murderer *did* attend the wake of his victim. One could argue the real murderer was already arrested, but Stan Brady was one of the men behind the man who pulled the trigger, and he had just walked out of the funeral home and disappeared into the night.

*   *   *

Two days after Jonathan Holmgren was cremated, with the children back in school, Evelyn went into the garage, opened the tool box and withdrew the small envelope containing the safe-deposit key. Still on alert, her conversation with Brady at the wake still on her mind, she periodically checked her mirrors for any sign she was being followed as she drove to the bank. There was no doubt a gray sedan followed her for the mile and half journey. The sedan parked in the same parking field at the bank as she did, but no one got out and followed her inside.

With nerves on edge she signed the box registry card. The attendant took her key, retrieved the box, and directed her to a private room. She locked the door, unlocked the heavy metal safe-deposit box, and removed the envelope marked "Evelyn - #1." When she was half-way through the four pages she broke down in tears. It took several minutes to recover, so long in fact the attendant knocked on the door and asked, "Are you okay, Mrs. Holmgren?"

She managed a weak, "Yes, I'll be done soon," and stuffed the letter back in its envelope. She put the envelope and the one marked "Evelyn - #2" into her purse and left the third small envelope, which contained the second safe-deposit box key, inside the box. She called for the attendant and accompanied him to the vault where he replaced the box and handed her back her key.

On high alert now it was easy to spot the gray sedan as it followed her home and continued past the house as she turned into the driveway. She made herself a cup of strong tea and sat at the kitchen table this time reading the entire letter, determined to keep her composure. She read it a second time still unable to believe its contents – the double life in the witness security program, Jonathan's real name and past crimes, the million dollars in the box in Brooklyn. Was this all real? All true?

The second letter was much shorter and dated a few months ago. In it Jonathan expressed his fears he was being followed, but an entry dated a month later said the tails had apparently stopped, and perhaps it was his imagination working overtime. But his description of one of the vehicles being a gray sedan triggered Evelyn's alarm bells once again, causing her hand to shake and almost spill her tea.

Drinking her second cup of tea and trying to assimilate and analyze all this new information, Evelyn Holmgren came to a tentative conclusion. Jonathan was intentionally murdered and whoever was responsible wanted their million dollars back. And they hoped the widow Holmgren would lead them to it.

She picked up the phone and called Allied Insurance. A company that still believed in friendly customer service, a live operator answered saying, "Allied Insurance, how may I direct your call?"

"Mr. Stan Brady in Claims, please."

After ten seconds the operator responded, "I'm sorry, there is no one in Claims by that name."

"Oh, could you try the other departments?"

Thirty seconds later the operator said, "I'm sorry ma'am we have no one by that name at Allied at all."

"Oh, I'm sorry. I must have gotten it wrong. Thank you anyway."

Taking the Yellow Pages from the pantry shelf she flipped through them stopping at the listings for Real Estate Brokers. Paging down to the local Massapequa Century 21 office she dialed the number and said, "Hello, I'd like to have a sales associate visit me tomorrow to list my house for sale."

She would go back to her family in Ohio. The proceeds from the house sale and the insurance policy would be sufficient to allow her not to have to think about the million dollars – *stolen* dollars – in that Brooklyn bank for a long, long time. Long enough, she hoped, that Jonathan's killers would give up the search.

* * *

After cheeseburgers and cokes at Mulvaney's, Spider and I left Mineola and headed south and east to Massapequa, with Spider behind the wheel. "So tell me, partner, how did Holmgren's wife take the news of her husband's death?"

"Evelyn Holmgren acted like most women do when hit with that news – she broke down and cried."

"And when she recovered, did you and Tom ask her the standard questions?"

"Of course, and her answers, as best as I can remember them, indicated Jonathan had no enemies who would ever want him dead."

"But of course at the time, you and Ferguson didn't know he was in the Witsec program."

"No, but you and I know now, and I'm interested to hear how Evelyn answers our sharp-pointed questions about dear old Jonathan, a/k/a Jerry."

"So am I."

Fifteen minutes later we pulled up in front of the Holmgren house and were met at the door by a gray-haired woman in her sixties. We identified ourselves and asked for Evelyn Holmgren. "Oh, she moved away," she said.

"When was that?" Spider asked.

"Not too long after her husband died. Wasn't that a terrible thing? Those poor children! And such a nice woman. Why…"

"Uh, ma'am," I said. "Do you know where she moved?"

"No, she was close-mouthed about it. Said she wanted to leave these awful memories behind."

"Who handled the real estate transaction?"

"Century 21, a nice lady named Alice…uh, I can't remember her last name."

"That's okay," Spider said. "Thanks for your help."

"Is there something wrong? You know, did something new come up on the case, as they say on TV?"

"No ma'am, just routine follow-up. Just like they do on TV."

We got back in the car and headed for the Century 21 office on Sunrise Highway. Luckily, Alice Gibbons was in the office. Unluckily, after reviewing her sales file on the computer and searching her memory, Alice could not recall Evelyn Holmgren ever mentioning to where she was relocating. We walked out and I said, "Post office, Spider?"

"Post office," he said.

And, of course, the post office had no record of a forwarding address which caused Spider to say, "Wanna bet she closed all her utility accounts and credit card accounts and left no forwarding address with them either?"

"No bet, partner, but we'll check anyway, won't we?"

"Right, but the afternoon is young. Ready to go see Betty Kernan?"

"Let's do it," I said getting back in the car.

* * *

Twenty minutes later we pulled up in front of 1721 Parkway Drive North, the scene of the crime, now coming up on seven months ago. This time an elderly man answered the door and after identifying ourselves and asking for Betty Kernan he said, "Moved out about four months ago. Me and the missus are renting the place now."

"Was Mrs. Kernan also renting?" I asked. "For some reason I thought her and her husband owned the house."

"No, the real estate agency handled the rental for some absentee landlord. Some corporation, not anybody named Kernan."

"Do you have any idea where she and their children moved to?" Spider asked.

"No, we never met her. The house was vacant when we rented it."

Spider and I looked at each other and I said, "Well, thank you sir for your time. Oh, what agency handled the rental?"

"Ames and Ames, up on Hempstead Turnpike in East Meadow."

"Thanks again," Spider said as we turned away. "Ames and Ames and the post office again?"

"Yeah."

Different agency, different branch of the post office, but the same disappointing results. Evelyn Holmgren was strike one, and Betty Kernan strike two.

"All we have left is our shooter," Spider said. "Let's hope he doesn't strike us out tomorrow."

* * *

Back at the squad we joined Father Finn in his office for coffee. "You guys got back here quick. Hope you didn't strike out."

"Good choice of words, Sarge. Two strikes, and one more swing to take. Here's what happened…"

Finn took a sip of coffee from his mug and said, "So you have no clue how to find Evelyn or Betty?"

"None that come immediately to mind," Spider said.

"Danny?"

"No, Sarge."

"Tell me, Danny Boy, how did old Willy Edwards, former first-grade detective turned private-eye, find *your* kids when your ex-wife spirited them away?"

Then it dawned on me. I slapped my hand to my head and said, "Duh! School records!"

"Ah! The light comes on," Finn said shaking his head.

"We'll hit the local elementary schools after we finish interviewing Kevin Kernan," I said. "They had two boys."

"So you will go upstate tomorrow and track down the school records the day after?" Finn asked.

"That's our plan."

"And then you'll be done working for the Feds and back working for the NYMPD?"

"Miss us, Sarge? Can't solve any cases without your two ace investigators?"

"My ass! Two prima donnas would be more like it. The duty chart's getting slim with vacations and guys in court all day. Wrap this up fast, okay?"

"Will do. Jeez, you scare me when you get angry."

"Yeah, Boss," Spider said. "I'd prefer the *friendly* Father Frances Finn figure from now on."

"Great alliteration, Spider!"

"Will you two get the hell out of my office and go prepare your interview of Kernan? Like now?"

* * *

That night Kevin Kernan reclined on his bunk in his jail cell in Wallkill state prison, hands behind his head, reflecting on the fact tomorrow would mark five full months completed toward his sentence. If he kept up his record of good behavior he would be out in nine more. Fourteen months was a small price to pay for what he got out of the transaction – his life, the life of his wife Betty, the lives of his step-children David and Steven, and the forgiveness of over sixty grand in unpayable gambling debts and forty grand on top of that. Of course, there was that little problem – he had to kill a man, some seemingly nice guy with a family, who apparently led an innocent, decent life. But Stan Brady had assured him the death of Jonathan Holmgren was more than justified. "Kevin," he said, "this Holmgren is *not* a good guy. He is a rat of the worst kind that must be eliminated, as retribution for what he did, and as a warning to others who might be thinking of doing likewise."

Brady would not get more specific, but he was emphatic about one point in the process. He told Kevin no matter what anyone said to him he was always to maintain the death of Jonathan Holmgren was a tragic accident and nothing more. And so far that had been easy, as the investigating cops apparently bought his story hook, line and sinker. But that one detective, Boyland, who was helping the state police guy, he was a crafty one. He looked as if he wasn't buying it at all. Good thing it wasn't his case.

* * *

A correction officer banged his truncheon on the bars of Kevin's cell the next morning at eleven o'clock saying, "Up and at 'em, Kernan, you got visitors."

Betty he figured, although her visits and letters had inexplicably tailed off recently. He would be happy to see her again. Married for two years, he was eager to pursue a happy future with her and her two kids. A family man at last. About time he turned his rotten life around. But hadn't the officer said *visitors*? "Officer, do you know who these visitors are?"

"Yeah, a couple of dicks from the NYMPD. Let's go, Kernan."

Kevin took a deep breath and followed the CO to the visiting area. Keep to the story. *No matter what these guys had to say, or offer, just keep to the story.*

Chapter 6

When we walked out of Sergeant Finn's office, I was stopped by a nervous Bernie Gallagher who shoved a handful of papers at me saying, "I did a few pages. Can you read them for me?"

"Sorry, Bernie, not now. Spider and I got a lot of work to do, but I should be free in a few days. In the meantime, I'd like you to learn some techniques, okay?"

"Uh...sure, I guess so," the huge detective said as a cloud of doubt creased his brow.

"Ever hear of the use of alliteration?"

"Uh...no."

"Spider used a great example of it a few minutes ago. He said, 'I'd prefer the friendly Father Frances Finn figure from now on.' Notice the five words in a row beginning with the letter F?"

"Yeah...?"

"That's alliteration. Remember Willy Edwards' famous double murder case?"

"Sure, Tassone and Perna."

"And the fictionalized account of that case began, '*Bettin' Bobby Bonasera bopped and bounced down Baisley Boulevard...*'"

As if a light had clicked on in Bernie's brain, a big grin lit up his face and he said, "Yeah, I remember that! The B's! I get it now."

I patted him on the back and said, "Great, now use that technique once-in-awhile to spice things up. And I'll teach you a few more tricks of the trade when I get freed up."

That seemed to satisfy Gallagher as he stepped spryly away, still smiling, papers clutched tightly in front of him. Spider grabbed my arm and whispered, "What in God's name was that all about? Don't tell me Dr. Death is writing a novel?"

"So he says, and it seems mine is the lucky brain he's picking."

"Why you? Oh, wait a minute, your journal of the *Dragon Lady* caper."

"Partly, but also because I read a lot of crime novels and I absorbed a lot of those writers' techniques, techniques I recognized thanks to a terrific high school English teacher back in the good old days."

"Lucky you," Spider said, "but I can't believe that dumb ox could ever write a readable novel."

"Bernie's not so dumb. He's solved more than his share of cases, you know."

"Yeah, by threatening his suspects with great bodily harm and breathing his foul breath right into their faces."

"Hey, we all have to play to our strengths in that interview room, which we should be now discussing."

"Do you think we should call Mike Havlek and let him know what's going on?"

"Yeah, no sense keeping the bad news from him."

Although Mike Havlek was disappointed Evelyn Holmgren and Betty Kernan were no longer in the area, he had high hopes they would eventually be tracked down through their children or by other tracing methods. He said, "I don't mean to put pressure on you two, but your interview of Kernan tomorrow is the only real thing that has any promise. You have to crack him."

"You have nothing going on with the other three cases?" Spider asked.

"Nada, but the other three victims have the same profile as Holmgren – all witnesses in multi-million dollar scams and frauds of one kind or another. Unfortunately, so far there are no clues from their deaths that lead to other than an accidental cause."

"How about the guy who drowned in his backyard pool?" I asked. "He could easily have been forced under water."

"Prove it, Danny."

"The guy who died in a fire in his home," Spider said. "What caused the fire?"

"Frayed electrical connection in the bedroom, and he was a smoker."

"That could have been intentionally manipulated without too much effort."

"Sure, Spider. Prove it."

"And the auto accident, Mike? How did that happen?" I asked.

"Bad brakes."

"Jesus, that's a classic and readily accomplished sabotage."

"Prove it was sabotage."

"Okay, I get it. Now let me ask you this. How many more witnesses under protection in the program fit this profile?"

"We are researching that and are about a quarter of the way through the database. We have two more, so far."

"Are you going to re-locate them again?" Spider asked. "To be on the safe side?"

"Yes, as soon as we can."

"Are you and the Marshal's thinking you might have a mole with access to the database?" I asked.

"Unfortunately, yes. We can think of no other explanation, other than the database being hacked from the outside. But there are no signs of that."

"You'll know for sure if one of those two you move gets whacked," Spider said.

"Yes, we will. We hope to prevent that by transferring the active database to a new operating platform and strictly limiting access to the director of the service and two or three of his immediate assistants. Any requests for information will have to be documented and approved by one of these long-time, trustworthy and dedicated officials."

"Assuming one of *them* is not your mole," I said.

"As they say, you have to trust someone. Good luck with Kernan. Call me right away – one way or the other."

"Superman sounded a bit on edge," Spider said after Mike disconnected.

"A bit? He's on the verge of panic, and I can understand why. Let's relieve some of his pressure and break this murderer Kernan for him tomorrow."

* * *

"You're awfully quiet," Spider said as he drove the unmarked sedan north on the Thruway.

"Just remembering the last trip I took up to Wallkill about eight years ago. You weren't driving, a correction officer was, and I was in a cold, creaky prison van. I was supposed to spend forty years there. And it was about this time of year – December – gray, dreary, depressing."

"I can imagine what you went through. Twenty months in jail must have been no picnic."

"Thank God for the perseverance of old Willy Edwards. If not for him, I'd still be rotting away in a cell."

"How's he doing?"

"Great. Still enjoying the retired life down South. Tara and I talk to him and Edna once in a while."

We continued at a leisurely pace, each alone with our thoughts, and mine turned toward my children – Patrick and Kelly. Pat, now sixteen, was a junior in high school and Kelly recently turned fourteen and was in her freshman year at the same school in Roanoke, Virginia. Their mother, my ex-wife Jeanie, died a few years ago of cancer, taking her unforgiving hatred of me to her grave – and I couldn't blame her one bit. After all, I ruined our marriage and our family for the Dragon Lady – and I ruined it willingly and deliberately, much to my surprise and dishonor.

Now, although I had technical custody of my children, I de facto ceded custody to their grandparents – Jeanie's parents – with whom they lived. Their hostility, originally on a par, or higher, than Jeanie's, had somewhat abated over the years in deference to the children, and whenever Tara and I visited they forced themselves to be cordial, if somewhat reserved. I knew they would never forgive me, and I couldn't blame them one bit.

My introspection was broken by a playful poke in the ribs and Spider saying, "Wake up sleeping beauty. We have arrived."

My eyes took in the menacing, stark prison building as we got out of the car and I involuntarily shuddered. Twenty months of my life wasted over a scheming, murdering woman. Stupid, stupid, stupid.

* * *

Fully focused on the task at hand we sat in a featureless, windowless interview room awaiting the arrival of the only lead, our only hope, for information in the death of four people. We were determined to leave with that information, even if we had to get down and dirty to pry it out. I'm not implying we would resort to torture or smacking Kevin around – those days are over, although Dr. Death's intimidating presence here might be welcome.

My thoughts were interrupted by the abrupt opening of the steel door. A manacled Kevin Kernan in an orange prison jumpsuit was guided into this dungeon by two correction officers. "Want the bracelets off?" one CO asked. "We'll be right outside until you're finished."

"Yes," I said smiling at Kevin who smiled back in return. Spider and I had discussed how Kevin would react to our presence this many months after his conviction. He could clam up completely demanding his Miranda rights again, but if he did so, he would drive our suspicion level way up. We figured he would play it the way he had played it up to now – a terrible, stupid accident and a willingness to pay for his stupidity. *I'm so, so sorry...* But Kevin had to be wondering what the hell we were doing here all the way up here from Long Island.

When Kevin was seated a CO asked if we wanted anything to eat or drink. I said, "Would cokes all around be okay?"

Spider and Kevin both agreed and the three of us chatted briefly about the weather and football until our sodas arrived. We all took a sip from our plastic cups – no metal cans in here – and, as Spider and I planned, I began. "Kevin, I'm sure you're curious why we are here."

"Sort of. I mean I've been here five months without anybody coming to see me, except my wife."

"Ah yes, Betty," Spider said. "We checked the visitor's log. She hasn't been up here in over two months. You two have a spat, or something?"

"A spat? No, not at all. She's busy with the kids, I guess."

"But she still writes?"

"Sure, I get a letter at least once a week."

"When did you receive the last one?"

"I...I don't remember."

"It was over three weeks ago," Spider pressed. "Wasn't it?"

"I guess so."

"Let me ask you something, Kevin. Is Betty having second thoughts about you and your story?"

Kevin thought a few seconds and said, "No, why should she? I told the truth and she believes me."

For the first time some concern showed in Kevin's face. I said, "Kevin, I have one important question, in fact if you answer this one question for us, we'll be on our way back to Long Island right now."

"Okay, if I can. What is it?"

"Who contracted you to intentionally murder Jonathan Holmgren?"

Kevin sat up straight in his chair almost spilling his cup of soda. "What? It was an accident!"

"Bullshit," Spider said.

"No, no, it was the way I said it happened. There's no evidence it happened any other way..."

"Because if there was any evidence we would have arrested you for murder, right?"

"Right, I guess."

"And if we didn't have the evidence *then*, but had it now, we should be arresting you *now* and taking you back down to Nassau County for arraignment."

"Can you do that? Wouldn't that be double jeopardy?"

"Now that is a interesting question, Kevin," Spider said. "To answer the legal aspect of your question, the answer is, no. We are talking about two different crimes—negligent murder versus intentional murder. Two different statutes. Double jeopardy doesn't apply. But your answer held out the suggestion we *did* have that evidence."

"It did?"

"Perhaps," I said, knowing we had reached a fork in the road. If Kevin were to ask for a lawyer it would be now or never. I sat in silence for a full minute staring at Kevin. Spider followed my lead.

Kevin let out a sigh and said, "I don't know how many times I have to tell you the shooting was an accident. If you think you can prove otherwise, lock me up again and take me down to court."

"Kevin," I said, "look at me. We have absolutely no evidence whatsoever you intentionally murdered Holmgren. None."

"Then why are you here? What's going...?"

"We are here," Spider said, "to get that evidence – from *you*."

"And we are not leaving until you confess your real involvement in the death of Jonathan Holmgren in all its gory details."

"But..."

"Shut up, Kevin. Shut up and listen to us closely. I am going to be truthful with you. My partner will be truthful with you. Listen to us, and then you can ask questions, okay?"

"Okay," he said thankful for an opportunity to relax and keep his mouth closed.

"The guy you shot was not who you think he was. He was a bad guy whose real name doesn't matter. He ratted out several big shots who had stolen millions of dollars from their investment firm and went to jail for a long time. Somebody put a price on Holmgren's head – a big price, we figure. And when they found him they concocted an elaborate plan to take him out. And you, Kevin, were the final piece in that plan."

"I..."

"Stop! "Spider said. "We're not finished. Your wife has figured it out. She realizes you're a murderer. She's finished with you, my friend."

Of course we had no idea if this was true, but we did know she had taken the kids out of school and disappeared. I said, "Do you know where Betty is now? Do you know where your step-kids are?"

"On Long Island where I left them," he said, doubt creeping across his face.

"No, they are not. They are gone. They don't want to live with a fucking murderer. Someone else is living in your house. Your kids are not in school. Give it up, Kevin. Stop protecting the bastards who hired you."

Kevin wiped a tear from his eye and lowered his head to his arms. We had him! I looked at Spider and we waited. A minute later Kevin raised his head and said, "I'm sorry Betty doubts me, and I'm sorry you guys don't believe me, but no one hired me. The shooting was purely an accident. How many times do I have to tell you two that?"

Damn! But we had a couple of more aces up our sleeve. I said, "Kevin, things are going downhill for you fast. Your family is gone, now let me ask you this – how long do you think they'll let you live after you walk out of here?"

That seemed to throw him off balance and he muttered, "What do you mean?"

"You know what a loose end is, don't you?" Spider asked. "You're a loose end, Kevin, their last loose end. You're expendable, in fact, your death is now necessary."

"Why?"

"Because you are the only living link to them. They can't afford to let you spill your guts to us."

"Like you two want me to do now?"

"Right," I said, "but we can prevent your death from happening. We can provide you with a new name, and a new start in life."

"You mean the witness protection program?"

"Yes," I said, thankful Spider and I had not mentioned Jonathan Holmgren had been in Witsec, and it hadn't protected him at all.

Kevin mulled it over, looking back and forth to me and Spider. "That's a generous offer, and if what you said fit the facts, I would certainly take it. But, whoever Holmgren was, I shot him by accident."

We couldn't believe he didn't crack, but I had played only one ace – a nice, soft red ace of hearts. Now it was time to play my final card – the death card. Here comes the down and dirty ace of spades, Kevin. "Okay," I said getting up from my chair as Spider followed suit. "I guess we are done here. Oh, with Betty in the wind who do you want us to notify?"

"Notify about what?"

"About your untimely *accidental* death in prison."

"Hunh?"

"Your death, I'm guessing, within a week after we leave here," Spider said.

"We'll make sure of it," I said. "What do you think we are going to say to those correction officers outside? I hoped to say, 'typical hard-assed con, wouldn't tell us a fucking thing.' And I would have said that if you had cooperated."

"But you didn't," Spider said. "So now we tell those CO's what a wonderful visit we had, and how you told us everything we wanted to know."

"And you know how fast jailhouse scuttlebutt gets around. Yeah, a week, or two at most, you'll be toast."

"Found hanged in your cell, or a shiv in the liver in the shower room, I would venture to guess," Spider said.

"And if it doesn't happen in two weeks, we'll be back up here. And when we leave we'll spread the word some more about how you're giving up everything you ever knew, especially about the guys who hired you to kill the guy on the Southern State parkway."

I went to reach for the door and Kevin said, "You two guys are a couple of real, no good rotten bastards."

"Well, not literally, Kevin. But in the context you most certainly mean, we most certainly are, and we most certainly don't give a shit who kills you, or how. Let's get outta here, Spider."

"Wait, give me a minute."

It was now or never, and we managed to keep silent as we nervously waited. It took him a full two minutes, an eternity for me and Spider, before he said, "Sit back down. I'll tell you what you want to know."

Chapter 7

We had completed as thorough a background check as possible on Kevin Kernan prior to our visit and hadn't come up with much at all. Service in the army in the middle-east where he qualified as a sharpshooter with his rifle, but nowhere near sniper standards. No criminal record. Two traffic violations, none alcohol related. No apparent drug use. Then a hit from the Seattle Vice Squad showed his name as a listed "KG" – a known gambler, but only a player – a player who bet substantial amounts inconsistent with his salary as a part-time construction worker. To ease Kevin into his confession I said, "Was it the gambling that did you in?"

"Yeah, I was into the bookies for over a hundred grand at one time. I hit a lucky streak and got it down to about sixty, and that's when I was approached."

"How did that take place?" Spider asked.

"I stopped off occasionally at a local bar near where I was working at the time and had a beer or two before I headed home. One of those days a guy grabbed the stool next to me, ordered a beer, and started up a conversation. After a bit he said, 'You're Kevin Kernan, aren't you?' I'm surprised he knew my name and he introduced himself as Paul Johnson. He asked if he could buy me a beer and we moved ourselves over to one of the booths. He told me he had a business proposition to run by me. I figured, what the hell, and over we went where he laid it all out."

"Gave it all to you right then and there?" I asked. "The whole plan?"

"Oh, yeah. Started right off with the fact of my gambling debts – he knew the *exact* amount. He said he would pay off my debt and give me forty grand cash if I would kill a guy."

"How did you react to that?"

"I wanted no part of it until he explained how they had rented the house across the country on Long Island for us, and how it would be seen as an accident, and how I'd go to jail for only a short time and come out debt-free with forty grand."

"So you went for it," Spider said.

"No, I hesitated. Said I didn't want to kill anybody no matter how much money was involved. But then Johnson patted my hand and said, 'You're not getting my message, are you?'"

"I asked him what he meant and he said, 'Kevin, if you don't do this we will kill Betty and her kids, and the guys you owe the money to will kill *you*. And I assure you your death will be a long, painful drawn out process. Now, do we have a deal?' What was I going to do? He had me in a box."

"What did this Paul Johnson look like?"

"Not like a typical mob guy, that's for sure. More like a businessman, early forties, dressed in a nice suit and tie, and a friendly face. Reminded me of the guy on TV who sells insurance for some big company – you know, bald, glasses, always smiling?"

"Yeah, I know who you mean," Spider said.

I handed a legal pad to Kevin and said, "Write down everything you told us. Include all the details with dates and times attached. And write up that description of Paul Johnson exactly as you remember him. I'll get us some sandwiches and drinks."

I left the room and the correction officers said they would scare us up some food in a few minutes. When I got back inside Spider said, "Kevin, how many times did you meet with Johnson?"

"Twice more. Once to finalize all the details, including the date of the murder, and once more to give me the money."

"He gave you the whole forty thousand upfront?"

"No, half of it. I'll get the rest when I get out of here."

"Did Betty know about you getting the money before the murder?"

"Yeah, she knew I had a gambling problem. I told her I hit a real good streak and was able to pay off what I owed – I told her it was only ten grand – and I had this additional twenty in winnings. And I told her I loved her and was through with gambling forever."

"Did she believe you?" I asked.

"I thought so. I hoped so."

* * *

We took a break as one of the correction officers brought in a tray of sandwiches, donuts and sodas. I stepped outside on purpose and a CO said, "Looks like it's going good for you guys in there."

"Not really. The bastard is running us through hoops. Wants to talk about the Giants and the Jets, and we want to talk about money and dope."

"What's he writing?"

"We got sick of listening to his bullshit and told him to write it all down. If you guys weren't right outside, we'd smack the shit out of the lying fuck."

"Don't let us stop you, but don't leave too much blood for us to clean up."

"Thanks. I better get back in there."

I told Kevin to stop writing and we all dove into the sandwiches. When we finished Kevin said, "Listen, I'm sorry what I called you guys before…"

"Hey," Spider said. "Forget it, it's part of the job. We understand why you said what you did. Now we all have to concentrate on moving forward."

"What happens next?"

"I laid the groundwork with the officers outside. I told them you weren't giving us anything, and I'll reinforce that when we leave. As soon as we get back, we'll get in touch with the Feds and have them get the process going."

"How long will that take?"

"I'm guessing two to three weeks. One day a couple of guys will show up and get you out of here and into your new life."

"You know, the worst thing I'm dealing with is the loss of Betty. I loved her, and her kids were great."

"Yeah, I know how much it hurts, but maybe you can patch things up with her before you get out. How are you doing on your statement?"

"Almost done. A couple more pages."

When Kevin finished, I read the first page and passed it to Spider. Kevin relaxed, finishing his sandwich and drinking his soda. When we both finished reading all the pages, and only having to ask a few questions for clarification I said, "Kevin, are you up for a show, a bit of an acting job?"

"What do you mean?"

"Spider and I are going to start yelling and cursing at you in a couple of minutes. We're going to overturn your chair and knock you to the floor and smack you in the face with these papers while calling you a fucking liar. Maybe I'll backhand you in the mouth a couple times, okay?"

"Yeah, I get it. Thanks… I guess."

I nodded at Spider and we went into the act and both guards looked into the room, but didn't enter. When we finished with Kevin sobbing and burying his face into his arms on the desk, we stormed out into the corridor. I said, "What a waste of our fucking time."

"Jerked you around, did he?"

"Oh, yeah, and these eight pages he wrote are probably similar bullshit. Guaranteed when we check out everything in here it will be all useless."

"What were you trying to get from him? I mean, didn't he confess to shooting that guy?"

I was surprised they knew about that, so I cautiously answered, "Yeah, there are no questions about that, but since we knew him from that case, the Narcotics Squad asked us to question him about his involvement in the drug trade. They think he may be a player and knows some mid-level dealers in cocaine."

"Which of course he denied," said one of the CO's.

"Of course," Spider said. "Now we are out of here. Thanks a lot for all your assistance and the food and drinks."

"Our pleasure. Have a safe trip back down."

"Thanks," I said, "and if you happen to be a little rough in returning that lying bastard to his cell, it wouldn't bother us at all."

* * *

We were back in our Mineola office by four o'clock and filled Sergeant Finn and Lieutenant Veltri in on our results. They were pleased in more ways than one. Veltri said, "You solved the case here. After you tell your Fed friend Havlek, you can rejoin us and let someone else solve his other problems."

"Fine with us, Boss," I said, but I knew Spider was as disappointed as I in getting pulled away from the larger investigation when it was getting interesting. Who was the mysterious Paul Johnson? Was he also involved in the other three *accidental* murders? Where were Betty Kernan and Evelyn Holmgren, and what would they have to say to me and Spider?

Eventually Father Finn read my face and, crafty old sergeant that he was said, "Don't take it hard, Danny. There's plenty of work here to keep your juices flowing. You and Spider did a great job, but the rest is outside our jurisdiction and you two know it. Now go call Superman and give him the good news. Then give him the bad news."

I dialed Mike Havlek's office down in D.C. but he wasn't there. "He's in Chicago," his secretary said. "Do you have his cell phone number?"

"Yes. Anything hot and heavy out there in the Windy City?"

"I better let him tell you about that."

When we reached Mike on his cell phone he said, "Let me call you back in five. I'm almost wrapped up here."

"What's up?"

"Another one. Fill you in later."

"Oh, boy. The plot thickens."

"I wonder if it was one of the two possibles they recently identified in the database?" Spider asked.

"We'll find out soon. Let's get another cup of coffee and wait by the phone."

It was a full fifteen minutes by the time Mike called back and he sounded tired and distraught as he related the untimely *accidental* death of one Marvin Ness in the Chicago suburb of Oak Park. It seemed Marvin jumped to his death from a window in his eighth-floor apartment located in a luxury twelve-story, high-rise building, leaving a handy suicide note behind. "Well, Mike," Spider said, "it sure sounds like a legitimate suicide. Anything in there suggests otherwise?"

"I'm in the Oak Park Police Department, and I finished going over the case with the detectives. They did a great job on it. This happened yesterday, so the scene is already wrapped up. But the photos tell the whole story."

"How did you find out he was in Witsec?"

"His wife told the cops at the scene. Also told them Marvin had absolutely no reason to take his own life. They lead a happy, financially secure existence, and had tickets that night for a production of the show *Kinky Boots* in Chicago."

"What did the suicide note say?" I asked.

"It was brief. *'I can't lead this phony life anymore knowing I betrayed all those people — my friends. Vivian, I hope you understand the depths of my despair. Good-bye, Milt.'*"

"Milt?"

"His real name is Milton Nachman."

"Was it his handwriting?"

"One hundred percent sure, according to his wife. It's on its way to Quantico as we speak with examples of his known handwriting."

"So, if this is not a suicide," I said, "it's a damn good cover-up. I assume Vivian disputes the contents of the note?"

"Vehemently. She insists he had to have been pushed out of the window."

"Any physical evidence to indicate that?"

"None that I'm aware of."

"Mike," Spider said, "was Marvin one of the two guys you and the Marshal's identified as a possible target?"

There was a long pause and Mike answered softly, "Yes."

"I don't want to criticize, but wasn't he supposed to be re-located?"

"Yes, but as I recently found out, the process is not an easy one. New documents have to be painstakingly created and appropriate locations have to be found. It's lengthy, and by its very nature, it cannot be shortened or circumvented."

"How long does the process take?"

"About a month, including the permanent new location."

"Shit! Maybe the Marshal's should grab the other guy and put him somewhere, a motel or something, until everything is ready."

"I'll mention that to them right away," Mike said.

"We may have a similar situation, and we'll tell you about it in a few minutes," I said, "but first let me ask you something about your alleged suicide. Did Marvin Ness have his shoes on when he jumped?"

"I don't know. What difference does that make?"

"Humor me, Mike. You have the pictures there?"

"Yes, about three dozen of them."

"Find the pictures of the body and describe what he was wearing, particularly his shoes."

Spider was looking at me with question marks in his big brown eyes when Mike responded, "He's splayed out on the sidewalk, dressed in a suit and tie, and wearing expensive looking brown leather slip-ons. Wait, only one slip-on, his other foot only has a dark-colored sock on it."

"Is the other shoe nearby?"

"I heard Mike shuffling through the photos. "No, I don't see it in anywhere."

"Check the photos of the inside of the room, especially in the vicinity of the window he jumped from."

More shuffling heard and Mike said, "Yeah, here's the other shoe, by the window, about two feet out from it, on the carpeted floor."

"Bingo! One shoe makes it murder!"

"What the hell are you talking about?" Mike said as Spider said, at the same time, "What the fuck…?"

"Come on, you two, you know I read murder mysteries, but I also watch a lot of crime shows on the boob tube. And many years ago, so many I think this show was in black and white, the TV detective solved the case because the alleged suicide had only one shoe on."

"I'm afraid I'm not following you, partner."

"I'm mystified," Mike said.

"This TV detective said a jumper *always* jumps with either both shoes *on*, or both shoes *off*. Never with one shoe on and one off, which indicates a physical struggle took place."

"You gotta be kidding me," Spider said.

"No, I did my own research on it. Studied hundreds of jumpers. The TV detective was correct, and whoever the writers were, they did a helluva job with their research."

"Well, I'll be damned," Havlek said. "I'll have to think about this and run it by my associates in the unit. But I think you may have something here, Danny Boy. Deep down, we all know this was no fucking suicide."

Mike was not a big user of profanity and I figured it was an indication of his frustration with now *five* dead Witsec people on his hands. I said, "How about some *good* news, Superman?"

"Please. Anything will help."

"I'm going to get more coffee. Spider will fill you in on all the details of our visit to my former home in Wallkill."

By the time I made a fresh pot and returned with our cups filled to the brim, Spider was wrapping up and it was obvious Mike was happy, no doubt the only bright spot in his day, no doubt the only bright spot in his entire investigation. "Great job, guys! At last, a break."

"Mike," I said, "I'm concerned for Kevin. You have to get him out of there and into the program ASAP. I'm fearful for his life."

"Why? You two did a great acting job, right?"

"Maybe, but you never know how convincing it might have been. I think you should move him up to number one on the priority list, and even then a month may be too long. Get him out of there fast to a safe house or motel."

"I'd like to get a sketch artist up there to have Kevin prepare a drawing of this Paul Johnson."

"No, Mike, no, no, no. A thousand times no. That would put the kiss of death on his head if we didn't put it there already."

"But this Johnson guy is all we have…"

"We have a good description of him from Kevin in his statement. We'll make a composite from that."

"Okay," he said, the reluctance obvious in his voice. "Now are you two going to find Evelyn Holmgren and Betty Kernan for me? And crack those two also?"

"Afraid not, "Spider said.

"What do you mean?"

"Bad news," I said. We've been pulled off the case."

"What? Why?"

"We solved the murder of Jonathan Holmgren, which was our case," Spider said. "In fact, it wasn't ours, as you know. But the rest of the murders, and I'm sure we agree they *are* murders, despite how elaborately contrived and plotted they were to appear like accidents, are out of our jurisdiction. They are yours, my Federal agent friend, as Veltri and Finn firmly told us. All yours."

There was silence on the speakerphone for several seconds. Mike said, "But you two are interested in this case now, right?"

"Right," we both said.

"So why not call your old buddy, who is my big boss, and have him pull the necessary strings to keep you on the case with me?"

"You mean Director Walter Kobak, correct?"

"Correct you are, Danny Boy. I was with you when you called him a few years back, if you remember."

"I do, but going over Pete's head by having Kobak call the PC is not something that would be career enhancing, you know. Mike, this is a big caper. Call Kobak yourself, or have your immediate boss call him. I'm sure he'll listen to your plea."

"You call me Superman, but I would need some real super powers to get you and Spider back on this case. Pushing hard may not be too career-enhancing for me, either."

"If you pursue this," Spider said, "what super powers are you planning on using? Are you going to stop a powerful locomotive?"

"Or leap a tall building in a single bound?" I said.

"Or stop a speeding bullet…"

"Maybe, you two jokers, I'll just say Shazam!"

"Jesus, Mike, that's fucking Captain Marvel. Superman never said Shazam."

"Regardless of which super hero I am, get ready my friends. I'm going to make that call, and you two are about to become my Batman and Robin."

"Mike, we can't wait to work with you if you can pull it off, but first you gotta get Kernan out of Wallkill and into Federal custody as soon as you can before he gets whacked."

"I'll see what I can do."

Chapter 8

I spotted Dr. Death walking my way two days after our conversation with Mike Havlek. I relaxed a bit when I saw he had no pages of a manuscript in his first baseman's mitt of a hand. "How's it going, Bernie?" I asked somewhat tentatively.

"Goin' good, Danny. I took your advice and I'm going to get those three chapters done before I bother you again."

"You're no bother, Bernie. You know that."

"Yeah, you're a great guy helping me here, but I wanna get this right, and I'm doing my research. I Googled alliteration and found out about other things like similes and metaphors. Interesting stuff, and I'm gonna use it. In fact, I didn't know I used a simile in my first sentence when I compared Jimmy the Nose to a wad of phlegm. See, I must have inner writing talent already, right?"

Bernie was juiced up now, and I was not about to disappoint him so I said, "I guess you do, my friend. You're well on your way. Now stick to it and churn out those chapters for me. I can't wait to read them."

Google? Similes and metaphors? Had I underestimated the intellectual capacity of Dr. Death?

Bernie's face lit up, but then his mouth turned down into a frown. He fumbled in his pocket and handed me a torn piece of paper. He said, "I took this message when you were in the crapper. It's some guy in the Commissioner's office. I hope you're not in any trouble."

"Thanks, Bernie, I hope so, too," I said taking the note from his fingers and reading the main number of police headquarters in Manhattan, with a five-digit extension number scrawled after it. I took a deep breath and dialed the number and punched in the five digits when directed by the mechanical voice. Two rings later a man said, "Inspector Magness, Commissioner's Office."

"Uh, Detective Boyland, Nassau Homicide here. I was directed to call."

"Oh, yes, Detective. Please hold while I connect you to Commissioner Carson."

The Commissioner? What had I done? Where had I screwed up? Those thoughts and others equally disastrous raced through my mind, as I'm certain they would race through any cop's mind, when about to speak to God. My distress was interrupted by a click and a pleasant voice saying, "Hello, Danny. Charlie Carson here."

Charlie? "Yes, si...sir," I stammered.

"Congratulations, Danny. I heard how you and your partner solved that murder on the parkway. Please pass on my congratulations to Spider as well."

"Yes, sir, I will. I...I didn't realize Lieutenant Veltri made the upper brass aware of this case."

"Well, he didn't. I heard it from another source."

He paused, waiting for me to ask about that source, so I did. "Who might that be, sir?"

"None other than Agent Havlek's boss, the Director of the FBI. I know you know who that is, right?"

"Yes, sir. Walter Kobak. Good man."

"A *very* good man, indeed. And Walt Kobak wants you and Spider. No, he *needs* you and Spider – badly. Want to help him out?"

"You bet we do, Commissioner, but Lieutenant..."

"I'll take care of Pete Veltri and Father Finn, Danny. Don't worry about that."

"Thank you, sir."

"And, Danny? You and Spider will make us proud. You and Spider will show those Feds what the NYMPD can do, right?"

"We sure will, Commissioner. I can't wait. And speaking for my partner, Spider can't wait either."

Spider was out in the field following up on an old case, and I couldn't wait to tell him about the call from the PC when Lieutenant Veltri yelled out of his office door, "Boyland! Get in here!"

Uh-oh. I hoped Pete didn't think we went over his head on this. I walked in and observed a grim-faced boss and a sour-faced Sergeant Finn. "Sit down," Pete said.

I sat silently until Finn opened the conversation by saying, "Have yourself a nice little chat with the PC, did you?"

"Uh… he called me first."

"You could have not returned the call," Lieutenant Veltri said. "Who the hell do you work for around here?"

"Yeah, you back stabbing traitor," Finn said. "Goin' over our heads like that. Well, go work with the Feds, you rat. You and your partner are through here."

"Sarge, wait a minute…"

"Wait? For what?" Pete asked. "Get out of my office and go pack your things."

I got up to leave, stunned by the animosity of my supervisors when I noticed a slight smile on Father Finn's face soon joined by a larger smile on the lieutenant's face. He said, "Gotcha, Danny Boy!"

"You two sadistic…"

"Ha, Ha!" Finn chortled. "Got you *good*. The PC called us *first*, you know. He's giving us replacements for you two jokers."

"So you won't be missed at all," Pete said, "as you and your partner throw in with your FBI buddies."

"How many replacements are you getting for us?"

"Two, of course."

"Not nearly enough to replace your two ace investigators. You should have asked for at least four," I said with a big grin as I hustled out of the office to Finn shouting, "Ace investigators, my ass, you two prima donnas…"

* * *

So as Inspector Clouseau used to say to his houseboy Cato, "Cato, I'm back on the case." Spider and I would go to Washington, D.C. the following week for a brain-storming session with Mike Havlek, his fellow agents in his unit, and the local investigators involved in the other four deaths. But first we were on our way to a small town called Hartland, a few miles from Columbus, the capital of Ohio. Specifically, we were going to visit the Hartland Elementary School and serve a Federal subpoena on the principal for the address of Evelyn Holmgren. We had previously served a similar subpoena on the principal of the South Elementary School in Massapequa to obtain the transfer records of Evelyn's children, John, age ten, and Laura, age eight.

So, still deputized as Federal agents, Spider and I drove our rented vehicle from the Hartland School to 118 Maplewood Street and knocked on the front door after waiting and observing the children enter a few minutes before. Evelyn opened the door on this chilly early December day and her smile faded rapidly as she recognized Spider who said, "Good afternoon, Mrs. Holmgren. My partner and I need to ask some follow-up questions concerning your husband's death. May we come in?"

She hesitated a bit before stepping aside to let us enter. She said, "You came all the way from Long Island just to ask me a few questions?"

"Yes," I said, "and I noticed you didn't ask how we located you. I'd like you to remember that during our conversation. If we can find you, the bad guys can also find you. The bad guys that murdered Jonathan, whose real name was Jerome Harrison, as I'm sure you well know."

Spider and I had planned this direct, hard-assed opening approach and it had the intended effect. Evelyn Holmgren put her left hand to her chest, let out a deep sob and sank down on a nearby stuffed chair. "The children," she whispered regaining her composure. "I don't want them to hear any of this."

"I understand," Spider said. "We'll wait while you check on them."

Evelyn came down from the upstairs part of the house and said, "They're doing their homework and I told them to watch TV when they finished. They are both great kids and miss their father terribly. He was a good dad to them, a good man. This whole situation has me totally confused – and terrified."

"But you did know about his real identity all along, didn't you?" I asked.

"No, not until I went to the bank after the funeral."

"Can you explain that to us?"

"Yes, but first can I get you something to drink? I could use a cup of tea or coffee. This is a bizarre story."

Happy that Evelyn Holmgren seemed willing to tell us all she knew, we stifled our eagerness and patiently waited while she put on a pot of coffee. Five minutes later, seated around the kitchen table, Evelyn told of the mysterious Stan Brady at the wake, of her visit to the safe-deposit box, and of the contents of Jonathan's letters and the million dollars in the second safe-deposit box. She concluded by saying, "That's why I ran from Massapequa. Whoever murdered Jonathan wants their money back, and if they killed him I have no doubts they'll kill me and my children. I guess I have to move again. Could you tell me how you found me? I left no forwarding address with anyone."

"We got the transfer records from your children's former school," Spider said. "But we had to subpoena them. The bad guys can't do that."

"Maybe not, but they could find out in other ways where I live. Do you agree?"

"Yes," I said, "but I'm now of the opinion they are not looking for you at all."

"Why?"

"It's been over six months since Jonathan's death. Based on what you said was in Jonathan's letter, I believe they have no knowledge he stole that money. They would have come after you right away."

"And," Spider said, "that guy – Stan Brady – seemed convinced of your lack of knowledge when he spoke to you at the wake. And assuming it was him who followed you to the bank, it confirmed his opinion you were not actively talking with us anymore"

"So, are you saying we are safe?"

"I believe so. Jonathan was murdered for his testimony which put a lot of big shots in jail. You didn't know him back then, and as I mentioned before, they likely didn't know he took that money."

"I was going to ask if we should request going into the witness program, but they found Jonathan anyway despite that protection."

Spider and I looked at each other and I nodded to him. He said, "Evelyn, we believe the program has been compromised. Danny and I have been assigned to a Federal group to investigate that breach."

"Have there been others?"

"Yes," I said, "but we have to trust you to keep that fact a secret. And that is why we are now going to ask you to search your memory and give us as detailed a description of this Stan Brady as you possibly can."

And when Evelyn Holmgren had given us a complete narrative description of Stan Brady, while she was ably sketching his face with a #2 yellow pencil, it was obvious to me and Spider that Stan Brady and Paul Johnson were the same person. We took her statement and when she signed it she asked, "What now?"

"As we mentioned," Spider said, "we believe you are safe here."

"What about the million dollars? I certainly don't want that embezzled money."

"We are going to suggest to the FBI agent we are working with that you go to Brooklyn and retrieve it."

"What?"

"Do you feel you are being followed? Any other suspicious things happening in your life?"

"No, and I have been extremely observant as you can well imagine."

"Then this will be the acid test," I said. "You go to the bank and we in law enforcement will cover you like a blanket the entire trip. We will ensure your safety and follow you all the way there and back. If nothing happens, you are home free."

"But I bet you hope something *does* happen, don't you Detective Boyland?"

"I'd be lying if I said otherwise. We have to catch these guys before more people get killed."

"I understand, and I'll help you all I can, if that's what you decide to do."

We thanked her, and after obtaining her contact information, we headed back to our modest hotel in town and had a couple of beers at the bar, satisfied with our afternoon's work. "Let's call Superman," I said taking out my cell phone and heading to a secluded booth. Spider followed with our beers and we dialed Mike. "Batman and Robin calling from the Ritz-Carlton," I said when he picked up. "It's great to be on the Fed's expense account."

"Yeah, you jokers. You better be in a Comfort Inn or a Motel 6, and your rental car better be a Ford, and you better not be going to Morton's Steakhouse for dinner."

"At least you sound in a better mood. What's new?"

"No more murders, thank God. But no leads, either."

"Well, we got some good info from Evelyn Holmgren. Let me fill you in."

Mike Havlek was pleased, especially the sketch of Brady/Johnson and Evelyn's willingness to cooperate in retrieving the money from Brooklyn. He said, "We'll set that up when you finish tracking down the next one, Kernan's wife."

"Yeah, we fly out in the morning," Spider said. "We had to leave that one hanging. The local public schools we checked so far didn't have the kids registered. We still have a couple more to go, and also the parochial schools in the area."

"Keep me in the loop, as always."

"Will do, Superman. Batman and Robin, over and out."

* * *

When we got back to work the next day, Spider and I went right at it. We did what most cops do – the basics, the grunt work, the leather pounding. We knocked on doors in the neighborhood, and after less than an hour, we hit pay dirt. An elderly gentleman named Ed Crockett confirmed the Kernan's two children took the school bus which stopped every morning in front of his house. Although he hadn't seen them for quite a while, he gave us descriptions of the two boys and assumed they must have moved. We thanked Crockett and resumed our neighborhood canvass, but discovered no additional information.

Early the next morning we got out of our car and walked over to a small group of children and women gathered by the bus stop. The obvious mothers of the kids eyed us suspiciously until we identified ourselves and asked for their help concerning the Kernan children. They all remembered them, but agreed they moved from the neighborhood a few months ago. The school they attended was the Linden Lane School. We thanked them and drove over to the school based on their offered directions.

We went into administration and identified ourselves. We were directed into a side office where we spoke to the administrative assistant and explained our predicament, and again we hit pay dirt. Mrs. Aronoff had a distinct memory of Betty Kernan coming in after her husband's commitment to prison – perhaps a month after – and removing the children from the school. She told Mrs. Aronoff they would be moving in a few days. Now for the key question, "Can you tell us where the school records went?" I asked.

"Now you know, Detectives, you need a subpoena for that information."

"We do know that, but before we go to the trouble can you tell us if the records were indeed transferred to another district?"

"Yes, I can. Give me a few minutes at my computer."

Spider and I looked at each other and crossed our fingers. Mrs. Aronoff looked up from her computer and said, "Their records are still here, and we have not yet received a transfer request."

Damn! "Mrs. Aronoff," I said, "can you put a reminder on your PC to periodically check to see if a request does come in?"

"Certainly, will once a week be okay?"

"That will be fine," Spider said, handing her his card. "As soon as the request comes in, we'll be here with the subpoena."

As we walked out of the school I said, "Let's call Kevin when we get back to the office. Maybe Betty wrote him of their new location."

"What are the chances of that? I mean she booked on him not long after he went upstate. I'm sure she knew the shooting didn't happen the way dear Kevin told her."

"Yeah, but let's give it a shot anyway."

Back at the office, Spider reached for the phone, checking our case file for the number of Wallkill prison. When he was connected he asked if they would be so kind as to bring prisoner Kevin Kernan to the phone, or allow him to call us at Nassau Homicide. "I'll have someone go get him, the correction captain said. "It may be a while, so don't hold on. I'll let him call you back."

Spider hung up and we waited. Fifteen minutes later the phone call from Wallkill came, but it was not Kevin Kernan speaking – it was the boss himself. Warden Thomas McArthur solemnly informed us Kernan couldn't come to the phone, "You see," he said, "Kevin Kernan is dead."

Warden McArthur went on to explain the correction officer sent to fetch Kevin found him in the indoor exercise yard, on the basketball court. Apparently, while driving to the hoop, he slipped, or was fouled, or was purposely pushed, into the round metal pipe supporting the backboard, suffering a head injury which was sufficient to cause his death. "Of course," the warden said, "a thorough investigation will take place to determine what occurred, and if there had been foul play, we will get to the bottom of it."

"Of course," Spider said looking at me. "Please keep us informed of the results of your investigation."

Spider hung up and looked at me. I had been listening to the conversation on the speakerphone. We both knew the death of Kevin Kernan would never be solved. No new leads on who was pulling the strings would ever be forthcoming from him. "What now, partner?" I asked.

"Well, Batman, I suggest we inform Superman."

"He'll be real happy to hear this. We struck out. We have nothing more to do on this case here, do we?"

"I don't think so."

To say Agent Michael Havlek was disappointed with our news was an understatement. "Shit! Fuck!" he shouted. "The only guy who could implicate this Brady in the Holmgren murder – dead!"

Spider and I glanced at each other with raised eyebrows noting Mike's increasing use of profanity as this case dragged on. We said not a word waiting for him to calm down. When he regained his FBI composure he said, "Okay guys, I'm going to get that meeting going in a day or two, so come down when you can."

"Sure thing," I said. "Cheer up, Mike. When we all get our heads together maybe something will pop for us."

"It had better. The Marshal's service is apoplectic on this breach, and they are bugging the Director for an arrest, and you know shit flows downhill."

"We understand the pressure," Spider said. "We'll get down there tomorrow."

Chapter 9

Spider and I got down to Washington the following afternoon and drove our rental vehicle from Reagan National to the FBI complex at Quantico. The Behavioral Science Unit included VICAP – the Violent Criminal Apprehension Program – and was where Mike was assigned. He greeted us warmly and we all got coffee. He said, "Later, after you check into your motel, Allison wants you both to join us for dinner at our home."

"Great," I said. "It will be great to see her. It's been awhile. How's she doing?"

"Doing fine. The doctor says the baby is developing normally and he foresees no problems."

"Boy or girl?" Spider asked.

"We don't know, and don't want to know. We like surprises."

"Only a few more months, right?"

"Due on income tax day, April 15. Four months to go."

"So let's solve this caper before then, so you can enjoy the birth of your child without a care in the world."

Mike said, "Thanks, Danny. I'm counting on you and Spider to help us accomplish that."

* * *

After we checked in at the Marriott and freshened up, we drove the twenty minutes to the Havlek's apartment in the Virginia suburb of Manassas where a relaxed-looking Mike greeted us dressed in slacks and a green and red sweater. He said, "Good timing, guys, Allison's whipping up some cocktails."

"Vodka martinis okay for you two?" Allison shouted from the kitchen.

Spider and I responded with a loud yes as we walked toward the sound of her voice to greet her. I noticed they had a lot of Christmas decorations in place, but the artificial tree had only the lights attached to it. I thought they were real early into this until I realized Christmas was just ten days away. I said, "Spider, you do any Christmas shopping yet?"

"Uh-oh. No. You?"

"No, but when we get back..."

"We better move our butts."

As we entered the kitchen Allison greeted us with a big smile and handed us our drinks. Mike joined us and all four of us raised our glasses – there seemed to be plain ginger-ale in Allison's – in a toast. "To being together once again," Allison said.

We took a sip and I said, "And one more toast to the coming addition to the Havlek family. To Superboy!"

"Or Supergirl," Allison said as we sipped again.

Allison guided us into the den and we sat around a low table where she had laid out a large assortment of cheese, crackers, dip, olives, artichokes and salami, and we all dug in as we chatted away and caught up with each other's lives.

"So tell me Lois Lane," I said, referring to her nickname around the Nassau Homicide Squad, "has Superman made you aware of what he and us are working on?"

"Of course. He knows better than to hold back on me."

"Ace investigative reporter we all know you are," Spider said, "please give us your insight and conclusions as to what is going on, and who is responsible."

She took a sip of her ginger-ale and said, "I haven't a fucking clue."

We all broke into laughter and Allison excused herself saying, "Let me check on dinner, it should be about ready. We'll talk serious later."

"Good idea," Mike said. "Contrary to my wife's statement, she does have some ideas worth kicking around, and I hope you two do also."

Beginning with a small salad, dinner roll and glass of Merlot, Allison set out a basic American dinner – baked potato, green beans and medium-rare roast beef. All at the table couldn't have been more pleased. After sampling the beef I said, "This is delicious, Allison. I see your appetite seems unaffected by the pregnancy."

"I had morning sickness for only two days in the beginning, now I'm ravenous. I have to watch the weight gain closely."

"Then I guess you'll skip dessert?" Mike asked.

"Not tonight. Special guests are here and I'm sharing in that apple pie ala mode you whipped up. I'll starve myself tomorrow."

"You made an apple pie?" Spider asked.

"Sure. Made it all the way from the freezer at the supermarket to the thaw-out process here in the kitchen."

I was happy to see Mike laughing and relaxed at the dinner table with his wife and friends, a welcome relief from the stress I had observed in him lately. I hoped we could get to the bottom of these murders – for I was sure that was what they all were – soon enough to prevent Mike from going over the edge.

After dessert was over, four satisfied people made their way back into the den. Mike said, "Would anyone care for an after-dinner cordial?"

We all declined, not wishing to cloud our minds further from the serious business at hand. I began, "Okay, here's my take on what we have so far. We have five deaths, which have elaborately been staged so as to appear to be accidental, but which are most likely intentional murders. The five victims are connected by two things, they were in Witsec, and they were there because they testified against big-time thieves in the corporate world. Okay so far?"

"Right on," Mike said. "Continue please."

"We don't know who's killing them or how their new identities were compromised. A turncoat in the US Marshal's service seems likely, because they are the only agency that oversees the program."

"Unless their database was hacked from the outside," Allison said.

"We'll know soon," Mike said. "They will have their entire database transferred to new servers in the next several days."

"But what if the hacker, if that was indeed the case, has already downloaded all the names and their locations?" Spider asked. "You said it takes one month at a minimum to re-do their identities and re-locate them, and we now have a few more who fit the profile."

"Correct. This is why the bosses in the Marshal's office are moving them temporarily to safe houses pending the completion of the process."

"And if one of them gets killed after the re-location?" Allison asked.

"Assuming the *new* database has not been hacked, we have a mole high up in the Marshal's office. The new restrictions to be put in place on database usage and searches will be such that a user will be easily traceable, and those users limited to only a few highly trusted people."

"Okay, but now for the *big* questions, my dear. Who is behind this, and who is this Brady guy?"

"Stan Brady a/k/a Paul Johnson is a go-between, or planner, for whoever is calling the shots. The composite sketch of him based on Danny and Spider's written description from the late Kevin Kernan, and Evelyn Holmgren's sketch and description, will be available soon."

"Do you plan on distributing it to the local investigators?" I asked.

"Yes, but they won't arrive until the second day. Tomorrow, I want the three of us to meet with the agents in my group who have been assigned to assist the local investigators. I want their take on the locals who are working with them."

"Call me crazy," Allison said, "or maybe it's woman's intuition, but I smell an organized crime connection here."

"Not crazy at all," Mike said. "I sensed the same thing, which is why Vince Genova, our OC expert in the New York office will be joining us tomorrow along with that white-collar crime maven from the Nassau DA's squad. What's her name again, Danny Boy? Halle Berry?"

I laughed and said, "Now you're dragging my wife down here?"

"Wonderful," Allison said. "I can't wait to have a long talk with Tara — woman's talk for a change."

After we exhausted all our theories and thoughts, we said good-bye to Mike and Allison and headed for the door. No one had to say it, but we all couldn't wait for tomorrow. This investigation was about to move out of first gear.

* * *

Seven of us – me, Spider, Mike and the four FBI agents assigned to the case – assembled promptly at nine a.m. in a nicely furnished conference room at the FBI's Quantico facility. Vince Genova and Tara should be on the ground at Reagan National and would be delivered to join us via an FBI pickup. Mike opened the meeting by making the introductions, saying we would all be on a first name basis for both ease and familiarity. "Fortunately," he said, "none of us has the same first name."

While we awaited the arrival of Vince and Tara we brought the four agents – Dennis, Travis, Mario and Richard – up to speed on our latest information. When we finished, a civilian employee poked her head in the door and said, "Mike, your last two guests have arrived and the coffee is done."

"Thanks, Sally. Bring our guests into the coffee room and we'll join them there."

I gave Tara a squeeze and a kiss and we all went back to the conference room, mugs in hand. Mike went through the introductions once again for the benefit of Tara and Vince, although the second time around helped me firm up the agent's names with their faces. I didn't know about the others, but it seemed as I hit my forties – I would be forty-four in a couple of months – I was having a bit of trouble with remembering names. Mike said, "In case you're wondering about the smooch in the coffee room, Danny and Tara are married, and when we go around the table for a short biography of each of us, you may find out why. Danny?"

Having thrown it to me first I said, "I met Tara when I first went into Nassau Homicide. She was a great investigator, and I learned a lot about the job from her. I also learned a lot about life, and love, and loyalty, when she stayed by me through a very difficult time in my life. So I saw the light and asked her to marry me."

"And you said yes?" said Agent Dennis Willett, a medium-brown skinned man. "Sister, isn't he a bit pale for you?"

Willett was smiling when he said that, and Tara smiled right back at him and said, "I figured why not try white this time since the first two darker-skinned men, looking a lot like you, cheated on me no end. You don't cheat on your wife do you, Dennis?"

Dennis knew he had met his match so he said, "Oh, no ma'am, not me. Strictly work, church and home."

"Where have I heard that bullshit line before?" Tara asked looking directly at me.

We all laughed and Mike knew the ice had been broken and the group had the beginnings of a rapport, of a clicking together as a team – a necessity, he felt, to have any chance of solving this difficult investigation. "Okay, let's get down to work," he said as he passed out the composite sketch of the one and only suspect we had. "This is a guy who has identified himself as both Stan Brady and Paul Johnson. Does he look familiar to anyone?"

They all shook their head in silence so Mike said, "Danny and Spider will fill you in on him."

When we finished, the plan was for the four agents to discuss the sketch with their local counterparts when they picked them up at the airport later in the day. Perhaps something might break, and we would have a positive start for the next day's meeting. I mean, we needed *something,* and needed it soon.

Vince Genova said, "The guy in this sketch looks nothing like a Mafia guy, but that doesn't mean a thing anymore, right Tara?"

"Right. Organized crime is now an equal opportunity employer. Some gangs still cling to their ethnic heritage, particularly the Latino street gangs, but most organized criminal enterprises are ethnically and racially mixed."

"In other words," Vince said, "the only thing that matters is the person's ability to earn money for the group."

"Are you saying these murders are being committed for a monetary gain?" asked Travis Kellogg.

"Yes and no. My guess is these murders are contracted hits for revenge on the squealers. But the mob, whichever one is involved, is carrying out the contracts, and most likely charging their client's big bucks considering the extraordinary planning involved in making them appear accidental."

"Which group has the patience and sophistication to carry out these hits and make them all look like accidents?" Mike asked.

"Vegas," Tara and Vince responded simultaneously.

"Interesting. Anyone else?"

Vince and Tara looked at each other, racking their brains. After a full minute Vince said, "Miami?"

"Maybe Miami," Tara said. "But I think on a scale of one to ten, Vegas is an eight, and Miami is a two."

"I agree."

"And who is the top dog in the Vegas mob?" Mike asked.

"Jordan Carter Bigelow."

"Man, if that doesn't sound like an uppity WASP businessman," Willett said.

"That's exactly what he is Dennis, but I'm not so sure he is uppity. He is, however, a smooth, Ivy-League educated, wheeler-dealer of the first class. And, we believe, a cold-blooded killer when the need arises."

"Personally?" Agent Mario Vollaro asked. "Does he get his own hands dirty?"

"We don't know."

"And who is hiring our Las Vegas WASP to do these nefarious deeds of murder?" Agent Richard Timmons asked.

"Maybe when we scoop up Brady/Johnson he will be happy to tell us," Mike said.

* * *

That evening, the person whose composite sketch and true identity was of paramount importance to the investigative team, strolled into a small Italian restaurant in a Maryland suburb of Washington, D.C. The early dinner crowd had departed, so John Rowan, the name he was using in this situation, was able to secure a two-person booth with no other diners in the immediate vicinity.

He checked his watch, noting he was ten minutes early, and ordered a glass of Chianti as he awaited the presence of Stefan Konopka who always arrived precisely on time. And sure enough, Stefan did not disappoint, walking through the door at eight on the dot. After Konopka sat down and also ordered a glass of Chianti, he bent a bit closer to Rowan over the table and said in a low voice, "The place is in an uproar."

"Tell me about it."

"They know they've been compromised with the deaths of the five so far, so they're installing a new, much more secure computer system and transferring the current database to it."

"How did they figure out the deaths were not accidents?"

"I don't think they did, but they feel five witnesses of similar backgrounds getting killed are too coincidental for them to be accidents."

"But this database change will not prevent you from obtaining additional names, will it, Stefan?"

"Not at all, Mr. Rowan, and I have the next three right here," he said patting his jacket pocket.

"Good, let's order our dinner."

"Same terms as before?" Stefan asked as he studied the menu.

"Yes," Rowan said, patting his jacket pocket, too. Five thousand per name now, and an additional twenty per name more when the mission is accomplished."

"This deal has been a tremendous help to my family. I want you to know how much I appreciate your generosity."

"You're welcome, and I'm sure we can continue our relationship until we have... uh, tied up all our concerns."

"I don't mean to pry, but do you know how many more names you will require?"

"No, and I know your financial needs are great, but we must take our time in fulfilling our mission. They must continue to appear convincingly accidental to the authorities. That takes time and planning, as you may well understand."

"Of course," he said. "Whatever you need, I will provide. You will call me with your next request as usual?"

"Yes. When these three are taken care of, I'll let you know. Here comes the waiter. Let's order."

After dinner Rowan said, "Stefan, do not hesitate to call me on the cell phone I gave you if you suspect anything that might disrupt our process. *Anything.*"

"I will be on high alert as always," he said as he mentally calculated his earnings thus far — $125,000 from the first five, $15,000 in his pocket now for these next three, plus $60,000 more when Rowan completed the task. $200,000! Tax free! His betrayals, of course, bothered him deeply, but not as deeply as the financial needs of his troubled family. He had no idea how many more Witsec names John Rowan would request, but for $25,000 each, he would be happy to provide whatever number that would be.

Chapter 10

After leaving the restaurant, Stefan Konopka got into his five-year old Dodge – still brand-new by his standards – and lit up a cigarette, inhaling deeply. He removed the thick envelope given him by Rowan and flipped through the hundred dollar bills, not bothering to count them. He was sure all one hundred fifty were there. Smoking two packs a day was not his worst habit – gambling was – and as it was about to destroy him and his family, John Rowan had magically appeared on the scene and pulled him from the raging ocean of despair.

Their first meeting, almost a year ago, had been scary indeed. Rowan laid it all out to him in detail – his $100,000 in debts, his two kids approaching college age (the good two), the one kid into dope and thievery (the bad one) and the one kid physically and mentally disabled (the unfortunate one).

All four of Stefan's children would cost him ten times more than he could ever earn at his civil service job, albeit a well-paying one with government benefits. So when Rowan laid out his plan, he jumped at it like a man jumps at a life ring tossed to him as he is going under for the third time. His gambling debts would be totally forgiven with the caveat he would gamble no more. He would furnish information to Rowan, available from his workplace, which would provide him with sufficient re-numeration to pay for college, get treatment for the dope problem, and provide comfort and care for the disabled child. And one more thing, no one would ever know about his lucrative former, and current, side occupation of document forgery.

How Rowan knew all this about Stefan troubled him deeply, but he reluctantly had to give up his side business, as well as the gambling, as a condition of his new employment. As Rowan had truthfully, but painfully said, "Stefan, your forgery talents are exquisite, but the more you earn from them, the more you gamble away. No more forgeries, no more ponies, no more sports betting. No more everything. This is not negotiable. Now, do we have a deal?"

Stefan had agreed, and they shook hands with Rowan passing him a thick envelope as he did. "This is your down payment, Stefan. I will call you on this cell phone I'm about to give you as to when and where we will meet again. I assure you it will not be in this bar, or any other bar, where your bookies do business. Also inside the envelope is a piece of paper with the five names and locations I need. I'm counting on you, Stefan. My…uh, associates would be *very* disappointed if you don't come through for us. Do you get my drift?"

The message had come through loud and clear. Stefan would end up a corpse just like the five guys on this piece of paper would. He most certainly did get the *drift*.

* * *

Marian Konopka, stoic and capable of bearing great suffering, was about at the end of her patience with her husband. She was not a screamer, or one to threaten. One week ago she had simply stated to Stefan if things didn't change drastically, she would leave him and sue him for divorce. She got specific – his gambling debts had ruined the family, specifically their children. Janet and Alice would not be able to attend college, Marty would kill himself with an overdose of drugs, and Madeline would die of neglect in a public institution. "What are you going to do Stefan?" she had asked.

She looked at her forty-nine year old husband of twenty-five years awaiting an answer. Stefan's hands shook as he lit another cigarette. His thinning hair, now mostly gray, and the baggy eyes and numerous creases on his face suggested a man more in his sixties. "I know I have a problem, Marian, and I do love you and the children – you know that, don't you?"

"As much as you love your betting? I don't think so. I repeat my question. What are you going to do?"

"I'll change, I swear. I'll stop the gambling and get a side job…"

"When?"

"Soon. Give me some time. Let me see if I can get a payment plan with the bookies."

"You have two weeks," she said getting up from the kitchen table. "Two weeks, then I go see the lawyer."

And with one week to go, salvation had come to him in the person of John Rowan. He took the deal. He *had* to take the deal. He knew the information he provided would result in the death of many people. He didn't care. He would live. Marian would not leave him. His children would survive and prosper.

When he came home the night of his first meeting with Rowan he handed the fifty one hundred dollar bills to her and said, "I did what you asked. I found a well-paying side job using my artistic talents. The bookies are happy I am going to pay them off, and they will not take any more bets from me, because I will bet no more. We will be fine. The children will be fine. I love you, Marian."

Marian, of course, had a dozen questions for her husband, but she chose to remain silent and let the drama play out. She said, "And I love you, too, Stefan."

* * *

John Rowan returned to his motel after his meeting with Konopka and relaxed in the stuffed chair. He did not turn on the television; he had some serious thinking to do. Now that he had the next three names marked for death, he first would verify their locations and plan their *accidental* deaths. This would take time, although he had two others on his team who were as capable as he in the process. But something nagged at him – and that something was Stefan Konopka.

Rowan arose from his chair, walked over to the mini-bar fridge, and selected a cold Heineken. He popped the top of the can and took a large swallow. Back in his chair he reasoned Stefan was now the weak link. Not that he thought Stefan would turn on him – he had too much to gain, and too much to lose. John Rowan was afraid the investigation would have to eventually shine its spotlight on Konopka and his department of legal forgers. For once the database was transferred and secured, where else would they look?

He took another swallow of beer and focused on another troubling issue. What if the Feds were now scouring the current database to discover possible future targets based on the profiles of the five already killed? Rather than wait until morning, he called his two accomplices and gave them one name each with instructions to move as fast as possible. He would handle the remaining target himself, but first he had to meet with his boss, and his boss *never* spoke on the phone.

After contacting Mitch and Rusty on his disposable cell phone and giving them their instructions, he made one more call after checking his laptop. "Yes," he said when the airline agent answered. "A one-way ticket to Las Vegas, please. On tomorrow morning's 10:18 flight out of Reagan National."

* * *

All four agents returned with their out-of-town local investigator counterparts by five p.m., and Mike Havlek decided to have everyone meet and greet over cocktails. That way, I guess he figured, we could get right down to business the next morning without the usual preliminaries.

We all mingled around the lounge and I went out of my way to meet and have a few words with the locals, and I was happy with my impressions. The four men ranged in age from their early thirties to mid-fifties and seemed to be on the ball and eager to assist in the overall investigation. Moreover, they all seemed happy with the agents they were paired with, a definite plus.

Spider, Tara, and I discussed the locals on the drive back to our motel, and although we both expressed our optimism with the entire group, Spider brought us back down to earth when he said, "Yeah, but are they going to tell us something new tomorrow, or are we all flying back home with what we came with?"

Tara and I nodded our heads. We'd find out soon enough.

* * *

We were all assembled by 8:30 a.m. the next day and got right down to it. Detective Tony Morrone of the Oak Park, Illinois PD brought us up-to-date on the Marvin Ness *suicide*. "The handwriting was definitely his according to the FBI Lab, but the widow still claimed he would never commit suicide."

"So why did he write the note?" Mike Havlek asked.

"We think he was forced to," said Morrone's FBI partner Dennis Willet. "His wife knew he was in the program, and she figured the guys he ratted out – and there were quite a few –caught up to him. She said – and Tony and I believe this makes sense –they must have threatened to kill her, their children and grandchildren if he didn't comply."

"Why the struggle at the window?" I asked.

"You mean your one shoe makes it a murder scenario?" asked Morrone with a little grin on his face.

"Yeah."

"Maybe when they took him over to the window his sense of self-preservation kicked in and he thought *no fucking way*."

"Okay," Mike said. "How many of us here believe Marvin Ness was murdered?"

Everyone in the room raised their hands in the affirmative.

"Good. Now please take a look at this."

Mike passed out the composite sketch of Brady/Johnson. He said, "This is our guy. Do any of you have an indication he was spotted by anyone you interviewed during the course of your investigations?"

They all took their time studying the sketch, but disappointingly, no one could place him, or a description of him by any witness, at all. Mike said, "When you go back to your jurisdictions, I'd like you to take several of these with you and re-visit your witnesses and the deceased's relatives. Your agent partner will go with you and stay until all leads are exhausted."

The next case to be discussed had occurred in Socorro County, New Mexico where the victim – a healthy forty-year old male – drowned in his backyard pool which had a maximum depth of four feet. The local coroner had labeled the death suspicious, but could not find any physical marks on the body to confirm a struggle. The Deputy Sheriff Investigator, Bob Lopez said, "Before I left for the airport the State Police Lab got back to me with the results of a video tape we took from a camera that scanned the pool as well as the rest of the back of the house. They caught two shadows – person-size shadows – leaving the side of the pool and heading toward the front of the house. You can see the body of the vic floating face down, but this whole scene was only five or so seconds."

"Any neighbors spot these guys?" Mike asked.

"No, but I will hit the neighborhood again when I get back."

"Looks like another murder, do we agree?"

Again, we all raised our hands in affirmation. However, the next two cases were not clear-cut at all. In Myrtle Beach the victim was driving his Benz on Route 17 when a large tanker truck, carrying non-flammable liquids, T-boned him at an intersection where the traffic light had malfunctioned. "It was ruled an accident said Detective Bert Perrinski, and I'm damned if I can make a murder case out of it. The truck driver was clean as a whistle, not even a traffic ticket."

"That in itself is a bit suspicious," Spider said. "And how about that signal light? How did that malfunction?"

"SCDOT said that particular light has been acting up on occasion for the last couple of weeks prior to the accident. It was scheduled for a complete electrical makeover due to occur about a week after the occurrence."

"A little shaky, but pending more info I don't think we can definitely say murder here," Mike said.

We all agreed and moved on to the final case which occurred in Dickinson County, Kansas. "The victim was burned to death in his home when he apparently fell asleep while smoking a cigarette," said Investigator Marco Pena. "So far it appears purely accidental – the vic was a heavy smoker, and the Arson Squad found no traces of an accelerant. Electrical system tested fine."

"He was alone in the house?" asked Agent Kellogg.

"Yes, his wife was away visiting her sister in Wichita. Their two kids are grown and live out of state."

"How convenient."

"Sure is, Danny, but that don't make it murder."

"No, it doesn't," Mike said.

We discussed all our investigations in detail right up to the lunch break. Suggestions were copied down, notes taken, theories explored, and cases compared. But as we left for the cafeteria we were all disappointed. The disturbingly sad fact was we were no closer to solving the cases than we were before we arrived.

* * *

After lunch, our new found camaraderie tempered by our gloomy mood, the group gathered once more for our final sessions. Joining us was the Director of the US Marshal's Service, Harold Sparr, and his Assistant Director in charge of the Witsec program, Henry Lindsay. Although both men smiled when introduced, and took pains to shake everyone's hand, it was obvious to me they were under tremendous pressure, most of it caused by the increasingly obvious fact it was one of their own who was providing the information that led to the deaths of these five people. "I know you haven't classified all five as murders," Director Sparr said, "but I am convinced of it, just as I am convinced one of my staff is responsible. No one wants that person caught and punished more than Henry and myself. Now for a bit of good news. Henry?"

Henry Lindsay came up to the podium to join his boss and said, "Right after Marvin Ness's death the four other members we identified as possible future victims were scooped up and placed in safe locations pending the completion of the permanent re-location process. As we continue to go through the database and move it over to our new system, we might discover more who fit the same profile as we get the rest of the database transferred."

Mike Havlek raised his hand and said, "Excuse me, Mr. Lindsay, can you tell us when the entire database will be transferred?"

"In two to three days. We seem to have gotten most of the bugs out, which always cause problems in situations as this, and things are moving much more rapidly. And, Mike, please call me Henry."

"Yes...Henry," Mike said. "And thank you for getting those four already identified over to us. We are processing their background information, along with the other five, hoping to find one common thread."

"You're welcome, and I will call you with any additional names we find."

Lindsay and Sparr had the lights dimmed and put on a slide show depicting the table of organization of the entire Marshal's service, and a more detailed chart of those who worked in Witsec. The slides included photos of various offices and work areas with names of those who worked there listed below the photo. Sparr said, "As you can well imagine, all our employees are thoroughly background checked, but we are doing it again. Our entire employee list has been forwarded to Mike with a request for the FBI to also screen them. As I mentioned, I want this murdering rat bastard bad."

The tough language coming from the dapper boss of the service was a surprise to me, but certainly indicated his state of mind. He said, "Henry and I will now take questions, and we will stay here until they are all answered."

"What is the total number of employees who work in your Arlington headquarters, and how many of them have access to the Witsec database?" Agent Kellogg asked.

Both men shuffled their feet and dropped their heads a bit. "Six hundred, give or take," Sparr said, "with about one fifty in Witsec." He hesitated a bit. "Seventy in Witsec, and twenty outside of Witsec, had access to the current database."

I suppressed an urge to whistle and shout out, "How fucking stupid is that?" But, noticing the agony in their faces caused by that admission, I stifled myself and said, "How many will have access to the new database?"

"Six. Four trusted input clerks, their supervisor and Henry Lindsay."

So they were closing the barn door after the horses left, but at least they were closing it tight. The questions went on to well after three p.m., and after Sparr and Lindsay left, we wrapped up the session. Vince, Tara and the eight agents and locals made their preparations to leave for the airport. I took Mike aside and whispered, "Spider and I are staying. I want to visit the Marshal's headquarters in Arlington tomorrow morning – only the three of us. Can you arrange that?"

"I'm sure I can. Care to tell me why?"

"Well, since we have little else, I think we should visit the scene of the crime, don't you? The scene where the original data theft took place and which led to five murders. Let's nose around, ask questions, take photos and put the fear of the FBI into that murdering rat bastard, whoever he is, as Director Sparr so eloquently put it."

Spider said, "Right on, partner."

"I like it," Mike said. "Let's go back to my office and I'll call over there."

Chapter 11

The next morning the short trip from Quantico to Arlington passed in silence, our somber moods not cheered up by the brilliant blue-sky of this beautiful northern Virginia morning. We entered the non-descript building, and after signing in, were met by Henry Lindsay, who greeted us warmly. He said, "I had the clerks work all night – damn the overtime – and we got the rest of the database transferred."

"How many more likely targets were you able to identify?" Mike asked.

"Two more, for a total of six. They fit the profile exactly, but we found three more that *might* fit – maybe we stretched the parameters a bit – but it doesn't hurt to err on the side of caution."

"When will you notify them?"

"It's in the works. By day's end there will be deputy marshals in their current homes making plans to house them somewhere temporarily, until they can be permanently relocated."

"Which means another new identity, right?" I asked.

"Yes, license, passport, the works."

"And since the database has been transferred and secured, they should be entirely safe and protected going forward?" Mike asked.

"I don't see why not."

"Unless," Spider said, "the source of the leak has nothing at all to do with the database."

"I know where you are going, and I don't like it," Lindsay said a bit huffily.

"With all due respect, sir," Mike said, "we cannot, at this time, rule out a mole – a high-ranking mole."

"Yes, I understand. Sorry for getting my back up there, but…"

"No one wants to think one of their own is a betraying bastard," I said. "We'll know for sure down the road when those six, or nine, if you include the possibles, are relocated, and none eventually get murdered."

Lindsay nodded and said, "Yes, we will. Now, shall we begin our tour?"

* * *

As we proceeded through the open office spaces observing the busily working employees, the number of people who had access to the old database floated around my head, as I'm sure it did in Mike's and Spider's. Seventy in Witsec, plus twenty others. Ninety possible suspects to be interviewed and thoroughly screened, a huge task, but one that had to be done.

Lindsay guided us through a locked door he accessed with his ID card and his thumbprint scan. The large room contained an amazing amount of sophisticated equipment – microscopes, cameras, slide projectors, computers, hundreds of bottles of varied color inks and dyes, and engraving equipment filled the workspace. All eight workers assigned to the unit were bent over their desks, most wearing magnifying eyepieces. Lindsay walked us over to one desk that sat at the end of the room on a raised platform. He said, "Gentlemen, this is Stefan Konopka, our shop foreman. His actual title is Master Document Maker."

We all shook hands with Konopka, and upon the request of Lindsay, he gave us a tour of the place and explained its workings. I was fascinated by the time and care spent in preparing exact copies of legal documents for those about to go into Witsec. "The birth certificate is the most important document," Konopka said. "With that a person can apply for a driver's license and a passport. But we don't want our clients doing that, so we do it for them."

"How long does the process take?" Spider asked.

"Once we get their photograph and new location information, which takes the most amount of time, about a week to ten days for all three documents."

"Wow, that's very fast."

"We have paper stock for every jurisdiction that issues birth certificates and driver's licenses. We also have metal dies for putting the raised seal on the certificates, and holographic equipment for the driver's licenses."

"And the passports?"

Stefan said, "My boss here has friends in the passport office. They send us the blanks, and we encode them and add the photo."

"So no one in the passport office would know the new identities?"

"No, sir."

"But you know them all, Stefan. Correct?" I asked.

There was a brief silence before he replied. "I know the ones I worked on personally, and I supervise all the documents my men produce. So, to answer your question, yes, I know them all."

"And when you complete a set of documents, do you enter the information into the database?" Spider asked.

"No, I give the documents personally to Mr. Lindsay, and he has someone input that information."

"There is no database terminal in this area," Lindsay said.

"And you don't keep your own records of the documents you prepared?" Mike asked.

"No, why would I do that?"

I noticed he was a bit perturbed. Realizing we were peppering him with questions that bordered on an interrogation, I said, "Curious, that's all."

Lindsay asked if we had any more questions, and when Mike and Spider remained silent I said, "Thank you, Mr. Konopka, you and your men are an impressive group of dedicated craftsmen. I don't know how much Uncle Sam pays you, but I bet you could make a helluva lot more plying your trade in Times Square."

"Perhaps, Mr. Boyland, but I am happy to be working on the right side of the law. I have no desire to end up behind bars."

We all shook hands and left the document shop for Lindsay's office. We thanked him for the tour and he told Mike he would keep him informed on the progress of confirming and relocating the remaining possible targets.

"What do you guys think?" Mike asked as we drove down I-95.

"I think we should move Stefan Konopka and his seven forgers right up to the top of the background checks," I said.

"So you didn't believe him when he said he didn't keep records of his work?"

"No fucking way."

* * *

Stefan Konopka went back to his desk and drew in a deep breath. Although Lindsay had introduced these three *gentlemen* as Mr. So-and-So, there was no doubt in his mind they were cops, probably Feds. He had to get to Rowan right away, and thankfully, it was lunch time.

Twenty minutes later, sandwich and soda in hand, Stefan bypassed the cafeteria and found his car in the parking lot. He turned on the ignition to generate some heat and dialed the cell phone Rowan had provided. His call was picked up on the second ring with a, "Yes?"

"Me," he said.

"What's up?"

"Three cops were nosing around my area today asking all kinds of questions about my operation."

"Did you handle it okay?"

"I think so, but maybe we better speed things up."

"You may be right. I'm out of town, but I'll call as soon as I get back and we'll set up a meet."

"Okay, but I think maybe you should bring the rest of the names with you if you have them."

"We'll see. Talk to you soon."

When he hung up, John Rowan knew what he had to do – convince his boss to let him finish the list as soon as he could, although the normally careful planning to make them seem like accidents would have to be sacrificed. And to also convince Monaghan to allow him to take out the connecting link – Stefan Konopka.

And when Stefan hung up he also knew what he would have to do. Stefan realized once he had supplied the remaining copies of the driver's licenses he would no doubt be whacked, but he had a plan – a carefully thought-out plan – and as soon as he collected the final payments for the last three, he would put that plan into action. He was, after all, the Master Document Maker, wasn't he?

*   *   *

Richard Mangan, the real name of Rowan/Brady/Johnson, and several more aliases, did not look forward to meeting his boss at all. Not only did Bradley Monaghan distrust the phone system, he distrusted *everything*, especially electronic monitoring devices – bugs – in all their shapes and forms, and Mangan grimaced in anticipation as he ascended the thirty-two story office/condo building to its top floor.

He greeted the movie-star-looking blond receptionist, Samantha, and she gave him a dazzling capped-teeth smile. "Good morning, Mr. Mangan. You remember where to go, right?"

"Of course," he said as he headed down the hall to room 3316. When he entered he was patted down by two men, and then they all proceeded to a gym-like locker room where he removed all his clothes and placed them in an unlocked locker. He took a bathrobe and slippers from the locker and one of the men said, pointing to a door at the far end of the room, "Go right in, Mr. Mangan. The doctor is awaiting you."

Richard knew while he was being examined by the doctor – a real one – the two men would be scrutinizing and electronically analyzing all his clothing, his shoes, his wallet, and his keys, for hidden listening devices. He understood the organization's precautions, but the body cavity search he was about to undergo, was a bit over the top.

When Dr. Feelgood finished checking every orifice in his body – his mouth, ears, belly button and rectum – he searched his external body with a bright light and passed an electronic device slowly over his entire frame, including under his scrotum. This was done, Mangan figured, to detect any possible hidden microchips capable of transmitting a voice signal. Satisfied, the doctor said, "Fine, Mr. Mangan, you can get dressed now."

"Thanks, Doc. Now seriously, how is my prostate doing?"

"Having urination or sexual problems?"

"No, but I'm in my forties, and I know these suckers start to enlarge."

"It felt perfectly normal. Don't worry about it."

"Thanks again," Mangan said as he headed for the door.

Ten minutes later, fully dressed once again, he was escorted into Bradley Monaghan's huge, plush office with its three-corner view of Las Vegas and its environs. "How are you, Richard?" Monaghan asked, getting up from behind his glowing ebony desk and coming over to shake hands. "No problems, I trust?"

"I hope not, sir, but I wouldn't bother you if things were going perfectly smooth."

"Good, you remembered my wish to hear about possible problems immediately – before they become big ones. Go ahead."

Mangan explained the situation and concluded, "I'd like your permission to speed up the process. Konopka will try to get me the remaining names as fast as he can as soon as you give them to me."

Monaghan walked over to stare out the window pondering the situation, a frown on his handsome face, but a picture of coolness in his green eyes and his perfect posture. He turned to Mangan and said, "Let me check with Mr. Big. Have Samantha show you to an empty office and ask her to order whatever food you want delivered there. She'll come get you after I've spoken with him."

Just as Mangan had done, Bradley Monaghan wasted no time in bringing the bad news to his boss. Jordan Bigelow assessed the situation, asked one question about how long the Marshals might take to relocate the remaining six and said, "Have your man do it. Killing them is the main thing. It may be better to do it like a regular hit rather than these staged accidents, which are taking too damn long. The sooner the better."

"Fine, Mr. Big, I'll transmit your wishes to him now."

"Oh, Brad?"

"Yes?"

"I appreciate you not pressing me for further details of this operation. You will know all there is to know in due time."

Samantha brought Richard Mangan back to Monaghan's office before his food had been delivered. "Richard, Mr. Big agrees we should speed up the process. Here are the last three names."

"Yes, sir. I'll get on it right away."

"No questions?"

"No, sir," he replied not wishing to unnecessarily jeopardize his fee of a hundred grand per kill with a big mouth.

"And Richard, after Konopka gives you those names and locations you know what must be done?"

"Yes, sir."

"I do not want to see you again until you come bearing news of the complete and total success of your mission. Understood?"

"I certainly do, sir. I will not disappoint you."

Richard placed the call to Konopka as soon as he left the building.

* * *

Stefan Konopka would have no trouble getting the last three names for Rowan – he had them stored on his home computer. He was a sixteen-year employee at the Marshal's service, with his last ten as the manager of his department. For those ten years he had copied the front side of every driver's license prepared by him and his co-workers. This was accomplished by secreting a digital camera in the projection unit that displayed the finished license magnified on a large screen where he would check it for minor errors in typeface or copy placement. Once a week he would remove the data card from the camera, place it in his sock and take it home to transfer the photos to his laptop computer, returning the card the next day.

Stefan had a lucrative side business necessitated by his gambling addiction and would use the license data to create phony ones for his on-line customer base, working strictly by referrals. That Boyland guy didn't know how close he was when he mentioned Times Square, for that was exactly where Stefan began his counterfeiting trade. But a close call with the New York cops, and a wife with a child on the way, dampened his thieving nature, and he fortunately found a steady position where his talents could be legally utilized.

Now it was beginning to unravel, and he visualized the future unfolding of events. He would meet Rowan and give him the names in return for another

$15,000. As soon as he left the restaurant he figured his days were numbered. Maybe Rowan would have guys waiting right there, or at his house when he arrived back home. But Stefan would outsmart them. He would park outside the restaurant, getting there early to ensure getting a close parking space, and scouting the area thoroughly for any surveillance. When he left, he would not drive home. He would check for tailing vehicles before driving to a motel a hundred miles away where his wife and children, complete with all their new documents, awaited him. The next morning they would all drive to a nondescript town somewhere in the Midwest, and live happily ever after in their own self-made Witsec program. That is, unless Marian said no.

* * *

Richard Mangan was in the airport lounge awaiting the boarding of his flight back to D.C. when his cell phone rang. Mitch said, "Can't find my guy."

"What?"

"Gone from the location. Looks like he moved out in a hurry a couple days ago."

"Shit!"

"What do you want me to do?"

Pausing a moment, Richard said, "Take this info down." He gave Mitch the location of the man he was supposed to hit himself saying, "Good hunting." He disconnected and called Rusty. "How are things going?"

"Not good, Boss. Looks like he booked."

So the cops figured it out, Mangan thought, but the fact the two had gotten away was not the news he wanted to bring to Monaghan. Nor would he. He needed a plan B, and the long plane ride back should be enough time to figure out what plan B was.

He hoped.

Chapter 12

After Richard Mangan left, Monaghan returned to his desk and sat behind it with steepled hands touching his pursed lips. In the old gangland parlance his title would have been *consigliere*, but now it was *first assistant* to the *chairman*. In either case, the position was the closest, and most trusted, to the boss. But something troubled Monaghan about this whole operation, the chief thing being he was unaware of the end game.

His orders were to employ the right people to terminate the targets whose names were on the list Bigelow personally handed him. And when that was accomplished, those *right people* would also be eliminated. The operational details were left entirely to him, and soon his mission would be accomplished. What then?

Whenever he broached the subject to Bigelow he would get a smile and a dismissive wave of the hand, "Oh, big things, Brad. Big things. Don't you worry, the details are still being worked on. Just take care of your end, and you'll be pleased with what follows. Extremely pleased."

Details still being worked on? By whom? Wasn't that his job? Why was he being kept in the dark? Then a thought hit him, and it sent a shiver throughout his body. After the *right people* were terminated, would he be next?

* * *

It was time for me and Spider to go home. There was nothing more we could do. The background checks on Stefan Konopka and his seven co-workers had come up with a big fat zero. No past criminal history, no credit problems – nothing. But that was to be expected as they were all thoroughly screened before their initial employment, and since that time no negative information had been added to their files. "Something still bothers me about this Konopka," I said.

"Like what?" Mike asked.

"I don't know. He has access to all the documents he ever worked on."

"So what? Spider said. "He has no access to the database. Doesn't have a terminal in his area."

"Yeah, I remember. Maybe he memorizes the stuff. Ah, I don't know. How about tailing him awhile?"

"To what end, Danny?"

"To follow him to a meeting with Brady/Johnson where he recites the names and locations of the targets."

"If he did, wouldn't all the deaths have been accomplished?" Mike asked. "Why are they being spaced out?"

"Well, only five have been killed. Maybe he can only memorize five at a time."

"Give me a break," Spider said. "You're grasping at straws."

"Yeah, I guess so. We'll just have to wait for the next occurrence, which won't happen for months – if it happens at all."

We shook hands, and as we left I said, "Mike, keep us in the loop. If anything breaks we'll be back here in a flash."

"I know you will, but I'm not optimistic about anything."

"Hey," Spider said. "Tell Allison we said Merry Christmas."

"And the same to you, Mike," I said.

"Thanks, guys," he said with a wry smile. "Merry Christmas, indeed."

* * *

The day after Detective Tara Brown Boyland and FBI Agent Vince Genova returned to New York they got together at Vince's Manhattan office to pool their knowledge and information about the Las Vegas mob. Vince spread out the latest updated organization chart on a large table. Pointing to the top photograph he said, "Their Don is Jordan Carter Bigelow, although he is officially known as The Chairman."

"Chairman of what?" Tara asked. "I mean what is their group called?"

"It's called the LV Betterment Group," Vince said.

"Give me a break! And what are they bettering, besides themselves?"

"No one, but they put on a good appearance, and they do donate to many charities and civic associations."

"Where does their money come from?"

"The standard mob streams of revenue – gambling, prostitution, narcotics and loan sharking."

"But aren't gambling and prostitution legal in Nevada?"

"In some areas, but not all, and they're tightly regulated. There is always a demand for both vices outside the legal realm."

They went over the photos on the chart with an eye toward getting lucky. Could one of the twenty or so mob members depicted be the elusive Brady/Johnson? Each photo had the person's name, rank in the organization, and date and place of birth. Tara said, "None of these resemble our guy at all, but the top guy sure is one handsome dude. Reminds me of somebody."

"Richard Conte," Vince said.

"Who?"

"An old-time movie actor from the forties and fifties – way before your time. Usually played a bad guy, but had great looks – dark hair and the cleft in his chin."

"And these titles they give themselves – first assistant, section leader, account executive – a big reach for legitimacy I presume."

"Notice anything unusual about their names?"

Tara scanned the chart once more and said, "No, other than most of them sounding generic. But I did notice a couple of brown-skinned brothers which, I guess, is somewhat unusual."

"Correct, but look again. None of the names, except one of the three obvious Hispanic ones, ends with a vowel."

Tara looked again and said, "You're right. Why do you think they discriminate against Hawaiians?"

They both laughed and Vince said, "There are paisanos in that group – seven to be exact – but they have changed their names – anglicized them." Pointing to a photo near the top he said, "This guy – Joseph Perner – used to be Joseph Perna. And this guy down here – Michael Fortune – used to be Michael 'the Razor' Fortuna."

"They seem to have done a decent camouflage job, but I bet they remain killers and crooks, one and all."

"Yes, and I think they have everyone fooled but us."

"Where do they hang out?"

"They own a big building on the Strip. It's not a hotel and has no casino. Strictly luxury apartments, condos and office space. The LV Betterment Group occupies the top two or three floors."

"Does your Las Vegas office monitor the entrance?"

"Indeed it does."

"Can you have them send us the past video discs for a look see?"

"I placed that request before you arrived."

"Proves once again, Vince – great minds think alike."

On her drive from Manhattan back to her Mineola office, something nagged at the back of Tara's mind, something with the photo array of the Las Vegas mob. It wouldn't come, so she knew to put the thought away. When it popped, if it ever did, it would pop when it wanted to. She turned her thoughts to her husband. He should be home later, and after discussing the case – she was real interested now – it would be time to catch up on some long-delayed lovemaking.

* * *

The meeting between Richard Mangan, known as John Rowan to Stefan Konopka, was set for that evening at a restaurant they had never utilized before, a local sports bar about twenty miles outside of D.C., in a quiet Virginia suburb. It was a relatively slow sports night with the ten television sets showing routine NBA and NHL games of minimal importance. Mangan had come up with his plan B, but he needed Konopka's assistance. He hoped his direct approach would secure that help – for both their sakes.

Although Konopka had convinced his wife to take part in his escape plan, he had been forced to scale it down. Marian would only agree to meet him at a much closer motel with the children and with enough clothing for a week. "You have to convince me we must leave our house permanently, Stefan," she had said. "Perhaps things may not be as bad as you think."

If she only knew. But having chosen to give her minimal details of his involvement with his "side job," he reluctantly agreed with her assessment and modified his escape plan accordingly. And maybe, prayerfully, Marian was right, and things were not as bad as he imagined. He would know shortly as he checked his watch and entered the restaurant at 7:00 p.m.

He had gotten to the area as planned an hour before and got a parking spot directly across the street from the restaurant's front door. He had gotten out of his car and walked the streets, checking for suspicious persons sitting in parked cars where they could observe bar. He had found none, and now, forty-five minutes later, he shook hands with John Rowan. John said, "Stefan, we have a problem."

"What...?"

"Let's order a drink and I'll tell you all about it, and how we can solve it."

Konopka began to sweat and hid his hands in his lap, clutching them together to quiet their trembling. When the waitress appeared, Rowan ordered a double Chivas scotch on the rocks and Stefan ordered a double Stoli the same way. Neither one spoke again until their drinks arrived. Rowan picked up his glass and motioned for Stefan to do the same. They clinked glasses and Rowan said, "To us, Stefan."

They both took a sizeable swig and set their glasses down on the table. Rowan said, "I'm going to give it to you straight and honest, and then we'll figure out what to do next, okay?"

"Okay," Stefan said, wondering what *they* would have to figure out next.

"There's a briefcase under our table which you will take with you when you leave. In it is the $15,000 for the remaining three names. I assume you have them for me, correct?"

"Right here," Stefan said patting his jacket above its inside pocket and relaxing a bit with the news of the money.

"Also in that briefcase is all the information you need to make me a complete set of documents for my new identity."

"Are you in trouble, John?"

"Maybe."

"Am I also in trouble?"

"Maybe. Here's what happened. As I was leaving to come back here, I found out two of the persons whose names you gave me last time, were not at their location. Since then, I discovered the other one also was not where he was supposed to be. All three houses were vacant and, of course, no known forwarding addresses."

"The cops are on to us."

"Yes and no. I believe they have figured out the likely targets by scrutinizing their database and comparing profiles. Depending on how wide or narrow their comparisons were, they could have come up with less than, or more than, the remaining six names."

"They obviously found the last three."

"Correct, and we'll know more when we get these three names out there for further necessary action."

"You mean you're still going through with this? Isn't that dangerous?"

"Yes, but not any more dangerous than disappointing my employer – *our* employer."

"Shit!"

"Apt description of our situation, my friend. How about another round before we order food."

"Good idea, but maybe I won't eat tonight."

"Let's not panic. Let's weigh our options."

"I'm listening."

"First option – you take the money, make my documents, make documents for you and your family and we both disappear. Of course, you destroy whatever means you employed to obtain the names for me. We can be gone within the week."

"I was counting on more money – a lot more money – when I made the break," Konopka said.

"That's still a possibility. In fact, that's option number two."

Their second drink arrived and Rowan encouraged Konopka to order something to eat and he signaled to the waitress telling her, "just a cold antipasto for now."

Rowan ordered a bowl of penne with red clam sauce and after the waitress left said, "Stefan, let's assume we can't find any of these six guys. The Feds have to provide them with brand new identities. And who makes those identities? You!"

"But they are onto us."

"No, they are onto *something*, but not us."

"Not yet."

"Correct. After you and your team make those new documents, get the information to me all at once. That's a quick thirty grand for you. Then never go back to work and disappear with your family using your new identities. I'll put on a few more guys, and we'll take care of the six as fast as we can. And each completion is another twenty grand in cash which I'll wire to you, or personally give to you."

"But then you'll know my whereabouts and new identity."

"And you'll know mine, won't you? You're making my new identity after all."

"But…"

"Stefan, it's you and me – *only* you and me. We have to trust each other completely. It's the only way we can make this work."

The waitress arrived with their food and Stefan thought of his additional take of over a hundred grand. In cash. Tax free.

"So what do you say, Stefan?"

"It's a deal," he said passing the three names over to Rowan.

"By the time you make my documents, these names will be checked out, and appropriate action taken – or not. I'll call you to set up our next meeting."

They finished their meal in silence, and after Rowan paid their bill, they left the restaurant, each wondering if they could pull this off and come out alive.

When Konopka arrived at the motel he greeted his wife and children with a big smile and hugs for all. He said, "You were right, Marian, things were not bad at all. Let us spend the night here, and after a big breakfast tomorrow morning, we will return to our home."

Marian broke into tears and hugged Stefan tightly. "Thank God," she said, "for us, and for our children."

Chapter 13

"Welcome home dear," Tara said as I came through the door.

"It's good to be back, but I'm disappointed with the investigation."

"I'll get us a drink, and you can fill me in on the details."

When I finished, Tara told me of her meeting with Vince Genova and her uneasy feeling about something in the Las Vegas mob's organization chart. I said, "I'd like to see it. I'm...we're...all going crazy trying to figure out what the hell is going on here. Why these five murders? What's the real connection among the victims? Is the Vegas mob calling the shots? And if so, why?"

"We have to stop thinking directly about this for awhile. Let all the facts swim around in our brain. We need a distraction, and I know what it is."

"Oh, and what are you planning?"

"Christmas shopping. We only have a week left, and we have to get your kids their stuff and drive it down to Virginia."

"Did you get me my gift yet?" I asked.

"No, as I'm sure you have not gotten anything for me. But if you join me in the bedroom I will give you a great pre-Christmas welcome home gift that will put a big smile on your face."

"Oh, you naughty little elf. Go, I'm right behind you."

* * *

We both went back to our jobs and planned to take two full days off together early the following week to do our shopping in Manhattan. And we both hoped by then Vince Genova had discovered something on the videos from the mob's building entrance in Las Vegas. We brought the bosses up-to-date on the case and Finn said, "When are you two going back there?"

"After New Year's," I said.

"You both don't look too happy," Lieutenant Veltri said.

"It's frustrating, Boss," Spider said. "Too many unanswered questions."

"I understand, but you two are too close to see the individual trees in the forest. Let me throw something out there, okay?"

"Sure, Pete," I said.

"When you get back down there with Mike, instead of looking at possible connections among the victims, which you already know…"

"Excuse me?" Spider said. "We already know?"

"Sure, they all ratted someone out who went to jail."

"Yeah, but…"

"Look away from the victims and look at the people they turned on. Find the connections with the big shots that went away. Why were they embezzling huge amounts of money from their firms and clients? Weren't their salaries, bonuses and stock options enough to keep them comfortable and happy? Why the need for greed?"

I slapped my hand on my forehead and said, "We never thought about that. Jeez thanks, Boss."

"Now we know why you're the boss and we're merely a couple of grunts," Spider said.

"Don't be too hard on yourselves," Father Finn said. "Sometimes even ace investigators like you two get too focused on one item."

"And don't press too hard on that either," Veltri said. "It may turn out to be a zero. Maybe call Mike now and run it by him. Maybe they can use their whiz-bang computers down there to turn something up."

When I got back to my desk, and before we had a chance to call Mike, Spider poked me in the arm and whispered, "Here comes the novelist."

I looked to my right and there he came – Doctor Death – bearing a big grin and a sheaf of papers in his big paw. He slapped them on my desk and said, "Done, Danny. Three chapters. You gotta read them for me."

"Sure Bernie, but not now," I said as I picked up the pages. "I'm busy on a case and have to make some calls. I'll take them home and read them tonight. I promise."

"Great, I can't wait to hear what you think about them."

As an afterthought I said, "And I'll have Tara read them also. *Two* opinions for the price of one."

"Terrific! Say hello and thanks to Tara."

"Will do, Bernie. She'll be thrilled with this, I'm sure."

With Bernie happily gone back to his desk, Spider and I placed the call to Mike. "Agent Havlek," he said in a weary voice.

"Ace investigators Batman and Robin reporting in, Superman. What's new?"

"Nothing, and I guess that's good news since no one else has been murdered."

"Are all the rest still safely squirreled away and protected around the clock?" Spider asked.

"Yes, and beginning tomorrow the US Marshal's document workers will begin preparing their new papers as a priority task."

"Good, now listen to a suggestion Pete Veltri just made…"

"I like it," Mike said when we finished. "I'll get on it right away, and tell Pete thanks."

"Listen Mike, I know you didn't agree with me on this Konopka guy, but I think you guys should start tailing him as soon as his section starts work on the documents. And call me paranoid, but as soon as they are all re-located provide them with round-the-clock protection. I mean a couple of your agents inside the house and some agents and locals outside the house."

"So you think Konopka is the guy who is going to give the new info to our mystery man of many names, who is then going to carry out the hits?"

I took a deep breath and said, "Yes Mike, that's what I think, because I can come up with absolutely nothing else at all."

"I agree with my partner," Spider said. "Unless you have a different theory."

"No, I don't, I'm sorry to say. What else is happening?"

"Tara and I are waiting on a call from Vince Genova. We'll stop in to see him next week one way or the other. I want to see Vince's mob chart of the Las Vegas operation. Something about it is bothering Tara. Maybe I can figure it out."

"Okay, let's all take a step back, relax a little, and try to enjoy the holidays."

Spider and I looked at each other with raised eyebrows and Spider said, "Good advice, Mike. We'll talk only if something important comes up. Merry Christmas to you and Allison, from both of us."

"Relax?" I said after Spider hung up. "Superman can't relax. Superman's lucky if he can *sleep*."

* * *

"You promised Bernie I'd do what?" my dear wife asked in a threatening tone of voice.

"Come on Tara, he's an old friend, and you worked with him for years."

"Old friend? I had to work with that smelly old degenerate for way too long. He was *never* my friend."

"I know, I know, but do it for me. Please."

"I'll tell you what. After dinner we'll sit down and you read it to me. That way we'll hear it together."

"Deal," I said.

We took our glasses of wine into the den and I took the chapters out of my briefcase. I put on my 1.5 diopter drugstore cheaters I had recently been forced to use to assist my forty-plus year old eyes, and began to read, noting the first sentence was intact as I had first seen it - *The revolving door of the criminal justice system spun crazily on its axis and spit Jimmy "the Nose" Harrington out onto the filthy sidewalk like a huge wad of sticky, brown phlegm...*

"That's disgusting!" Tara exclaimed.

"Yeah, let's hear some more."

"Ugh. Oh, you look sexy in your new specs. Why not take them off and take off the rest of your clothes and..."

"Tara," I interrupted, "please, let's get through this first, okay?"

She grunted something and I began reading again - *It was not the first time that the Nose had been behind bars. The nasty, mother-fucking, perverted cocksucker was a regular inhabitant of the slimy cells of Riker's Island...*

"Oh, my God," Tara said, "I can't listen to any more of this crap."

She was right, of course, so I said, "All right, I'll read the rest and give him my opinion, and I'll tell him you agreed with me."

"Thank you," she said getting up from the sofa. "I'll clean up the kitchen while you enjoy the maniacal mutterings of Doctor Death."

The narrative got worse and there were far too many typos and cross outs, yet ironically there was *something* in that mess of profanity and incoherence, something *real*. But, as the editors would say – *it needs a lot of work*. Now, how do I gently explain the facts of life to Bernie Gallagher without getting my desk turned over on me? Yes, the smelly giant had done it once before.

* * *

Fortunately, Doctor Death was catching cases the next day and was out of the office on a routine homicide when I got into the office. After I told Spider about Bernie's attempts he said, "What are you going to tell him? You better go nice and easy so he doesn't turn your desk over on you again."

"You remember that?"

"Everyone here remembers that, and you were only kidding with him. This is serious shit to him."

"I think I have a way out."

"What is it?"

"You'll hear it when I tell him later. When you're standing at my side. When I'm also standing, and not sitting behind my desk."

"Hope it works, partner. Whatever it is you got up your sleeve."

"Me, too."

About an hour later Vince Genova called and said, "We got your guy in Vegas. Some excellent video. We're making stills now."

"Tara and I were going to stop by to see you next week, but we'll be on our way in a few minutes. Spider, too."

"Fresh coffee will be waiting."

"Saddle up, Spider," I called out. "We're heading into the city. Call Tara and tell her we'll pick her up in five minutes. I'll go tell Finn."

"Weren't you guys supposed to give this case a rest for a couple of weeks?" the good sergeant asked.

"Yeah, but…"

Finn put his hand up to stop me. "I know," he said, "I used to be an ace investigator myself one time."

* * *

"What did Bernie say when you told him *our* opinion of his drivel?" Tara asked as Spider steered us toward Manhattan on the Long Island Expressway.

"He was out on a case. I'll tell him when I see him."

"Postponing the inevitable."

"I got it covered. I'll let the big guy down gently."

"I hope so. Don't want no husband of mine with a bunch of broken bones."

True to his word, Special Agent Vince Genova presented us with fresh coffee and we got right down to work. Vince said, "We went back a full year on both the Miami mob's building and the Vegas building. Nothing at all in Miami, but we got three hits on your guy in Vegas."

"Three?" I said. "How far apart?"

"The first was about ten months before the first of your murders was committed, the second was three months after that, and the last visit was two days ago. Watch."

Vince darkened the room and played the video on a four by four foot screen. We viewed the front of a man walking into the front door of the building housing the LV Betterment Group, his face clearly visible by the hidden camera. Vince froze the tape.

"That's our guy, Brady," Spider said.

"No doubt about it," I said. "Looks just like the composites we made."

Vince showed us the videos of Brady's next two visits and then brought the lights back up. "Great work, Vince," I said. "Let's call Mike right away."

"Of course," he said, "but what are we going to tell him?"

We all looked at Vince in surprise and he said, "We have Brady entering a building. Period. There are a lot of offices in there other than those belonging to the mob. Once he went in that door, we have no idea where he went."

"He went to the mob to get his marching orders and to report on his results," Spider said.

"Prove it," Vince said.

"We don't have much of a parade here," Tara said, "and you're raining on it."

"Just being factual, Tara."

We all reflected on the *facts* as we sipped our coffee and I said, "Let's run it by Mike. He needs something positive, even if it goes nowhere."

Mike Havlek appeared happy with the findings. "At least it's some indication of a connection. Now how do we locate Brady? Can we stake out the building in the hope he will return soon?"

"No," I said. "Follow Konopka. He'll lead you right to him. Brady won't go back to Vegas until he, and whoever works for him, kills all the remaining targets."

"Talk about a big deductive leap," Vince said.

"Got anything better we should do? We are all open to suggestions."

Vince looked at me, narrowing his eyes and said, "Danny may be right. Follow Konopka."

After Mike hung up, Vince put the organization chart of the Vegas mob on the conference room table and we all looked it over. I said, "Anything pop yet, Tara?"

She studied it hard and said, "Vince, this Bigelow, what was the movie actor's name he resembled?"

"Richard Conte."

"From the Forties and Fifties?"

"Correct."

She stared hard at Bigelow's picture and suddenly her face lit up with a smile. She covered the writing below the picture with her hand and said, "Each of you please guess how old Bigelow is."

We all looked at the picture and I said, "Forty-nine."

"Yeah," Spider said. "No more than fifty, fifty-two."

"Vince?"

"I know where you are going, and if I didn't know what your hand is covering, I would agree with Danny and Spider."

"But you *do* know his real age."

"Yes, the date of birth you are covering is June 17, 1942. Which makes Jordan Carter Bigelow seventy-five years old, but somehow I never picked up on this before. His date of birth is a statistic, like his telephone number. Maybe I am getting too old for this job, missing something like that."

We all stared at the photo in disbelief as Tara removed her hand. I said, "Don't be so hard on yourself, Vince. We all miss the forest for the trees once in a while, as my boss recently reminded me and Spider. How current is this photo?"

"One month ago. Taken as he entered a local Las Vegas restaurant."

"So we have the head of the mob, who is seventy-five years old, and looks twenty-five years younger," I said. "What does that do for our investigation?"

"I haven't a clue," Vince said.

"Maybe he's a dedicated fitness guru," Spider said, "and had cosmetic surgery."

"Which appears nowhere in the extensive dossier we have on him," Vince said.

"Then how does he do it?"

"Maybe he found the fountain of youth," Tara said. "Let's ask him. I could use a drink or two of that stuff myself."

Later on, many weeks later on, I would have occasion to remind Tara of that fanciful statement she had just casually made.

Chapter 14

Bernie Gallagher was sitting at his desk when Spider and I returned to the office from Manhattan. He jumped up and ran over to me with an apprehensive look on his broad face and said, "Well, whaddja think?"

"Let me get some coffee, and I'll meet you at your desk in a couple of minutes."

"Okay," he said scurrying away.

In the coffee room Spider said, "You're on your own on this one, partner."

"You're backing out on me you cowardly rat? Some partner."

"You said you could handle it. Good luck."

I took my mug of coffee and Bernie's chapters and pulled up a chair across from him at his desk. I said, "Not bad, Bernie, but it needs some work."

"Like what?" he asked, his eyes growing hard.

"You have too much good stuff packed in too small a space."

"Hunh?"

"It's non-stop action and non-stop profanity. You have to space that stuff out."

"I don't know how to do that."

"Let me help you. First you have to read more novels like the type you want to write. Then you have to decide if you want to write a novel or a true crime story based on your actual cases. You have a lot of them; I know that for a fact. The case where you got the nickname Doctor Death comes to mind."

"Yeah," he said starting to smile.

"And here's how you would write that." I handed him a copy of Allison's prize-winning newspaper series based on the Frankie Chandler case – my case – from awhile ago. "Read this, Bernie. It's all factual, but it has a great grasp of story-telling woven into it. That's a good model to use."

"Thanks, Danny, but what if I wanted to stay with the novel?"

"Read these ten books and get ideas on how it's done." I handed him a sheet of paper with the titles of books by Lehane, Grisham, Connelly, DeMille, Patterson and five others listed on it. "And when you find the one you really like – what you would like to write – read a few more from that author."

"Seems like a lotta work."

"It is, Bernie. Writing a book isn't easy. You have to learn the techniques. Re-write those three chapters, and you'll be on your way to fame and fortune."

He brightened up a bit and said, "Thanks for the advice, Danny. Are you back in the squad for good now?"

"No, I'm taking a couple days off this week and next, and then me and Spider are flying back to D.C."

"How long before you wrap up that caper and get back here again?"

"I wish I knew, Bernie. The damn thing gets more complicated as we go along."

I left a somewhat dejected Doctor Death looking at what I had given him and spent the rest of the day cleaning up some old cases and typing up supplementary reports. Tara and I would shop tomorrow for a final few items then head down to Virginia to see my kids for Christmas – a trip I was, and was not, looking forward to.

* * *

As I said before, I had been in the Nassau Homicide Squad for a little over a year when I caught my first big case, the case that ruined my marriage and destroyed my family. After my conviction was overturned I was re-instated to the Force, but Jeanie had divorced me and moved to Virginia with the kids. She never spoke a word to me again and turned Pat and Kelly against me. I deserved no better, but I persisted and gradually developed a relationship with my kids as the years went by. The ties got stronger after Jean died of cancer, but her parents, who I allowed to raise our children, still harbored animosity towards me. And, truth be told, I couldn't blame them one bit.

So, as we drove down Interstate 81, Tara said to me, "How do you think the Schneider's will treat you this visit?"

"Well, Bill and Doris invited me into their backyard when I visited at Patrick's request that one time. Since then I arranged to meet the kids away from there."

"They haven't softened since you allowed them to raise the kids?"

"I don't feel quite the bitterness in their voices now when I call to speak with the kids, but I don't have high hopes for this visit. We'll pick Pat and Kelly up and take them to our hotel on Christmas Eve day and give them their gifts there."

"And the next day we get to spend Christmas alone in a hotel in downtown Roanoke, or drive to Washington early?"

"I'm sorry about that, but I'm glad you came with me, or we'd both be alone."

"Maybe the Schneider's will relent and invite us for Christmas dinner," she said poking me in the ribs.

"Do you still believe in Santa Claus?"

* * *

We pulled up in front of the house at the prearranged time of two o'clock and, as we got out of the car, Patrick and Kelly came running out of the front door, a shopping bag in Pat's hand, to greet us. We all exchanged "Merry Christmases."

Bill Schneider then walked out the door and said, "When are you bringing them back?"

"After dinner," I said. "No later than ten."

"Okay. Uh, if you have no plans tomorrow, Doris and I would like to have you both over for Christmas dinner."

I was speechless, and as I fumbled for words Tara said, "We'd love to, Mr. Schneider. Thank you."

"About two o'clock?"

"That will be fine," Tara said. "Merry Christmas."

Bill Schneider paused for a moment. "Merry Christmas, Tara…you too, Danny."

"Merry Christmas, Bill," I said as he turned to walk in the front door, and I thought I had seen his shoulders flinch a little when I said it.

We had a great time with the kids and they thoroughly enjoyed our gifts – computer games and gift cards to their favorite stores. And they had both chipped in to buy Tara a beautiful sweater and a waterproof golf jacket for me. We caught up with each other's lives and Patrick showed a lot of interest in the case I was working on. "Wow," he said, "a lot different from the Frankie Chandler case."

"Yes, they are all different and difficult in their own special way. This one, though, seems particularly baffling."

"Are you going back to Washington after Christmas?"

"Yes, on January second."

"Um, do you think you could get me up to visit the FBI Lab and Headquarters?"

"You're really interested in seeing it?"

"Oh, yeah!"

"Me, too," Kelly said.

"I can arrange that. We'll run it by your grandparents tomorrow. Now, are you two ready and hungry enough for dinner?"

"Yes," they said.

"You pick the place, and it better not be Burger King or Pizza Hut."

"Gam Wah's Asian Kitchen," Patrick said. "I'll show you how to get there."

"You both like Asian food at your age?"

"Love it," Kelly said, "and you can eat all you want. Dessert, too."

"By all means show us the way," Tara said.

Four stuffed and satisfied people sat in the car as I drove back to the Schneider's house, arriving a few minutes before ten. Pat and Kelly walked up to the front door with their gifts and turned and waved good-bye as they entered the house. "I'm a bit tense about tomorrow," I said to Tara as we pulled away.

"I understand. What happens, happens. Let's be optimistic and hope for the best."

* * *

As it was Christmas, one of the two days we fallen Catholics attend mass, I convinced my Baptist wife to join me for the service. The ten o'clock mass was jammed to the aisles, and I figured as long as I was there, I'd offer up some prayers and some money, of course, for those near and dear to me. I prayed for happiness for my children and my wife. I prayed for good health and long life for Willy and Edna Edwards and for Bill and Doris Schneider. And, yes, I prayed the soul of my ex-wife, Jean, was no longer tormented and filled with hate. Lastly, I prayed for forgiveness for my past betrayal of her.

We packed up our things at the hotel and checked out around 1:00 p.m. I said, "Do you mind stopping at the cemetery on the way over to the Schneider's?"

"Of course not," Tara said deducing I was in a penitential mood.

We stopped at an open roadside florist and bought a Christmas wreath for Jean's grave. It was a gray, chilly day and I placed the wreath at the side of her headstone, noting the large, fragrant Christmas grave blanket spread out in front of it. I bowed my head and said an *Our Father* and Tara reached up to wipe a tear from my cheek. "What a rat I was to abandon her for Niki."

"The past is the past. Niki Wells is dead, and Jean Boyland is dead. And I'm here for you – now and always."

I hugged her and said, "And I'm happy for that. I don't know what I would have done without you."

"Well, for starters, if I wasn't there with you to shoot that bitch, she'd have shot you to death."

"Not doubt at all. Ready to go to the Schneider's?"

"I'll be truthful; I'm not looking forward to it."

"Me neither."

* * *

We arrived a few minutes after two and were greeted by the Schneider's with a warm smile – no hugs or handshakes – and an offer to take our coats. The house was tastefully decorated, and the scent of the fresh pine Christmas tree mixed with that of the roasting turkey, brought back memories of joyous Christmases past. Bill offered us drinks, and Tara and I opted for white wine as did Doris. Bill had a scotch and soda and the kids had cokes, and Doris brought out trays of goodies to nibble on. She said to the kids, "Don't you two fill up on those now. We have a big dinner ahead of us."

"Don't worry, Grandma," Patrick said. "I can handle it."

I looked at my son and agreed with him. At sixteen he was five foot ten, but a skinny 130 pounds. The older he got the more he resembled me – dark hair, brown eyes, and the same shaped face with the cleft in the chin. I wondered if that resemblance bothered his grandparents.

Kelly, on the other hand, was a duplicate of Jean – blonde, blue eyes and petite with a dimpled smile. I wondered if *that* resemblance bothered the Schneider's, too.

"Did you go to Mass this morning?" Doris asked.

"Yes, I did and I dragged my Baptist wife along with me kicking and screaming."

Bill chuckled and said, "You should feel right at home here in Virginia, Tara. We're in the Bible belt – I swear there's a Baptist church on every corner."

"So I noticed. We had a hard time finding St. Clement's in downtown."

"We go to Saint Teresa's," Doris said. "It's much closer and near to the cemetery. We stop there often."

I was feeling a little uncomfortable with the way this conversation was going. Were they setting me up for a good old-fashioned tongue lashing? I said, "Yes, we stopped there before we came over. I assume you put that beautiful grave blanket there?"

Doris seemed startled and said, "Yes, we did but why...?"

"Because she was my wife and the mother of my two children and I once loved her very much. I usually stop there when I come to visit the kids."

"And I assume you pray for forgiveness while there?" Bill asked.

Doris shot him a stern look, but Bill's tone of voice had not been stinging or harsh. "Everyday, Bill, whether I'm at the cemetery or not."

I'm not a mind reader, but I believe Bill was thinking, *Well, I'll never forgive you, you son-of-a-bitch*. He looked up at me and said, "A little more wine, Danny?"

"Sure, Bill."

With the tension level now way down, we all enjoyed a sumptuous Christmas dinner of roast turkey, stuffing and too many vegetable side dishes. Our stomachs full, we all had to wait almost two hours before swooping down on the homemade apple and blueberry pies. As we were sipping the last of our coffee Doris said, "Are you driving all the way home tonight?"

"No," Tara said. "We're staying at a friend's house near D.C. He's the FBI agent Danny and I are working with on this case."

Patrick's ears perked up and he said, "I didn't know you were also involved, Tara."

"Oh, yeah," she said and proceeded to tell her part in this investigation.

Patrick said, "Gramps, I asked Dad if I could visit him at FBI Headquarters when he was back working on the case after the New Year. Would that be okay?"

"Don't forget about me," Kelly chimed in.

"I don't see why not," he said.

"In fact," Doris said, maybe Bill and I could drive them up and see some of Washington ourselves."

"You're welcome to see the FBI facilities as well," I said. "I'm sure you would find it fascinating."

"Can you get us in to see the cool parts they don't show the regular tourists?" Patrick asked.

"Pat," Tara said with a chuckle, "your Dad has friends in high places in the FBI."

"Oh?" Bill said.

Tara told them of my relationship with Walt Kobak and that led to the story of the Romen Society investigation, which seemed to fascinate them. By the time we finished talking, it was past six o'clock and we all said our good-byes. On the way out Bill shook my hand and gave Tara a small hug. Doris kissed me on the cheek and hugged Tara. The ice, it seemed, had finally been broken.

Chapter 15

We arrived at Mike and Allison's a little before nine that evening, and they welcomed us to their home with the offer of a drink. "So, how did it go with the Schneider's?" Allison asked.

"Terrific, but we'll get to that later. What's new on the investigation?"

"You're not supposed to talk about that until after Christmas," Allison said with a sly grin. "How about after breakfast?"

"No way, Miss Ace Investigative Reporter. I'm not built that way and neither are you, Mike or Tara. Come on, Superman, spill it."

"Can I have a sip of my drink first?"

"Sure, one taste," Tara said. "Make it quick."

We all laughed, raised our glasses and took a sip. Mike said, "Okay, here is where we are. We have all nine people we identified as possible targets safely squirreled away in safe houses – finally."

"What do you mean by *finally*?" I asked.

"Some of them put up a stink and didn't want to move. We had to convince them they were truly a target. And when we said the safe house was only temporary and new documents for a second location had to be prepared… well, most were not happy campers."

"I can understand that," Tara said. "How is the documentation process going?"

"At a snail's pace, unfortunately."

"I thought this was going to be a priority."

"It was… is, but with Christmas right in the middle of things, and the fact these document makers seem limited to a maximum of nine to ten hours of work…"

"How come?" I asked.

"They start making mistakes. Henry Lindsay is staying on top of the process, and Konopka showed him five errors made by his men in the first three days."

"Ah, yes, our Master Document Maker. Are you tailing him?"

"Around the clock. But so far he goes to work and goes straight home. We figure when he gets all the documents done, he'll make the copies and hand them off. That is, if he's our guy like you believe him to be."

"He's our guy, you can bank on it. When will they be done with them?"

"Around the third or fourth of January."

"Good. Spider and I will be back here on the second. Oh, did your computer section come up with anything based on Pete Veltri's suggestion?"

"All the information is supposed to be on my desk by December 27."

"And when you get that information, you'll call me and Spider, won't you?"

"Of course."

"And did your whiz-bang computer people check out those ninety Marshal's service employees who had access to the original database?" Spider asked.

"Yes."

"And they all came up clean as a whistle or you would have told us otherwise, right Mike?"

"Right, Danny."

"So I say again…"

"Yeah, yeah, I know," Mike said. "Konopka's the guy."

* * *

"I was right," John Rowan said to Stefan Konopka on their throw-away cell phones. "The people in the second batch of three names you gave me were all gone. Their houses vacant. Their whereabouts unknown."

"So, they are onto us – definitely."

"Don't panic, Stefan. The Feds are the ones who are in a panic. They have these people temporarily stashed away somewhere pending their permanent relocation. Your group can expect to be called upon soon to make their new documents. They may give you more than my six depending on their database research."

"I don't want them too soon. I'm still working on my family's documents."

"And mine?"

"Already completed, just as you asked."

"You're a good man, Stefan. Keep the thirty grand I gave you for the six names, although they didn't pan out. And there will be an extra twenty for you for my documents."

"Thank you," Konopka said wondering how much Rowan was getting himself to afford to be so generous.

Three days later, as he was eating lunch in his car, Stefan called Rowan and said, "I was notified by my boss we have nine sets of documents to make as a number one priority. We start one hour early tomorrow morning."

"How long before my six will be ready?"

"A week to ten days."

"We won't talk until we're ready to make the transfer. Fifty grand for everything. Let's hope me and my guys can take care of those six ASAP."

"I hope so too, John," Stefan said thinking of the additional thousands that would come his way if Rowan was successful.

* * *

Stefan Konopka noticed the pickup truck following him on the third day after his group began work on the priority list of nine names. He had been alert for this for a long time and now, with the limited traffic on the road at this early morning hour, he easily spotted the tail.

The pickup truck turned off about halfway to his job but was then replaced by a van with tinted windows. The next day two sedans were used, and the day following the van and pickup truck were back, only this time tailing him to his home. Now that he was sure, he had to call Rowan.

The next day, afraid to call him from his home or from his cell phone while he was going to and from work, Stefan was going to call Rowan as he ate lunch in his car, but then thought better of it. Suppose they had a directional device pointed at his vehicle? Suppose they had bugged it? Turning his collar up against the bitter cold December wind as he walked to the rear of the lot, he dialed Rowan on the throw-away cell phone.

"What's up?" was all Rowan said when he answered.

"I'm being followed. I waited three days to be sure."

"We figured they'd do that. No need to panic. How are the documents coming?"

"Still on schedule, but how am I going to get them to you?"

"Let me think it over. I'll get back to you sometime tomorrow, okay?"

"Yes, John."

After Rowan disconnected he thought long and hard on all the variables involved. This was the end game. He had to get this right, and he realized killing Konopka right after the exchange was no longer a good idea. In fact, having Stefan quit his job and disappear was also no longer feasible. *He had to get this right.* A lot of money would come his way if he completed the six hits. Enough to last him a long, long time.

* * *

Stefan's cell phone rang at the prescribed time and he hurried out of his car and strode several paces away before he answered. "Are you in the clear?"

Stefan looked around. He was at the edge of the parking field now and observed no one sitting in their cars. "Yes," he said.

"Okay. Let's assume they are watching your house and car around the clock. Can they observe your back door?"

"No back door. I have a side door, and I guess they could see me leave it if they were positioned right."

"Could they see you if you climbed out a rear window into your backyard?"

"No way, the yard is surrounded by bushes and a fence."

"Can you hop the fence and make it out to the next street?"

"Yes."

"I checked out the area today. By the way, I noticed no one observing your house, and I made several passes. Here's my plan. Tell me what you think of it. We have to do this right, Stefan."

"Yes, we do. My family's documents are complete, except for the address. I'll have to discuss it with Marian, and I'm dreading that."

"Maybe you don't have to run away, or quit your job after all."

"But the moment one of those guys gets killed, they'll know!"

"Know what? They may suspect you, or your co-workers, but they will never be able to prove anything as long as you deny you were involved. Can you handle that interrogation if it happens?"

"I don't know…yes, I can. I must."

"Good, now here's what we'll do…"

* * *

"Superman on line two for Danny and Spider," Bernie Gallagher shouted. "He wants you to get Pete and Father Finn all on a conference call."

"Thanks, Bernie," I said. "Spider, I'll get the bosses and meet you in there."

When we were all seated around the table with the speakerphone and all the hellos were said, Mike Havlek got right into it. "I got the results on our eleven big shots and pored over their files, and so far the only thing they have in common is the amount of money embezzled. The amount stolen ranged from ten to thirty-five million."

"This is what the head guy alone took?" Pete asked.

"Yes, and of these eleven, five are still in prison – minimum security Federal pens for white-collar criminals – serving various terms."

"And the other six?" Spider asked.

"Served their time and are rehabbed back into society, and dutifully paying their monthly reparations."

"How far does this go back?" Father Finn asked.

"Almost ten years. That was when the first guy was caught. He spent five and a half years in the can."

"So the five still in might be getting out soon?" I asked.

"Yes, the guy in the Holmgren case gets out in six months. The longest has four years to go."

"Any other connection you can see?" Veltri asked.

"Not so far. Maybe after we talk to them…"

"Where's Holmgren's guy?" I asked.

"Allenwood. They're expecting you and Spider at eleven tomorrow morning. I'll fax the file over right after I hang up. Uh, is that okay with you, Pete?"

Veltri said, "I was wondering when you were going to ask my permission, but we all know that's not necessary. Batman and Robin will be at your service as usual."

"Thanks Pete, and guys, we won't interview any of the others until we hear back from you."

* * *

Snow threatened as I drove west on I-80 toward the Allenwood Federal Correctional Institution at Montgomery, Pennsylvania. Spider studied the case file of Howard Sunshine, former Chief Financial Officer of the Matterhorn Group, an investment brokerage firm still in business in California. "Anything particularly interesting?" I asked as I eyed the ever-darkening clouds in the western sky in front of us.

"If you mean is there anything here that would indicate Sunshine ordered the hit on Holmgren, the answer is no. There is no violence in his history, he made a full confession in court as part of his plea deal, and he has been a model prisoner."

"What did he spend the all those millions on?"

Spider paged through the file a minute or two. "He told the court he blew it on gambling and a party life style."

"Broads?"

"Doesn't say. His wife was in court with him."

"Yachts? Ferraris? McMansions?"

"Doesn't say. Maybe we should ask him."

"Yeah, or maybe he's got it buried somewhere safe awaiting his release."

"Maybe."

* * *

We were shown into a conference room with clean floors, relatively new wooden furniture, and large windows. It was quite a contrast to the dreary, depressing atmosphere of Wallkill.

"Nice digs, Spider."

"Yeah, I guess if you're going to do a non-violent crime, no matter the amount, a low-security resort in the country is your reward."

"Frankly, I don't get it. This guy stole twenty million bucks – and he may have ordered the hit on the guy who sent him here. He belongs in Wallkill, too."

"Here he comes," Spider said as the door opened and an uncuffed Howard Sunshine was escorted in by one correction officer, who then left the room.

We introduced ourselves and Sunshine said, "When I was told you were coming to speak to me, I was a bit apprehensive. I called my lawyer and he told me it was okay, but if you gave me my Miranda warnings or treated me harshly, I was to remain silent and call him."

"Excellent advice," I said. "I hope his fee didn't eat up too much of the millions you stole."

Sunshine said, "I wish his fee came from that. I still owe him money, and I have to begin making restitution as soon as I get out of here."

"I don't envy you that," Spider said. "That will take a long time."

"Yes, I'll never outlive the payback, but that's the price you pay when you steal."

He turned away from us and coughed into his hand.

"Any of those millions still around?" I asked.

"Unfortunately, no. I blew it all on the good life."

"Didn't you have a good life with your position? The CFO of a big company must pay a large salary."

"It did, plus options and an expense account. But it wasn't enough to satisfy greedy old me. I didn't want the fancy cars or houses or boats, but I did love to gamble, and I did love the high-class, expensive women."

122

"But your wife stuck by you, right?" Spider asked.

"Yes, thank God for that. She was the only one who did," he said coughing again.

Spider continued the routine questioning – I had already determined this guy was lying through his teeth – and I perused his file. Third generation German/Jewish, original name Sonnenschein – then I zeroed in on his date of birth. Howard Sunshine was sixty-two years old. I interrupted Spider's line of questioning and said, "Mr. Sunshine, it appears prison life appeals to you, except maybe for that cough."

"Excuse me?" he said coughing a bit longer this time.

"I look at you and I see a handsome middle-aged man with a youthful demeanor, a fit-looking body, and no wrinkles on his face. You appear to be forty to forty-five years old, but your date of birth indicates you are sixty-two. How do you do it?"

"Good genes, I guess," he said, but I detected wariness, and a bit of tension in his demeanor. "However, I do follow a strict regimen of diet and exercise. I've wasted many years of my life in here, and I want my remaining ones to be healthy and disease free."

"Do you take a lot of vitamins?" Spider asked.

"A few," he said crossing his legs, a sign of deception. He coughed again, violently this time.

"Well," I said, "whatever you take, and whatever regimen you follow, should be put into a book and published when you get out of here. Maybe you'll make that money back. But I must say, that cough doesn't sound too good."

"You flatter me, Detective Boyland, but I know you didn't come here to do that, did you?" he asked, ignoring my comment about his cough.

"No, Mr. Sunshine, so let me get to the point of our visit. Does the name Jonathan Holmgren ring a bell?"

"No, it doesn't."

"Holmgren was shot to death in his vehicle, and it appeared at first it was accidental. But as Detective Webb and I delved deeper into the case we found the shooter was hired to do the murder by a guy named Stan Brady."

Spider produced the composite photo, slid it over to Sunshine and said, "Recognize him?"

"No, never saw him before."

A truthful answer in my opinion, so I said, "The victim's name was not Holmgren. The victim was in the Witness Security Program. His real name was Jerry Harrison. Does that ring a bell?"

"Of course, and we all know why. Mr. Harrison's testimony put me here."

"Would you know anything that may help us find the people, Stan Brady in particular, who are responsible for Harrison's murder?"

"No, and I hope you don't think I had anything to do with it. I didn't."

"Is it possible, unbeknownst to you, some person engineered the murder of Jerry Harrison as a favor to you?"

"Who would do that? And why?" he asked coughing again.

"We don't know, Mr. Sunshine. Maybe not as a favor, but as a warning to others who might similarly testify?" Spider said.

"We are at a loss for an explanation," I said, "that's why we came all the way from New York."

"I wish I could help you, but I know nothing at all about the circumstances of Harrison's death."

I looked at Spider and he shook his head. I said, "Well, thanks for your time, Mr. Sunshine. We'll be on our way."

"All I have is time, Detectives, and I'm sorry I couldn't help you."

On the ride back I said to Spider, "I believe he doesn't know anything at all about Holmgren's murder."

"So do I, but he was lying about that twenty million. It didn't go to gambling and broads, and that whole thing about his looks – the good genes crap."

"Once again I agree a hundred percent with you, partner. Now tell me, how does a sixty-year old white-collar guy get to look like a forty year old leading man?"

"Maybe the same way Jordan Carter Bigelow got to look like Richard Conte?"

"Bingo! And the price for that miraculous transformation is?"

"Ten to thirty-five million bucks."

"Bingo again, Spider."

Chapter 16

We hit the rush hour traffic around New York and decided to go straight home and call Mike from the office first thing in the morning. I dropped Spider off and called Tara who had just arrived home. We agreed to have a cocktail at home and then go out to eat where I would tell her of our interview with Howard Sunshine. At the restaurant, when our glass of wine came, we touched glasses and I said, "To us."

"To us," she said. "Now get to it, and tell me what's new."

"Like the homicide dick you once were, I see you still got the fire in your belly."

"Yes, and I always will. This case has more unanswered questions than I have ever run across in all my other ones."

"Wait till you hear my story. I'll add a hundred more."

I didn't finish until our dessert arrived what with Tara's interruptions, mostly with questions I couldn't answer, and she said, "What now?"

"I tell Superman tomorrow and I know what he will do, or should do."

"Which is?"

"Interview all the other ones in prison, and those released, and see what they have to say. And, more importantly, see how they look."

* * *

The next morning with Veltri and Finn once more in on the conference call, Spider and I related the results of the interview. "Intriguing," Mike said. "Here's what I think we should do…"

"Write up our interview and fax it to you so you can use it as a guide when you send teams out to question all the others."

"Correct, Batman. When can I expect it?"

"Give us a couple hours, and Mike, something we should have done – have your guys take a picture of the subject."

"Good idea. Now please tell me – any of you – what the hell is going on here?"

"Maybe someone did find the fountain of youth," Father Finn said.

Uncharacteristically, no one laughed, and I pondered over the same choice of words Tara had recently used – *the fountain of youth*.

* * *

On the night of January 4, Stefan Konopka arrived home from work, again having observed the two tailing vehicles. After dinner he went down to his workshop, withdrew a flash drive from his pocket and plugged it into his well-worn laptop computer. When the download was complete, Stefan printed out the six copies of the driver's licenses and set them aside. He removed the flash drive and went to work on the PC, removing the battery and hard-drive. Using hacksaw, hammer and pliers he broke the hard drive into small chunks and put them in a paper bag. He kept the battery, and broke up the rest of the laptop, which he would later place in the regular trash.

Stefan turned his attention to the flash drive. He knew he should destroy it, but the thousands of driver's licenses contained on it could be a financial windfall if he had to go back to his illegal side business. He wrapped it in several tight layers of plastic wrap, placed it in an empty metal tin of breath mints, and wrapped that in duct tape. Satisfied, he placed it in his pocket along with the copies of the driver's licenses and went back upstairs to watch television with his wife.

Two hours later Stefan arose from bed without disturbing the gently snoring Marian. He took his clothes and shoes and went downstairs and dressed. He added a heavy coat, a hat with pull-down ear flaps, and a pair of gloves. Opening a back window, he climbed out into the backyard. He checked his watch – ten minutes to go. Withdrawing a small garden trowel he had secreted in the bushes and aided by a tiny flashlight, he walked to the back of the yard and began to dig a hole between the rear stockade fence and a clump of dead azalea bushes.

The frozen ground did not yield easily until he got down almost four inches, then he went another ten inches and placed the flash drive container at the bottom of the hole. After filling the hole up and patting the earth down, he surveyed the area to his satisfaction and checked his watch once more. Placing the trowel and flashlight in his coat pocket, he climbed the four-foot side fence, following it along his neighbor's property edge, and out into the street. He turned left and walked the half block to the corner. A car started up a block away and pulled up next to him. Stefan got in the passenger's side and the car drove away.

"Everything go okay?" John Rowan asked.

"Yes."

Rowan parked behind a darkened gas station and they got down to business. Stefan handed him an envelope saying, "Here are the six copies of the driver's licenses and all your new personal documents. He reached into his pocket and withdrew the bag containing the chopped up hard drive explaining the flash drive and hard drive were mixed together inside.

"Great work, Stefan. Here's your money."

He handed an envelope to Stefan containing the promised $50,000 all in hundred dollar bills.

"Thanks, John, and I hope you can take care of business right away."

"So do I. Here's a new cell phone for you, and in with the money is my new cell number. Let me have your old one, and I'll dispose of it along with these pieces of your computer."

"I guess I can afford a new laptop now," Stefan said as Rowan dropped him off and drove away.

Stefan was back in bed forty minutes after he had left it, and Marian was still sleeping in the same position. So far, so good. But would they grab him when the killings began? He would have to deal with it when the time came, no sense worrying about it now. But worry he did, and sleep did not visit him for many hours.

* * *

Ten days later Danny, Spider and Mike Havlek sat around a table in a room at FBI Headquarters and began reading the reports prepared by the teams of FBI agents assigned to interview the executives who had been arrested for embezzlement. It took almost two hours for each of them to read them all. When they finished Danny said, "I have to go to the bathroom. Too much coffee."

"I'll join you," Mike said.

"Weak bladders?" Spider said with a grin. "I'll make a fresh pot while you two take care of business."

Back at the table Mike said, "Here's what I conclude from these interviews. All the subjects were cooperative up to a certain point, and none seemed to tell an outright lie, but they didn't tell us squat."

"Basically," Spider said, "they admitted their mistakes, claimed they turned their lives around, are paying, or will pay, their reparations, and will live happily ever after."

"And amazingly, all now appearing fit, healthy, happy – and twenty to thirty years younger than their actual age," Mike said.

No one asked the question that had been, and still was, in all our minds. *Just what the hell was going on here?* I changed the subject saying, "At least our Witsec people have been re-located, and no attempts have been made on their lives – so far."

"So maybe you were wrong about Konopka?" Mike asked.

"Yeah, maybe, but we still have agents and marshals inside and outside of each of their homes, right?"

"Right."

"So maybe the hit men are unable to get to them?"

"You're assuming Konopka, or someone else, somehow got the new locations to the hit men already," Spider said.

"Yes, I am. Are we still tailing him?"

"Yes," Mike said, "but I think we should discontinue it. He's had over a week to pass off the information – if he was our guy."

"Dammit. We're striking out all over the place. Maybe we should grab Konopka and sweat his ass a little."

"On what grounds, Danny?" Spider asked.

I knew there were none, but I was frustrated and wanted to take some action, somewhere – anywhere. I shook my head and mumbled a few curses. I said, "Let's order a sandwich and think about it awhile."

* * *

Richard Mangan/John Rowan/Stan Brady was getting more nervous and upset with each passing day. He had chosen two of the targets for himself and assigned two each to Rusty and Mitch. Their orders were to kill their targets as close in time together as possible – get it done fast – no phony accidental deaths anymore. But after a couple days of observation, the situation became apparent. All six targets were covered – well-covered – by law enforcement people around the clock. None of them commuted to a job it seemed, but whenever they left the house to shop or run an errand, they were accompanied by men and women in plainclothes. Mangan would have to make the *consigliore* aware of the situation soon – and he was not looking forward to that meeting. He'd give it a few more days. Maybe after two weeks the cops would break it off.

* * *

"We have to force the situation," I said as I swallowed a bit of my turkey sandwich.

"What do you mean?" Mike asked.

"Pull all the outside law enforcement surveillance off, and leave two guys inside the house."

Spider and Mike got it right away. Spider said, "And when a hit man breaks in and makes his move we grab his ass and make him talk."

"Yeah," Mike said, "but all we'll have him for is a burglary first degree."

"Let him kill our target first," I said. "Then we got him for murder, and he'll want to talk for sure." I was kidding of course, but Mike Havlek, straight-arrow FBI agent, didn't think so.

"Danny," he said, "we couldn't allow…"

"I know, Mike. Only fantasizing here."

At the end of a long day we decided to drop the tail on Konopka and pull all outside surveillance off the nine witnesses. Realizing the increased danger posed by this reduction, we decided to add a third agent inside the house of each of the nine. Mike made the necessary calls and when he finished he turned to me and Spider and said, "Now what?"

"We wait," Spider said, "because I don't believe we have anything else to do."

* * *

Two nights later, Thomas "Mitch" Mitchell called Richard Mangan and said, "It looks like they're gone."

"Thanks, I'll get back to you."

He had made the same observations on his selected target. He punched in Rusty's number. When Russell "Rusty" Ferrand confirmed the same situation Mangan said, "Sit tight. I'll get back to you." He called Stefan Konopka and said, "Are they still tailing you?"

"I don't think so. I haven't noticed them the last two nights. Uh, how are…"

"When it's done, I'll let you know."

Richard Mangan was suspicious. Could this be a set-up? Suppose they hit their first target and the house was full of cops? But if he didn't get results soon, Bradley Monaghan might get pissed off. Should he go see him and explain the situation? Would his failure lead to his own death? He needed a drink – badly.

As he sipped his second scotch his cell phone vibrated in his pocket. The text message said simply, "LV." Monaghan wanted him in Vegas. He finished his drink, paid his tab and drove to his motel. After booking his flight for the next day he called Mitch and Rusty and told them to continue to monitor their locations, but to take no action until he called them back in two days.

As he undressed for bed Mangan mulled the situation over. Six targets scattered across the country. If all three of them were successful in simultaneously killing their first target, it would take them at least a day to get to their next. By that time the security would be ramped up again, or maybe the targets relocated once more. Maybe he should hire three more guys and do all six hits at exactly the same time. Or maybe Bradley Monaghan had some other plans for him. As he put his head on the pillow and pressed the light switch, he knew he would be in for a restless night.

Chapter 17

What had prompted Bradley Monaghan to summon Richard Mangan to Las Vegas was the result of a conversation, a long, fantastic conversation, he recently completed with Jordan Bigelow. Mr. Big told Bradley some amazing things— some unbelievable, almost impossible things – and the faithful consigliere was contemplating those things as he sipped twelve-year old bourbon and stared out of his floor-to-ceiling window at the stark desert landscape.

When Mr. Big invited him into his office two hours ago, he began the conversation with, "Brad, you have been a faithful right-hand man to me for many, many years, and I know I've recently been somewhat mysterious about certain information I possess. I appreciate the fact you never pressed me about what I have kept hidden from you, but I'm ready to reveal that to you now."

"Mr. Big, I always trust your judgment and will never question your decision what to tell me, or what not to tell me."

"Thank you, but before I give you the good news, I have a few questions for you."

"Sure, Boss," he said, wondering where this conversation was going.

"You're almost fifty years old, correct?"

"Yes. In two months I hit the big five-oh."

"And you've been regularly seeing our staff doctor and following his advice on exercise and diet?"

"Yes, I have."

"And I know you recently received a clean bill of health. No signs of heart disease, cancer, diabetes, or other illnesses, correct?"

"None, Mr. Big."

"Great news. Oh, by the way, I know the cure for cancer."

"What? You...you... do?"

"Of course. So do you. So does everyone."

"Uh, I'm not sure I understand."

"Don't get it in the first place," Bigelow said with a big smile.

"Good one," Monaghan said smiling back.

"With cancer, and all those other terrible diseases that plague mankind, some of which may never be cured, *prevention* is the key. Keep yourself from getting the goddamn condition in the first place."

"Makes excellent sense," Monaghan said, getting extremely curious now.

"Now for my next question. Listen closely, and think a moment before you respond. And I ask this question in all seriousness and sincerity."

"Yes, Mr. Big," Brad said, wondering what the hell was coming next in this bizarre conversation.

"Brad, how would you like to live to be 150 years old?"

When Bradley Monaghan found his tongue, he managed to respond, "Yes, I guess, but...."

"I don't mean being in a wheelchair or drooling in a nursing home. I mean living a full, vibrant, healthy life doing what you like to do. Let me explain...."

Ninety minutes later, after hearing about the work of the Summerlin Research Institute, his head swimming with questions, doubts and outright incredulity, Bradley Monaghan said, "It sounds fantastic...and wonderful."

And then came the topper. Jordan Bigelow slid a document over to him. There was an enigmatic grin on Bigelow's face as Monaghan picked up the parchment and glanced at it. "Your birth certificate?"

"Correct. How old am I?"

Bradley studied the date of birth and suddenly his eyes opened wide. "This can't be true. This means you are seventy-five years old. You don't look more than forty-five, maybe fifty at the most."

"I have been with Summerlin since its beginning over twenty-five years ago. I was one of the original members invited by the Board of Directors to join the organization. They waived the original fifty million dollar initiation fee for me, based on the fact my organization would take care of any complications or problems that might arise along the way as their project proceeded to fruition."

"But I don't have fifty million…"

"It's taken care of, Brad. It's my gift – and Summerlin's gift – to you. And by the way, the fee is a hundred million now. But before you can join the program you have to clean up all your unfinished business, and take care of one new item for me."

"Of course. What is it?"

"The eleven rats you have your people exterminating put eleven members of our group in prison with their testimony. Originally, seventy people were asked to join the group and fifty-nine came up with their initiation fee, but these eleven all fell a bit short. That is why they embezzled various amounts from their firms and, being novices in crime, they were all caught. Embezzlement is a difficult crime to conceal from your co-workers, shareholders, board members, actuaries and accounting firms, so they tried to monetarily take care of those associates who became suspicious of their activities. Eventually, those people came under scrutiny and spilled their guts when they got arrested."

"So you volunteered to take care of those rats as a favor to the eleven members?"

"Yes, to let them know they have not been forgotten and to show them our group's power and reach."

"As you know, we are in the process of eliminating the last six as we speak. I'm awaiting word from my main man in the field."

"Good, but I have one more target for your man, and this takes priority over everything else. His name is Evan Donaldson and he lives in Connecticut. He is one of the eleven."

"But hasn't he paid his dues and received the promise of a long life?"

"Yes, but in Donaldson's case, that will not happen. This past week teams of FBI agents visited all eleven and asked some disturbing questions. They are starting to put the pieces together and connect the deaths of the informants to them. They also remarked how young they all appeared and took pictures of each one."

"I can't imagine any one of them would ever divulge anything about Summerlin," Brad said.

"None did, including Donaldson, because at this time he has not been informed by the Institute he has Stage IV pancreatic cancer and, even with their most advanced treatments, he will not make another year."

"So when he finds out his fifty million hasn't bought him anything, he becomes a weak link and a potential rat himself?"

"Precisely, and we can't allow that to happen."

"But I thought they can prevent cancer with their treatment protocols."

"Not always. Some cases slip through the cracks. Some cancers are extremely difficult to detect, pancreatic cancer being one of them. It's a shame, but a fact of life."

"I'll summon my guy and have this taken care of right away, Mr. Big."

"I know you will. Here's Donaldson's address," he said slipping a piece of paper over to Monaghan. "And Brad, please call me Jordan from now on. We know each other many years, and I'm sure we will know each other for many more. Maybe a hundred more."

* * *

When Richard Mangan walked through the front door of the building which houses the LV Betterment Group, his coming and going were duly recorded by the surveillance camera connected to the digital recorder. Unfortunately, as we later discovered, his visit would not be found by the FBI until a week later, when the disc was eventually reviewed.

Spider and I were again going to request Vince Genova to have the building live-monitored, but we never broached the idea to Mike simply because we had forgotten to mention it as we were all caught up with the surveillance of Stefan Konopka and the protection of the nine Witsec people. But two days after Mangan's visit to Las Vegas, when me, Mike, and Spider sat around waiting for something to pop, Mike said, "Maybe we should have

Vince Genova call out to Vegas and have a couple of guys watch that building for a while."

"Good idea," Spider said, glancing at me in obvious embarrassment.

* * *

Richard Mangan was going to be a busy man over the next few days. First, he would personally whack Mr. Evan Donaldson and be $100,000 richer. Next he would hire three more men to augment Mitch and Rusty, who would not be happy to learn they would earn only $25,000 for one hit, instead of $50,000 for the planned two hits each. But Monaghan insisted he wanted this over with ASAP, so they all had to suffer some monetary pain.

Assured by Mitch and Rusty their periodic checks had still not detected any law enforcement presence in the area of their assigned targets, and having the same experience himself, Mangan wasted no time in hiring the three extra hit men, and furnished them the address of their intended target. He also provided each of them with a handgun, none less powerful than a .40 caliber semi-automatic, or a .357 magnum. His instructions to them were to check the surrounding area for two nights for any signs of cops. If everything looked kosher, he would set a date where all six of them would hit their targets at the exact same time. Kill fast and get out fast. Return the gun to him later at a prearranged place and time, and collect the $25,000 plus expenses.

The kill date he had in mind was now two days away, and satisfied things were all in place, Richard Mangan drove his rental vehicle to Stamford, Connecticut. Monaghan's instructions to him had been specific. Donaldson was not to be killed on his premises, but kidnapped and shot at a remote location. He had said, "We don't want police involvement right away. His wife would be certain to call the agents who recently interviewed him. Make him disappear and then take care of the other six rats."

* * *

Grabbing Evan Donaldson should be a piece of cake, Mangan figured – and it was. Monaghan had provided him with pictures, job location, work location and work hours. As Donaldson got off the train from Manhattan at the Stamford Metro North station, Mangan followed him to his car, shot him twice in the back of the head with a silenced .22 caliber revolver, and placed his body on the back seat. He drove Donaldson's car to a secluded place and moved his body into the trunk. After parking the car in the long-term lot at Norwalk airport, he hailed a cab back to the Stamford railroad station, where he retrieved his rental car, and headed south on I-95. The whole operation had taken less than ninety minutes.

The following night, after checking his Maryland target's home one last time, Mangan put the plan into motion by texting his five hit men with the message "127 – 1130P" which they had been taught to understand as January 27 at 11:30 p.m. Tomorrow night Richard Mangan would be a whole lot richer.

* * *

At 12:52 a.m. on January 28, the phone in my motel room woke me out of a sound sleep – one of the few I had recently enjoyed. "Hello," I mumbled.

"Danny, it's Mike," said an agitated voice.

"Huh? Who....?"

"Danny, wake up! It's Mike Havlek. Get Spider and get in here. All hell has broken loose!"

That got my attention and cleared the fog from my brain. I said, "What do you mean?" as I stumbled out of the bed.

"Shootings at our Witsec people's homes. I don't know how many, or have any real details yet. You and Spider get in here, and we'll sort it all out."

"We're on our way." I dialed Spider's room and we agreed to meet in the hallway of our adjacent rooms in five minutes. It took us another ten minutes to get to Quantico, where we found a bleary-eyed Mike, and seven or eight equally bleary-eyed agents, on various phones speaking and scribbling notes on yellow pads.

"More stuff coming in all the time," Mike said. "Coffee's on the way. Pull up a chair."

By 3:00 a.m. we had it all sorted out. It seemed a lone gunman broke into the home of six of the nine targets, at the same time, with the intent to kill that target. Their plans were thwarted – in all six instances – by the well-trained FBI Agents and Deputy U.S. Marshal assigned as protection. Two hit men were surprised and captured without a shot being fired. One other managed to get away by leaping through a window, although the following gunshots may have wounded him, as a few drops of blood were noted in the snow. Wild shootouts occurred in the remaining three homes resulting in the deaths of one hit-man, the wounding of two others, and the wounding of four law enforcement persons – two seriously.

The dead hit-man was Thomas "Mitch" Mitchell. One captured unharmed was Russell "Rusty" Ferrand. And one captured, slightly wounded in the left thigh, was none other than the long sought after Stan Brady. "Let's all get some sleep," Mike Havlek said. "Brady and the two others are being flown here tomorrow. The other guy is in surgery in Kansas City, and it looks like he's not going to make it."

"Finally," Spider said. "Finally we get to talk to the elusive Stan Brady."

"If he does talk to us," I said. "We'll save him for last."

* * *

Allison Havlek was now six months pregnant and still actively working at her Washington newspaper. When Mike returned from the office, she arose from a troubled half-sleep and said, "What happened?"

"I can't tell you."

"Why not?"

"Professional standards. It's a huge story. The PR department is working on a press release now, and they will distribute it to all branches of the media at one time tomorrow morning."

"It *is* tomorrow morning, so tell me now."

"Negative, my dear. No scoop for ace investigative reporter Allison Hayes who everyone in D.C. knows is my wife."

"No scoop for me?" she said with a smile. "Then maybe no sex for you."

"That's okay," he said playfully patting her stomach. "You aren't too sexually attractive anymore."

"You son-of-a-bitch!" she yelled, throwing a pillow at him. "You forget I will be thin and beautiful again in a few months."

"Can't wait," he said with a leering grin. "Now I have to get a few hours sleep. Wake me up when you're ready to leave for work."

"Give me *something*, or I'll never let you sleep."

"We got Stan Brady. He's being flown here tomorrow for interrogation."

"Terrific! How..."

"S-s-s-s-h. Sleep now, okay."

"Okay," she said, happy her dedicated husband had gotten a much-needed break in this weird case. Maybe it would be over soon, and she could have him back full-time as the baby's impending arrival got nearer and nearer.

Chapter 18

The six home invasions had taken place on a Friday night, and as Stefan Konopka sat at the kitchen table late Saturday morning anticipating his once-weekly huge breakfast of bacon, eggs, potatoes, and toast, Marian said, "While you were in the shower there was some terrible news on the TV."

"What happened?"

"A lot of shootings in one night. Different places all over the country."

"Strange," Stefan said as a stab of worry ran through his brain. "Were they connected?"

"I don't know, but I'm sure it will be on the all-news channels all day long."

When he finished breakfast, Stefan's two teenage daughters, Janet and Alice, eyes still heavy with sleep, plopped on their chairs at the kitchen table. He said, "Welcome to the daylight, my two lovely princesses."

Janet said, "Madeline is in her wheelchair playing video games. She'll call on the intercom when she wants to come down."

"Have you seen your brother?" Stefan asked, wondering if his wayward fifteen- year old son had come home the night before.

"No," Alice said, "but I heard the TV on in his room."

Stefan walked into the den and picked up the remote. Paging through the news channels, he had the complete picture of what had happened the night before in twenty minutes. He gulped and wondered if John Rowan himself had been captured – no names of either the victims, or the would-be killers, had been released – and, if so, would he give him up.

He continued to watch and think of all the probabilities. Someone *had* to talk. Law enforcement officers had been shot. If Rowan was not caught, someone would have to give him up. But maybe, with a lot of luck, John Rowan was dead, the one who the news media said was shot to death. He could not count on that however, and he had to initiate his plan – soon.

* * *

At noon that Saturday, the first captured hit-man arrived under heavy guard, hand-cuffed and shackled. He was brought into an interview room, unshackled and hand-cuffed to a U-bolt on the desk. Mike Havlek walked in and sat opposite him. Spider and I watched through the one-way glass. This guy, whose prints identified him as Christopher Tedesco, looked like a hard case – close-set, dark eyes and a scowl on his dark- whiskered unshaven face. "Is your name Christopher Tedesco?" Mike asked. I knew what Tedesco was going to say and he did. "I got nuttin' to say. I want a lawyer."

Not that I'm clairvoyant, but Tedesco knew we didn't have much on him. Mike knew what to do next. "Okay, let me read you your rights." When that was completed he said, "I am not going to ask you any questions, but I'd like you to listen to what I have to say. Then we'll get you some lunch."

Tedesco shrugged his shoulders and faked a yawn. I looked at Spider and said, "Got the urge to smack that gorilla upside the head?"

"Oh, yeah. More than once."

"You broke into a house armed with a gun and were captured before you had a chance to use it." Mike said. "The crime you committed in the state of New York is Burglary in the First Degree, punishable by up to fifteen years in prison. Due to the nature of the case, you will get the max plus five more for the loaded gun. But here's the kicker, Christopher, this crime, once you are convicted of it, will make you a four-time loser. You are looking at forty years, which may well be the rest of your life, behind bars. Do I have your attention?"

Tedesco shuffled in his seat and said, "Whaddya want, and what's in it for me?"

"I want you to identify the man who hired you, tell us where you got the gun, and give us all the details of what you were hired to do. If you say you will do that, I'll get the New York DA to offer you a plea bargain for ten years maximum."

"In writing?"

"Yes."

"Can I have a lawyer advising me?"

"Yes."

"Look, the guy who hired me gave me his name, but who knows if it's real?"

"Can you pick him out of a group of photos?"

"Yeah."

"If I put him in a line-up, will you be able to pick him out?"

"Sure."

"All your information must be verified by you sitting for a polygraph examination. Are you willing to do that?"

"The lie box? Sure, why not?"

"Then we have a deal, Mr. Tedesco," Mike said.

* * *

By the time Mike finished with Tedesco, both the second guy and Stan Brady had arrived and were placed in cells. I was chosen to talk with Russell Ferrand who, surprisingly, had no criminal record. I shouldn't have bothered as Russell clammed up and demanded his rights and a lawyer. Even after I gave him a spiel similar to what Mike had given the other guy he said, "Listen Boyland, stop wasting your breath. I broke into that place to steal their shit. That's it. Period."

"Yeah, Russell, you live 400 miles away. What were you expecting to find in there, the Hope diamond?"

"Just passing through, and it looked like an easy score. Now I am done talking."

"Suppose I can get you ten years instead of fifteen?"

Ferrand, who we later discovered had murdered seventeen people in the course of his career, smiled and said, "No dice."

Now it was time for the elusive, mysterious man of many names. Stan Brady's prints came back to what we assumed was his real name, Richard Mangan. As he was being brought to the interview room Mike said, "This is it guys. We have to crack him. I want all three of us in there with him."

And crack him we did, or to be honest, he cracked himself – much to our great surprise. Mike started off by saying, "Is Richard Mangan your real name?"

"Yes, but as you know by now, I've gone by several others."

"Stan Brady and Paul Johnson?" Spider asked.

"Yeah, that's two of them. The five guys I hired know me as either John Rowan or Bill Morton."

We almost fell off our chairs at his matter-of-fact admission of guilt. I said, "You admit you hired these guys to kill people in the Witness Security Program?"

"Yeah, and here's my situation. When I was caught last night, as the southern sheriff used to say on TV, I knew I was in a heap of trouble – a big heap of trouble. So, ever since, I've been figuring a way to save my ass and minimize the pain."

"Speaking of pain," Spider said, "how's the leg doing?"

"Bandaged up nicely. A clean wound in the thigh muscle, no bone hit. A little uncomfortable, that's all."

"Want some aspirin or something?"

"No, thanks for asking."

"Mr. Mangan," Mike said, "would you care to elaborate on your situation?"

"Sure. You got me for an attempted murder of a Federal agent, and you got me for arranging to kill five other people. I don't want the death penalty, which I know is a possibility under Federal law. That's it."

"And what can you give us for that deal?"

"I can give you all the names of those I hired."

"We got them already," Spider said.

"Didn't one get away? Or was the TV man in error?"

"Yeah, one got away."

"I can give you his name."

"Is that all you have for us?" Mike asked.

"For a promise of twenty years maximum, I can give you a lot more.

"Such as?"

"I can give you the names of the men who killed the previous witnesses. Oh, I did one of those myself. And I can give you the name of the man in the U.S. Marshal's service who kindly provided us with all eleven names and their locations."

I wanted to blurt out, "Stefan Konopka," but I forced my lips tightly together. "What else, Richard?" Mike continued.

"The name of the man who hired me to kill those eleven people, how much he paid me to do it, and how much I paid out to the people I hired."

"Can you tell us why these people were targeted?"

"Not specifically, except they were considered rats."

"You mean people who informed or testified against others?" Mike asked.

"I assume so, but I was not informed of the particular circumstances. Basically, I was given a list of names to kill."

"Now, for the $64,000 question…" I began.

"The answer is no. I cannot set him up. You're going to ask me if I will wear a wire and get the man who hired me to admit his part in this scheme. Can't do it. Impossible."

"Why won't you do it? That would surely get you your twenty year deal."

"Not that I *won't* do it. I *can't* do it. First, I'm caught and everyone knows it."

"No, they don't. When you give us the name of the guy who got away clean we'll grab him, but we'll tell the press – without mentioning names –the one guy is still out there. Your contact will think it's you when you call him."

"I know where you're going, but you still don't understand. I botched the job. I'm as good as dead and maybe as good as dead in jail, too. I'll need a guarantee of protective custody in there."

"I'm not convinced, Richard," Mike said. "We know your contact is in the Las Vegas mob. We got you on video going in and out of their building several times."

"Well, I know you guys are sharp, but let me tell you what I go through after I walk through those doors…"

"Shit!" I said after Mangan finished. "By the way, who is your contact in the mob?"

"Now, now, Agent Boyland, that was a good try, but all the details will be provided when our deal is done with the AUSA and my attorney present."

"You're pretty sharp yourself, Richard. Agent Havlek will put the wheels into motion. Let me say I appreciate your candor, but based on your history, I have no sympathy for you – a smiling, friendly, cold-blooded fucking murderer."

"No argument there. I am what I am."

"You mean what you *were*," Spider said. "You're toast now."

"One more thing before we leave you," I said. "Do you think the inside guy who gave you the locations of the Witsec people will rabbit when he hears what happened last night?"

"Most certainly."

"Yet you won't tell us who he is now?"

"Sorry, but not until….."

"I know, I know. Until the details are worked out and signed." I looked directly into Richard Mangan's eyes looking for any hint of recognition when I asked my next question. "Richard, would his initials be S.K.?"

Mangan winked at me! He said, "You guys, as I said before, are sharp."

* * *

After depositing Mangan in a holding cell, Mike Havlek alerted the troops. He had four teams of agents dispatched to Stefan Konopka's home, with orders to pick him up if he tried to flee, but to let him get about a mile from his home so as not to alert his family and neighbors.

Stefan Konopka had been glued to the TV set all day, but no mention of the hit-men's names had yet been made public despite the complaints and pressure from the media. He had to conclude they caught John Rowan, and he was now spilling his guts to save his bacon. He went into the kitchen and poured himself a scotch on the rocks and asked Marian if she wanted a cocktail. "Isn't it a bit early?" she asked, looking up at the clock on the wall which read 4:16.

"Yes, but after what I have to tell you, you may want one too."

"Are you in trouble, Stefan?"

"Yes, Marian. A lot of trouble. I will tell you everything, and tell you what I think we….I… should do."

Marian did pour herself a double vodka on the rocks well before her husband had finished his story. When Stefan paused she said, "You did terrible things and they will certainly come for you. What will I and the children do?"

"You will continue to live here while I disappear for a while. I have anticipated this situation and have provided for you. Tonight when I leave, I will bury over $100,000 in the backyard, by the azalea bushes near the back fence. Whether the police catch me or not, they will be sure to search the house. Do not go near the money until this completely blows over."

"Where will you go?"

"I don't know yet. I have new documents, and I will fill in the address when I find a place to settle down. I also have documents for you and the children, if you decide to join me some day. I won't blame you if you don't."

"I can't make that decision now, my head is spinning."

"I will go upstairs and pack my things. Where are the children?"

"Out with their friends, except for Madeline, of course."

"That poor child. I hate to abandon her as I hate to abandon you, and she has been dealt such a rotten hand…."

"We'll manage, Stefan, but what will you do for work?"

"I have a few thousand to take with me until I get established. Unfortunately, my talents do not lend themselves to a legitimate occupation."

"So you will create documents for those in need? Illegal documents?"

"I'm afraid that's all I can do to make enough money to take care of you and the children. I have no other skills."

Marian sighed and said, "Stefan, I love you….and I hate you. I have to get dinner started now."

Stefan poured himself another scotch and took it up to their bedroom where he spent the next hour packing his clothes into two large suitcases. He had to take all he would need now knowing he would never be back here again. He had finished closing up the suitcases when he heard Marian shout, "Dinner, everyone!"

Around the table Stefan paid particular attention to his children, joking with them and asking about their lives. Even his son, Marty, seemed jovial and not presently under the influence of a controlled substance. After helping Marian clean up the dishes, Janet, Alice and Marty made a beeline to their rooms to prepare for going out this Saturday night. As they left through the front door a few minutes later, Stefan said, "Remember, no later than eleven o'clock."

"Dad," protested Alice, the oldest child. "I'm seventeen!"

"And when you're eighteen, you can stay out until midnight. Now go have fun."

He would miss his family terribly, but his situation was his own doing after all.

Much later that night, when he had made sure to kiss all his children goodnight, he lay awake in bed next to Marian who also stared, wide awake, at the ceiling. At two a.m., he said, "It's time, Marian. I'll go bury the money now and come back to get my bags."

Retrieving three large, sealed plastic bags from the basement, he once more climbed out the same downstairs window into the cold, dark backyard. Fortunately, a late January thaw made the digging much easier now. He retrieved the small package containing the flash drive, widened the hole and made it substantially deeper. By the time the bags of hundred dollar bills were safely buried, no more than thirty minutes had elapsed.

Back in the bedroom, he hugged Marian and kissed her cheek. He said, "I know I haven't been the best husband, but…."

"Be quiet. I know you tried, and I love you for that. Godspeed and good luck." She touched his cheek and grabbed one of the suitcases.

Stefan looked out the front window at the quiet street. He went to the side door, opened it cautiously, and placed the two suitcases on the stoop, looking to his left and checking the street once more. Satisfied, he grabbed the bags, walked out into the cool January air over to the driveway, and placed them in the trunk of his car. He backed out and turned left on his street. Two hundred yards away, an FBI agent sitting with his partner in a chilly sedan, picked up his radio and said, "He's on the move. Now turning right on Sugarberry. Just put his headlights on. We'll do the initial tail."

"We'll take it now," another FBI agent announced as Konopka pulled into an all-night, self-service gas station which was about a half-mile from his home. The supervisory agent on the detail said, "All units converge quietly on the gas station. We'll take him when he gets a bit farther away, but before he gets to a major highway. Roger that?"

They all acknowledged, and ten minutes later, surrounded by four cars and eight FBI agents, Stefan Konopka came out of his car, hands above his head as ordered, tears running down his cheeks, and meekly surrendered.

Chapter 19

If there was one other person in the country, other than Stefan Konopka, who had been extremely disturbed by the news of the shootouts, it was Bradley Monaghan. He sat alone in his office on Saturday morning glued to the TV. At first the authorities had reported on the individual shootings as if they were unrelated burglary attempts. But when the reporters dug into the stories, they were able to put the facts together – six still un-named people, each guarded by a team consisting of a Deputy U.S. Marshal and two FBI Agents. These people were more than randomly chosen burglary targets and, of course, Bradley knew who they were and why he was now unable to stop a cold sweat from enveloping his body.

It was eleven a.m. and Bradley called the Las Vegas Chamber of Commerce, whose monthly luncheon he was scheduled to attend. He told the chamber president he had to beg off making an appearance as an urgent business matter required his attention. "Would it be okay if I spoke at next month's meeting instead?" he asked.

"Of course, Mr. Monaghan," replied the president, knowing full well to whom he was speaking. "I'll inform the group of the change. I'm sure they'll understand."

After Monaghan hung up, he returned to the TV news and pondered the situation, wiping his dripping forehead before the sweat ran into his eyes. First,

Mangan and he had agreed the six targets would be addressed only after he had taken care of the priority assignment in Connecticut. So at least that had been accomplished, he figured. But what had gone wrong last night? Why had Mangan proceeded with the attacks when agents were inside? Unless he did not know they were in there, an assumption he might have made on the fact none were observed outside the premises. Who was the one who had escaped? If it was Richard, how would he know? And if it wasn't Richard, was he now dead? Or, much worse, in custody spilling his guts?

Jordan Bigelow was across the country on Long Island for three days of treatment at the Summerlin Institute. Was he aware of what had happened? Too many unanswered questions. He had to stop and relax. Take a deep breath, Bradley, and try to assess your situation. What's the worst case scenario? He refilled his coffee cup and took out a notepad. After ten minutes of writing, he realized the worst case scenario was very bad – Mangan had been caught and talked. Mr. Big was furious the operation had been botched. Mr. Big would have him whacked.

Another ten to fifteen minutes and the best case scenario appeared on his notepad. Mangan had gotten away, or if captured, refused to talk. Mr. Big was happy the priority assignment had been taken care of, and not too upset about the botched operation on the six others, allowing Bradley to continue on in his position and to become a member of the Summerlin Institute. *Yeah, sure.*

He couldn't summon Mangan, there was not enough time. Realizing the odds were heavily against his survival, he emptied out his wall safe of all its cash, checked his office for any incriminating documents, packed up his laptop, and drove to his apartment. Performing similar tasks there, he loaded up the trunk of his black Mercedes S-500 and drove off, heading east, with absolutely no idea where he would spend the night, or where his ultimate destination would be. He regretted he had not had the foresight to have Richard Mangan's informant make a new set of documents for himself.

* * *

It was two in the afternoon on Sunday when Stefan Konopka was brought from his cell to the interview room to face Mike Havlek, Danny Boyland and Spider

Webb. Stefan raised his eyes, immediately recognizing them from their visit to his workplace. "I see you remember us," I said.

Stefan nodded. He said, "I do not wish to answer any questions, and I want a lawyer."

Spider dutifully read Konopka his rights, and after both cards were signed I said, "Stefan, I won't ask you any questions. I'll tell you what I believe your situation is, and how your punishment may be lessened if you cooperate. Then we'll bring you back to your cell and let you decide if you wish to play ball. You call for us if you do."

Konopka nodded again and we spent the next ten minutes laying out the case against him, the most damaging evidence being the flash drive found in his possession. It had been downloaded revealing the copies of the driver's licenses of over 3,000 people in the Witsec program. We concluded by saying his cooperation – a complete confession and the identification of the man who he sold the copies to – could result in a reduction of his sentence from life in prison to twenty-five years.

"I have a question," Stefan said after we finished. "What have I done that justifies a sentence of life imprisonment?"

"The information you sold led directly to the deaths of five people," Mike said. "And to the attempted murder of six others on Friday night."

"I don't think you can prove that."

I decided to get tough with Konopka. "Listen you dumb fuck, we don't give a shit what you think. I'm wondering why I'm wasting my time here with you. How do you think we caught you? Great police work? No, we caught John Rowan and he gave you up. Yeah, we know all about him, so we don't need your help at all."

"Detective Boyland is right," Spider said. "We don't need you. Just thought we'd try to give a break to a hard-working family man who screwed up big-time. Let's get him the fuck out of here."

Stefan wanted to cooperate, but he knew if he confessed everything, including how much money he was paid, he would have to divulge its whereabouts. For the sake of his wife and children, that was something he was unwilling to do. He said, "Take me away, I have nothing more to say to you," hoping they were lying about John Rowan.

We all stood and I said, "Think it over, Stefan. You have plenty of time before your trial is scheduled."

"I will, but I won't change my mind."

* * *

The search warrant executed at Konopka's residence turned up no additional evidence. The three of us joined five other agents and spent the entire day of Monday there. Marian Konopka seemed genuinely upset and shocked at the allegations against her husband. We questioned their children when they came home from school. They too showed surprise, and all broke into tears at the news of their father's arrest. And the poor little girl in the wheelchair, crying all day as we searched the house. A heartbreaking scene for sure. Stefan Konopka may have been a thief, but he had a good side. I said, "Do you think Marian knows where the money is?"

"For sure," Mike said. "Probably buried in the backyard, since it's nowhere in the house. Should we order up the backhoes?"

I looked at Spider and Mike and said, "Nah, I don't think so."

"Yeah," Spider said. "No doubt it would be a wasted effort."

Mike said, "I agree. Let's get out of here."

* * *

On Tuesday morning my cell phone rang and it was my son, Patrick. "Hey Dad," he said. "We've been following the news. That's your case, right?"

"Right. Things are finally breaking our way."

"When can we come over for a visit like you promised?"

"We have a few more things to tie up and reports to write and file. Give me another week, Pat. I'll call you when we can do it."

"Terrific! I can't wait. And Dad…?"

"Yes?"

"Great detective work."

"Thanks, Pat. I appreciate that."

Spider had walked in at the tail end of my conversation, and after I hung up he said, "Your son?"

"Yeah, wants to make a visit up here. I told him this should all be wrapped up soon."

"Really?"

"Well, all that remains is Mangan's deal to finalize, right?"

"And when he gives us the guy in the mob who hired him, don't you think we have some more investigative work to do?"

"Like flying to Vegas and talking to him?"

"Correct."

"And when he politely tells us to fuck off, what do we have on him other than an admitted killer's word?"

That made Spider reflect a moment. "I have to think about that. We should all think about that – you, me, Tara, Mike, Vince Genova, and Allison."

"I agree, because I'm at a loss on how to proceed."

We went into Mike Havlek's office to discuss this situation. He was on the phone and motioned for us to sit down. His side of the conversation went like this – "How long was he missing? When did they find him? How many bullets?" A long silence. Followed by, "Yeah, we'll handle it."

"Who's dead now?" I asked as Mike put down the receiver and turned to us.

"Evan Donaldson."

"And why should that concern us?" Spider asked. "Oh wait, that name sounds familiar…"

"Donaldson was one of the big shots who went to jail based on testimony from one of our Witsec guys. He went missing a few days ago, and his wife called the FBI team that had recently interviewed him. They contacted the locals who determined his car was not at the Stamford railroad station. They later found it in the Norwalk Airport parking lot with Donaldson in the trunk, shot to death."

"Holy crap. Are they shooting *these* guys now?"

"Maybe we should ask our friend, Mr. Mangan," I said.

We brought Mangan into the interview room. He looked around and greeted us with a smile. "How's it going, Richard?" I asked.

"Going great. I met with the US Attorney and my lawyer yesterday, and my agreement is almost completed."

"I don't think you told us everything," Mike said.

"Oh?"

"Evan Donaldson?"

"Yeah, I fucked up there."

"You killed him?"

"Yeah."

Mangan never ceased to amaze me. I said, "And you admit that so readily? Aren't you concerned this might screw up your deal?"

"Yeah, but like I said, I fucked up. I shot him with the gun they found on me when I was arrested. Big mistake."

"So you realize we would have tied the killing to you in a few days?"

"Your guys in the FBI lab are the top ballistics experts in these parts, aren't they?"

"They sure are," Mike said. "Now who ordered the murder?"

"I'll tell my lawyer to work that info into the agreement. Maybe it's worth a few more years off my sentence."

"Or maybe the AUSA will be fed up with you and rip the deal up."

"Que sera, sera," Mangan said with a shrug of his shoulders.

"Oh, by the way," I said, "we got Stefan Konopka. He spilled his guts about you, and told us the whole story of his betrayal."

"No kidding? Can I read his statement?"

We all had enough of this wise-ass and had him brought back to his cell.

* * *

Two days later we met with Assistant United States Attorney Christine Silvera to review Mangan's plea deal agreement. He would tell us all we wanted to know, and he would get twenty years max for all his crimes. Most of us in law enforcement hate these plea bargain deals, but realize the criminal justice system would grind to a halt if every case went to trial. We didn't mind the ordinary street burglars copping out, but multiple murderers were something else. They stuck in your throat like a fishbone. This one stuck fast.

The next day, with his lawyer and AUSA Silvera in the room, Richard Mangan did tell us everything we wanted to know. He confirmed he hired three additional guys to augment him and his two regulars. He named them and told us how to locate the one who had gotten away. He told us the make and caliber of the guns he provided to them and then, the biggest piece of information we wanted – who hired him.

"His name is Bradley Monaghan," he said. "I don't know his exact title or position, but he has to be a big shot. A *capo* at least, if they still use that terminology."

"Why do you think he's a big shot?" Mike asked.

"Corner office with big windows. Knockout looking secretary. Expensive office furniture. The works."

"Why did Monaghan want these guys whacked?"

"Because they were rats he once told me."

"That's it? What about Donaldson?"

"Never gave me a reason, but it must have been important because he said for me to take care of him first, before the other six."

"How much did he pay you?"

"Fifty up front and fifty more after the hit was done."

"A hundred grand?"

"Yeah, and when you collar him please collect my second fifty for me, okay? I'll buy you all a steak dinner."

Ignoring the remark I said, "And how can we collar him? All we have is your word against him."

"For another five years off my sentence I'd let you wire me up and get some admissions on tape, but like I said before, that won't work for a lot of reasons."

"Tell us again," Mike said.

"The examination process I have to go through before I get in to see him. He never talks on the phone. – I tried once to call him and he wouldn't take the call. The next time I saw him, he reamed me out. Man, was he mad."

"Then how does he contact you?"

"Sends me a two-letter text message. 'LV' means get on the next plane to Vegas. Uh, but you know none of this matters."

"What do you mean?" I asked.

"Monaghan has to be long gone. I would be."

"Why would he run?" Mike asked.

"He hired me to kill six people. I fucked up, so therefore *he* fucked up. He's number one on the hit parade now. He's the guy you need to grab and make a deal with before he gets whacked."

"And where do we find Bradley Monaghan?" Spider asked.

"Beats me. You guys are the hot shot detectives."

I saw Spider's left hand begin to close into a fist, and I grabbed his left arm lightly. He got the message and relaxed.

We went over a few more details, including Konopka's part and how much Monaghan paid him, and how he sucked him into the scheme. I said, "Just as you did with Holmgren, you prey on people with big gambling debts."

"Yeah, Monaghan was good with that type of information."

When we had asked Mangan all the questions we could think of, we left the room and let the lawyers conclude the agreement.

Back in Mike's office he asked, "What now?"

"Go on your computer," I said, "and bring up the phone number of the LV Betterment Group."

Mike raised his eyebrows in surprise, but a few clicks later he jotted it down on a piece of paper and slid it over to me. I picked up my cell phone and dialed it, and when the operator picked up I said, "Mr. Bradley Monaghan, please."

"Oh, I'm sorry," she said. "Mr. Monaghan is no longer associated with the LV Betterment Group."

"I didn't know he left; he told me to call today to schedule a civic association meeting."

"I'm sorry, but as I said, Mr. Monaghan is no longer here."

"When did he leave?"

"A few days ago."

"Do you know where he works now, or how I can contact him? He's such a great guy, and a respected contributor to our group."

"No, sir. I'm sorry, but I have no contact information for him at all."

"Well," I said with a sigh, "that's too bad. Like I said, he's a great guy."

"Yes. Good-bye sir."

"Guess a trip to Las Vegas would be a waste of time about now," Spider said.

"I'll get a couple of Las Vegas agents over there with Monaghan's picture," Mike said. "Maybe they can dig something out on where he might have gone."

* * *

Spider and I brought pizza over to Mike and Allison's place the next day for lunch and we got Vince Genova and Tara on the phone. After bringing them up to speed on the latest information Mike said, "So tell us all about Bradley Monaghan."

"His official title is...was...First Assistant to the Chairman, but in reality he is second-in-command, the underboss, if you will, and also acts as consigliere," Vince said.

"And he's forty-nine years old by his official date of birth, and he looks his age," Tara said.

"Do you two agree with Mangan's assessment and I guess ours now too, that Monaghan has fled?" Mike asked.

"Oh yeah," they both replied.

"Any idea where a top mob guy would run to to escape the reach of all the organized crime cartels in the country?"

"*Out* of the country," Vince said. "No doubt to the island or nation where his cash has been wired to over the years."

"And he'll be safe there?" Spider asked.

"Depends on how much Bigelow knows about his personal financial arrangements."

We batted a few more ideas around and basically came up empty. I said, "On a positive note, we did solve our case. We got the mole in the Marshal's Service and we caught the mysterious killer, and we saved six lives."

"And when Pete Veltri is told these facts, he'll want you two back in Nassau Homicide forthwith," Mike said.

"Can you give Pete any reasons why we shouldn't go back?" Spider asked.

"Not off-hand."

"I can give you one good reason," I said. "I want to arrange a grand tour of the FBI facilities for my kids and in-laws. And we don't have to tell Pete Veltri we are somewhat at a dead end here."

"Great idea, Danny. I'll arrange that tour as soon as you get me the date. And maybe by that time one of us six brilliant investigators will think of something to further this investigation."

"I love your optimism, dear," Allison said as she picked up her second slice of the aromatic, steaming pepperoni pizza, the food even a six and a half month pregnant woman could not resist.

* * *

We had solved the case all right, but I knew none of us were satisfied. And we wouldn't be satisfied until we found the reasons these embezzlers looked so freaking young, and how they got that way, and who was the brains behind this scheme. Could Bradley Monaghan tell us? We had put him into the NCIC system as fast as possible with a Federal warrant for conspiracy to commit murder. We noted he was a flight risk out of the country which automatically sent his photo and identifying information to all international airports, ship terminals and railroad departure points that led to foreign shores. Now all we had to do was wait, and hope, and pray we got lucky.

Chapter 20

The Summerlin Institute of Research sat on sixteen acres of highly valued land on Nassau County's North Shore in the village of Sound View Point. The protrusion of land jutting out into Long Island Sound, called East Egg by F. Scott Fitzgerald in his novel *The Great Gatsby*, is still home to many millionaires living in huge mansions. One such millionaire – in reality a multi-billionaire – had turned his fifty-two room house into a vast, humming research center with one defining objective – to extend man's life span as far as possible by preventing all disease – including the disease of aging.

Courtney Summerlin had earned his billions by applying his vast mathematical knowledge, learned at the Massachusetts Institute of Technology and Harvard, to the hedge fund industry. His techniques had not only made him rich, they had made many of his investors into multi-millionaires. Court, as he was known to family and friends, was not obsessive about his wealth. His tastes were not extravagant, and other than buying the vintage 1920's estate on the Gold Coast, he lived modestly and donated millions to the charities of his choice.

Court, a billionaire by age forty-seven, was somewhat taken aback with his new found wealth, but first used it to assure the financial security of his wife and two children, his parents, and all his relatives and in-laws. All his personal needs were satisfied and would be for as long as he lived. And that was the fly in the ointment – someday he would die and his earthly pleasures, restrained as they were, would cease to be. And, although brought up a believer in the Christian faith, he always wondered if there was an existence after death. He hoped there indeed was, but he would like to postpone that discovery for as long as possible.

One afternoon, soon after he turned sixty-six years old, Court was sailing with his wife, Laura, on a brisk early May day. He remarked how much he enjoyed the simple pleasures of life, those money couldn't buy. Laura said, "Your money bought this sailboat, my dear, and the huge house we live in."

"And I could have bought this modest craft on a professor's salary. A lot of people I know, with much less money than we have, opt for those huge yachts with crews. Totally unnecessary. They're missing the point."

"Which is?"

"Enjoyment. Laura, can it get any better than you and I out here on the sound, sailing this boat ourselves, with deli sandwiches and cold beer?"

She snuggled up to her husband and said, "No, Court, I don't believe it can. And speaking of sandwiches, this fresh air has stimulated my appetite. What will you have, ham and Swiss, or roast beef?"

Court opted for the roast beef and said, "What's on the agenda for tomorrow?"

"Nothing, other than you working on your hedge fund for ten hours, as usual."

"Now, now, I only put in four hours this morning on the business."

"And you'll do six more after dinner."

"Maybe not, I'm thinking of cutting back, maybe selling the whole thing."

Laura sat up in surprise and stared at her husband. She said, "And what would you do to occupy your time?"

"Sailing, golfing, traveling."

"Ah, yes, the simple pleasures of life. Nice thoughts, but you would be bored to death. I know you love life, and nature, and seeing the world, but that's not enough for a man like you."

"What do you mean by *a man like me?*"

"You need another goal, an objective. Something big. You scrimped and saved and developed The Summerlin Fund. Your goal was to make it successful and make a lot of money. You did, but if you cash out, believe me, you'll need a substitute."

"I guess you think you know me after forty years of marriage?"

"I most certainly do."

"So what do you think this substitute goal should be?"

"Something difficult and big."

"Like finding the cure for cancer?"

"Yes," she said, thinking of her dead mother.

* * *

Over the next several months Court Summerlin eased out of his hedge fund, turning over more and more responsibilities and shares to his three junior partners. With the decrease in workload, he increased his efforts in research on disease – particularly cancer – although no one near and dear to him, other than his mother-in-law, had succumbed to that horrible disease. However, cancer's incidence and prevalence on Long Island gave Court cause for concern, and Laura had planted a seed in his mind. There seemed to be clusters of breast cancers on the North Shore much higher in occurrence than statistically expected. Was it something in the air? The water? No one knew, and after months of investigation, Court Summerlin came to the distressing conclusion, despite millions upon millions of dollars spent on this disease, doctors and scientists were no closer to finding a cure than they had been twenty years ago.

Perhaps, he thought, the money wasn't being spent wisely, or targeted in the right areas, but he clearly remembered one dedicated instance, an all-out effort to cure one type of this deadly disease – pancreatic cancer.

Shocked and saddened by the premature death of Marc Lustgarten, his friend and vice-chairman of his company, cable-media mogul Charles Dolan established a foundation in Marc's memory for the sole purpose of finding a cure for that deadly disease. Putting his money where his heart and soul were, he jump-started the foundation with ten million dollars of his own money. Using his charming and relentless powers of persuasion, he enlisted financial assistance from his many friends and associates in the media business, and from outside it. And the response to the gentle arm-twisting from the well-respected Dolan was overwhelming.

Memorial Sloan-Kettering Hospital in Manhattan, and The Lustgarten Foundation's fund raising arm, promised every penny donated would go directly to research – all administrative costs and salaries would be picked up personally by the benevolent Charles Dolan. He had done everything within his power to find a cure for this one particular form of cancer and now, almost twenty years later, that cure still eluded the researchers. The cure rate stood at no better than seven percent after five years, and the length of life was marginally increased beyond the initial six to twelve months. But the magic bullet had yet to be found. Court Summerlin had met Dolan on several business and social occasions, and knew how deeply disappointed he was a cure had not been found. And while thinking of Dolan and Marc Lustgarten, Court Summerlin had an epiphany – maybe everyone involved in cancer research was focused on the wrong target. Maybe cancer, in all its forms, could *never* be cured. Maybe the money and research should be directed at prevention. *Maybe the cure for cancer was simply not to get it at all.*

So Court turned his energies to prevention efforts which he found were mainly employed by the alternative medicine practitioners, those who pushed natural remedies and nutrition to fortify the body against disease and aging – the ones called "quacks" by the established medical profession. But the more Court studied, the more he became convinced a total health disease prevention approach was a much better alternative to conventional medicine, which only targeted a condition or disease *after* a person contracted it, and targeted it with super-expensive drugs, some with side effects worse than the disease. Following Chuck Dolan's example, Court founded The Summerlin Research Institute and, with expert advice from alternative medicine practitioners, nutritionists, naturopaths, and some conventional medical doctors who were open-minded to this approach, he put one hundred million dollars into the pot.

The home base of The Summerlin Research Institute was Court's fifty-two room estate, of which forty-two rooms were now devoted to laboratories, conference rooms, libraries, cafeterias, and small residence units. In later years, separate dining, residence and research facilities were built adjacent to the main house, and the entire property was surrounded by a six-foot tall, New England-style stone fence.

As Court approached his seventy-fifth birthday, his health began to deteriorate due to diabetes and heart disease. Although he had believed in, and adhered to, the healthy regimen developed at his institute, his doctors informed him his lifestyle changes had come too late to significantly alter his condition. Court had set a goal for his research staff – develop an elixir, a potion of nutrients and disease preventative additives, which could be taken in a daily dose with one's morning orange juice. This elixir would allow a normally healthy person to live a disease-free life for up to a minimum of 150 years. A long-range goal it indeed was, but now, after only ten years of work, they had a group of subjects all aged around sixty, who looked and tested as if they were twenty years younger.

One evening Laura said, "Court, you've done such wonderful work, it's a shame you can't benefit from it."

"I'm content our children will, and mankind in general. Too bad I couldn't have begun this project twenty years sooner."

"How are you feeling?"

"Tired, but the docs tell me I'm not going to die anytime soon."

"Maybe you should cut back your work a bit?"

"I have. Basically, I'm going only to worry about the finances – and I have a couple of assistants to help with that. The board of directors and I all agree on our goals and research protocols. There will be plenty of money remaining well after I'm gone. I will die a happy man someday."

"And I will die a happy woman, Court. You will go down in history as a great pioneer in this field."

"That would be comforting, but I don't believe there is anything more valuable to leave than a loving family and some benefit to human kind."

* * *

Fifteen years later, both Court and Laura Summerlin were resting in their graves, and their two children had moved out to their own homes and families. They remained devoted to, and part of, the program started by their father. The institute had expanded once again, and the stone fence was augmented with CCTV and alarm systems. The focus of the board of directors had changed – and not for the better. As Court Summerlin's fortune left to his beloved institute began to shrink, the board, with only one original member left who vehemently protested, decided to provide the institute's services not to mankind in general, but only to the select few, those rich enough who could post a fifty million dollar initiation fee.

As the character of the board changed from benevolent to malevolent, they realized they would need some "muscle" to enforce their new goals. Jordan Bigelow was invited to join the program. His initiation fee was waived in perpetuity in return for his services as needed. Bigelow was accepted and given three targets to eliminate and make their deaths appear accidental – Desmond Wolfe, the recalcitrant member of the board, as well as Courtney Summerlin, Jr., and Maryann Summerlin Hastings, the founder's children.

The accidental deaths, spaced out over two years, raised no suspicions of foul play, and the board was highly pleased with Jordan's performance. But now, many years later – today – when the news of the six failed attempted murders reached the board, they were not pleased at all. They were, in fact, furious and Jordan Bigelow would be called on the carpet to answer for his blunders.

* * *

Bradley Monaghan sat in his cheap motel room – cash, no I.D. required – and pondered his situation. He assumed the worst and figured Mangan had given him up, and now he was a wanted man. He had to get out of the country, and get out with his cash, which was well over the ten thousand dollar limit. Damn! He should have followed Bigelow's advice and stashed his money in an off-shore account; he should have gotten Mangan to get his inside guy to make him a set of documents; he should have done a lot of things, but now he had to face up to his situation and try to deal with it as best as he could. He put his head on the pillow and tried to sleep.

It took him two hours, lying on his back and staring at the ceiling, before sleep had come. But during those two hours, the beginnings of a plan formed in his mind. And the first thing he had to do in the morning was to get rid of his beautiful S-500 Mercedes-Benz, which was on every highway patrolman's hot sheet in the country. After he rose from his fitful sleep, he Googled Benz dealers in the vicinity of his motel in Albuquerque, and picked the biggest one. Using the map search function on his cell phone, he easily located it. A half hour later he checked out of his motel.

The receptionist at the dealership directed him to a sales rep, and Bradley got right to the point. He said, "I have a mint S-500 out there with less than 17,000 miles on it. I'm in a bind and need cash. Here's what I propose. Figure out what you can sell my car for, and give me ten grand less than that amount. Then write me a lease for a C-Class sedan. I may be in a temporary squeeze, but I still want to drive a Benz." He gave the salesman his warmest, sincerest smile and waited.

The salesman worked on his computer for an agonizingly slow five minutes. He said, "I'll be right back. I have to see the boss."

When he returned he said, "We can give you $87,500, assuming it passes inspection."

Monaghan thought it might be a bit low, but not bad. "Deal," he said.

"We'll give you a check and you can cash it at our bank. I'll call them so there will be no problems. And while you're gone, I'll write the lease."

Two hours later, minus some cash for the lease payments, Bradley Monaghan was again on his way east, after stopping for lunch at Burger King. He still didn't know where he was headed, but now felt a tiny bit safer. He drove at or below the seventy miles per hour speed limit and arrived in Amarillo, Texas at six p.m. He checked into another cheap motel, paying cash once again.

He worked a solid two hours to complete his plans. Satisfied, he drove to a nearby restaurant for a much-needed cocktail and dinner. Tomorrow, he would get an early start and should reach Dallas by early afternoon. His research on his laptop provided a list of countries which had no formal extradition treaty with the United States. Unfortunately, most of them held no attraction at all. Only two were promising – Croatia and Dubai. Having stopped at a couple of Croatian ports on a cruise he had taken three years ago with his now ex-wife, he liked what he had seen.

So, Croatia it would be. He would deposit most of his cash in an international bank in Dallas, drive to Dallas-Fort Worth International Airport, leave the Benz in long-term parking, and take the 6:40 p.m. flight to London, paying cash. He would then fly on to Zagreb, establish residence, and have his cash wired to him, as needed. That was as far as his planning went. He would be out of the country in a matter of hours. That was the critical thing. He would worry about the rest of his life after he got to Croatia.

The chilly, blowing January air in North Texas was an immediate waker-upper for Monaghan as he stepped out of his motel room door at 6:30 a.m. He would get his coffee and some breakfast at a fast-food drive-thru window, and be on his way. Forty minutes later, he turned off Interstate 40 on to Interstate 27 south, and set the cruise control for sixty-five in the seventy mph zone.

Texas Highway Patrolman Bobby Longworth, sitting in his cruiser a hundred yards up on the entrance ramp at Exit 52 near Plainview, noticed the silver-colored Benz go by and saw his speed detector register sixty-five mph. He raised his eyebrows. Nobody drove that slowly on this interstate, especially in a Benz. He glanced down at his hot sheet and saw a Benz was indeed wanted, but that Benz was a black S-500. But, with not much else to do on this bright, sunny morning, he figured he might as well check it out.

As he approached the Benz, he noticed the temporary tags from New Mexico, and his curiosity rose a bit higher. The fifteen-year veteran flipped on the overhead rack lights and tapped the siren. He saw the driver's head snap up suddenly. Poor guy, caught him by surprise. Oh well, let's see what we got here.

By the time Patrolman Longworth reached the driver's side window, Bradley Monaghan had somewhat regained his composure and had his wallet out. When Longworth said, "Good morning, sir," Bradley responded, "I didn't realize I was speeding, Officer."

"You weren't. May I see your driver's license and registration documents?"

"Sure, I just leased this car. The papers are in my glove box. Here's my license."

While Bradley was fishing around in the glove box, Longworth glanced at the license. Oh, boy! The name fit. This was the guy associated with the black Benz. Monaghan handed over the temporary registration and Patrolman

Longworth took the papers back to his vehicle. After confirming he indeed had the wanted man in the car in front of him, albeit in a different vehicle, he got on his radio and called his dispatcher in Region V – Lubbock. After the dispatcher ascertained the locations of the nearest highway patrol vehicles, Bobby suggested a plan, and it was approved by all.

Monaghan took a deep breath as the officer returned. He handed Bradley back his documents and said, "Why are you driving so slow? A Benz is made to run."

"Well, Officer, first I didn't want a $200 speeding ticket and second, this baby is brand new. I have to break it in before I step on it."

"How many miles you got on her?"

Bradley glanced at the odometer and said, "Three hundred forty-seven."

"Plenty broke in, and these cars don't need breaking in anymore, what with the synthetic oil and all. Tell you what, I got a lunch date in Lubbock I don't want to miss, if you know what I mean. How about you follow me down that way and you can open her up, make up some time for me stopping you?"

"Are you kidding me?" Bradley said. "And when I do open her up, you give me a very expensive ticket?"

"No, sir, I wouldn't trap you like that; you got my word on it. Ready to go?"

"Okay," Bradley said, hoping this guy was on the level. "I'll try to keep up."

"We'll go about forty miles before I have to get off. When I exit, you slow down. Try to keep it a bit below eighty. We usually don't ticket anybody on this road unless they push it past eighty-five."

The Benz responded beautifully as Bradley followed the big police cruiser. After hitting 120 mph, the patrolman settled in at 100 mph, and less than a half hour later he slowed down as the Lubbock exit approached. As Monaghan slowed behind him, something caught his eye in his rear-view mirror. It was the flashing red and blue lights of another cruiser closing on him, and now Patrolman Longworth's lights were also flashing. Another cruiser pulled up alongside him, and they all slowed, and slowed, and then they all stopped. Bradley was completely, tightly boxed in.

Chapter 21

Mike, Spider and I had flown out to Lubbock the night before, and we were at the county jail bright and early the next morning to interview Monaghan and take him into our custody. After speaking with Highway Patrolman Bobby Longworth – we loved his tale of the capture – and the investigator assigned to the case, we joined Monaghan in an interview room where he sat at a desk with his right wrist shackled to a U-bolt. He looked up at us and said, "I have nothing to say. I retained a lawyer, and he is on his way."

"Okay," Mike said. "We'll wait until he gets here. What's his name?"

"I have nothing to say."

We left the room and I said, "Don't you love these assholes? I think Bradley will have plenty to say when we get done telling him the facts of life."

We hung around with the Texas cops in their squad room swapping war stories and drinking coffee, and a quick thirty minutes later we were informed by the desk sergeant a Mr. Leo Davison, the attorney retained by Monaghan, was present. We went out to meet him and after introductions were made, he requested to speak to his client alone. "Sure," Mike said. "No problem, but you sure don't look like the typical mob lawyer we were expecting."

That shot a big look of surprise across Davison's face. "I'm a local criminal lawyer. What do you mean about the mob?"

"We'll tell you when you are done speaking with your client. Oh, here's a copy of our warrant, so you can discuss the exact charges with him."

"Thanks," he said, taking the papers from Mike and heading into the interview room.

He was out in fifteen minutes and said, "Gentlemen, my client vehemently denies the charges, and he will fight rendition back to Washington."

"Okay," Mike said. "Let's all go talk to him."

"I will not allow you to question my client..."

"Shut the fuck up, Leo. Let's go, guys."

Spider and I looked at each other in surprise. Mild-mannered FBI Agent Clark Kent had apparently reached his limit of civility in this stressful case. Davison meekly followed us into the room. This was going to be Mike Havlek's show, and he went right at Monaghan. "Listen to me, you piece of shit. You're going to tell us what we want to know, or you'll be a dead man. That's it in a nutshell."

"I must protest these threats against my client..."

Mike turned toward him, his eyes flashing with anger. He said, "Your client is in the Las Vegas Mob. He is the number two man in the organization. He retained you because he cannot retain his normal mob lawyer. The top man, Jordan Bigelow, wants to kill your client as soon as it can be arranged. He wants to kill him because he fucked up badly, and because he wants to silence him. So, if your stupid client doesn't open up to us, and put his miserable life into our care and custody, he will be dead in short order. So talk to him again."

With that, Mike motioned us all out of the room, leaving Leo Davison with a *what the hell did I get myself into?* look on his face. It did not take long, five minutes at the most, before an ashen-faced Davison opened the door and motioned us back inside.

Mike said, "Here's the deal, Bradley. You roll on Bigelow and we put you in Witsec. We got Mangan, and we got the guy in the Marshal's Service who was giving the info to him. The game's up. We'll read you your rights, and you voluntarily come back to D.C. with us where we cut the deal with the U.S. Attorney's Office."

Monaghan looked into Mike's eyes, and whatever he saw there, made him nod his head in obvious defeat. "Okay," he said.

Mike turned to Davison and said, "I don't think you want to listen to this, or represent Mr. Monaghan in this matter anymore, do you counselor?"

A look of relief washed over Davison's face, and he arose from his chair. "You are correct, Agent Havlek. Is that all right with you, Mr. Monaghan?"

"Sure, but your fee…"

"My fee is waived in this case. Good-bye,"

After Leo Davison hustled himself out of the room, we formally read Monaghan his rights, assured him his arrest would not be publicized, and he would be placed in protective custody once we got back to D.C. via a private FBI plane. Apparently satisfied, he told us everything we wanted to know and spent an hour writing it down for us, although we had audio-recorded the interview to be on the safe side.

We had him put back in his cell under suicide watch and we thanked the Texas cops for all their help. "He a real bad guy?" Patrolman Bobby Longworth asked in his Texas drawl as we prepared to leave.

"What guy is that, Bobby?" I said.

"I understand, Danny. Paperwork will be collected and sealed in the Captain's safe. Press will not be notified. And I bet the big boss of the Texas Highway Patrol would love a nice letter from the FBI when you wrap it up."

"Be glad to, Bobby," Mike said, shaking his hand and giving him his card. "Thanks again, and call me if you have any problems doing what you said."

"I'm sure there will be none. Adios, partners."

*　*　*

We were back in the lobby of the Lubbock Marriott by four o'clock and sitting in the lounge relaxing with cocktails. We needed something strong after what Monaghan had told us. After all, most of it bordered on the unbelievable.

"Living to be a hundred and fifty, or longer?" Spider said.

"And in decent shape, too?"

"I wonder how far along they are at this Summerlin Institute with their plans," Mike said.

"We are ace investigators," I said, sipping my scotch. "We will find out."

"How?"

"Let's talk about it."

"I think we should re-interview the eleven…I mean ten embezzlers," Mike said. "They stole the money to help raise their initiation fee for Summerlin. Maybe we can crack one or two."

"With what leverage?" Spider asked.

"I don't know, but we'll review all the written reports of their first interview once again to see what we can pick up."

"And of course we have to locate and arrest Jordan Bigelow who I bet is no longer on Long Island and not back in his Las Vegas office."

"And we should pay a visit to that institute in the near future," I said.

"Let's sleep on it for now. We are in the end game. We'll have a good dinner and a good night's rest. When we get back to D.C., we'll get all our heads together – Vince, Tara, Pete Veltri and anyone else involved. We have to do this right."

"I'm sure we will, Superman," I said smiling and raising my glass to Mike.

"This is some weird shit we're getting into now," Spider said.

"Weird indeed," Mike said. As he downed his martini in one final gulp.

* * *

Jordan Bigelow had flown from Las Vegas to JFK Airport in New York on the Friday morning of the six hits scheduled to take place that night, and the car service had delivered him to the front door of The Summerlin Institute by five p.m. The next day, he would begin his regular scheduled, four times yearly, three-day intensive longevity treatment protocol. In addition to a complete physical examination and various tests, he would be infused with a variety of nutrients, vitamins, minerals, anti-inflammatories, and gene modifying solutions, all designed to extend his lifespan and turn back the bodily damage visited upon him by environmental toxins, genetic mutation and harmful radiation.

Jordan's day began at 7:00 a.m. on Saturday and, except for purified water breaks, he was not scheduled for his lunch break until noon. So when the Chairman of the Board of Directors of the Summerlin Institute, who was always on hand to greet Bigelow, heard and saw the newscasts of the events of the previous evening on the TV in his office, he became extremely concerned.

As the day wore on and the remaining five members of the board had been notified and were now also glued to their televisions and telephones, their consternation began to grow. By three that afternoon, they were gathered in their surveillance-proof director's meeting room to decide what to do about this dangerous situation which, when fully played out, could bring down their Institute and all their future hopes and dreams.

Their decision was made easier by the fact Jordan was already on the premises. "He finishes at four o'clock," the chairman said. "I'm scheduled to have cocktails with him at 5:30, followed by dinner in the executive dining room. Perhaps you should all join us after dinner to hear what Mr. Big has to say about this fiasco."

"Would I be correct, Mr. Chairman," said one of the directors, "regardless of what he does have to say, he will not live to see the sunrise?"

"That is a strong possibility, Robert, but not yet a certainty. We'll decide after we hear him out."

* * *

The first thing Mike Havlek did when they got back to Washington and had Bradley Monaghan safely tucked away in a cell, was to reach out to the FBI's Research Unit and order up whatever information they could find on longevity studies by the scientific community. He asked for an expedited delivery, and the unit pulled out all stops and hand-delivered a two-inch thick packet a day and a half later.

After a brief glance through the voluminous material Mike said, "I'll have copies made for us. It will take time to get through it all."

"I have a suggestion," Spider said. "We have a loose end to take care of in New York, the million dollars in the safe-deposit box. Now would be a good time to have Evelyn Holmgren retrieve it, and we will be there to provide surveillance and back-up."

"We will?"

"Yes, and we'll bring copies of this research up for Tara, Vince Genova, Pete Veltri and Father Finn. After we all digest it, we'll meet at Vince's office at the FBI Headquarters in New York to lay out a plan of action."

"Sounds like a great idea," I said. "Mike?"

"Yes, let's do it. And I'll make a copy for Allison to leave with her. Oh, the autopsy report just got faxed over to me – Evan Donaldson's."

"Anything unusual?"

"Here, Danny, this is your area of expertise. I didn't read it."

I had read dozens of these ME autopsy reports and knew where the important information was in the pages of rhetoric. Only one thing stood out other than the cause of death, which was by two bullets in the head, and that was Evan Donaldson had Stage IV pancreatic cancer. At the time of his murder, he had only about three months to live. I remarked on this to Spider and Mike, saying something about all the money he spent to live to be a hundred and fifty, but to be screwed over in two ways.

"Shouldn't those millions have guaranteed him not to get cancer?" Mike asked.

"I don't know. Maybe the answer is in this stack of paper."

"But I bet the answer as to why Mr. Big ordered the hit on him is *not* in those papers," Spider said.

"Probably not, and he didn't tell Monaghan either. So I guess we'll have to ask Jordan Bigelow ourselves when we catch up to him."

"Do you think he'll run?" Mike asked.

"Good question," Spider said. "According to Monaghan, Bigelow flew out to the Summerlin Institute on Friday and may spend a few days in Manhattan before he flies back to Vegas. But he's the last guy we should talk to, I think."

"I agree. We need to do our research and other interviews first. Let's start packing."

* * *

Jordan Bigelow was a relaxed, contented man after his first day of treatment. The cocktails, and now this excellent dinner with the chairman, nicely complemented his satisfaction. "Jordan," the chairman said, "after dinner, I'd like you to join me and the directors in the boardroom to discuss some further business."

"Certainly, Randall, and I will bring good news with me for us. By now Evan Donaldson has been taken care of, and also those final six rats. I'll check with Bradley now for the details and bring you all up-to-date at the meeting."

"No, no," Randall Baxter said with a big smile. "You can call him on the speakerphone from the boardroom, so we can all enjoy the details together. That is after we partake in an after dinner aged port and a fine Cuban cigar."

"Good idea. We can toast to a long, long life – seventy-five more years, at the minimum."

"Indeed we can, Jordan. Maybe a hundred more!"

When they were all assembled and smiling in the boardroom, Jordan Bigelow dialed Bradley Monaghan's cell phone. The call went immediately to voicemail. A slight frown crossed Bigelow's face as he scrolled further and dialed Monaghan's home. Same thing. Was he at the office this late? Again his private office number went straight to voicemail. The office switchboard provided the standard greeting that the LV Betterment Group was closed for the weekend and would re-open at eight a.m. Pacific time, on Monday morning.

"Where the fuck is he?" grumbled Bigelow as he hit the disconnect button.

"Let's hope he is not in jail blabbing his guts out about us," Baxter said as he stared at Bigelow with cold, hard eyes, the smile gone from his face.

"What the hell is that supposed to mean?"

"It appears your man, Monaghan – and therefore *you* – screwed up big time. That's what it means. Take a look at this."

They turned to the big screen TV on the end wall and Baxter pressed a button on the remote he was holding. "This is a compilation of TV news reports that have been all over every network today while you were being treated."

Bigelow turned white as the clips ran one after another, the ramifications of the arrests hitting home. He had to assume, and he knew Baxter and the other board members had assumed, some of these arrested were talking. And the fact Monaghan seemed to be in the wind meant he ran before they got to him, or he too was indeed in custody. "I'll get to the bottom of this," he said. "I'll take care of the idiots who fucked up."

"We all feel it's too late for that, Jordan. We can't afford to have any association between you and Summerlin exposed to the authorities. They will come for you, and you will cut a deal."

"Never!"

"Correct." Baxter said, pressing a button under the arm of his chair. "You will never cut a deal."

Three burly men entered the boardroom and grabbed Jordan Bigelow out of his chair. One hand-cuffed him behind his back and another slapped a piece of duct tape over his mouth. He was dragged out straining and kicking. Within a few hours, the dismembered sections of Jordan Bigelow's body, weighted and wrapped securely, were dropped overboard at various locations in the middle of Long Island Sound.

Randall Baxter addressed the board members as soon as Bigelow was dragged out of the room. "We have always anticipated one day we would have to explain ourselves to the authorities, or the IRS. Let us review our situation, and finalize what we will convey to them. Then we'll get Victoria in so she can be fully prepared to deal with whoever arrives."

Chapter 22

Something was nagging at me as I read some of the material on the plane ride back to New York. As Tara at first couldn't put her finger on what was wrong with the Vegas mob's organizational chart, I couldn't pinpoint the clue floating around inside my brain. I put the papers down, rested my head back, and closed my eyes.

"Tired, partner?" Spider asked from the window seat next to me.

"Nah, just trying to think of something bothering me about this case."

"Well, we do have another loose end, you know."

I perked up, opened my eyes, and turned toward Spider. "Yeah?"

"Betty Kernan. We never heard from that school official if she ever requested her kids' school records."

"She probably never did. Mrs. Aronoff seemed reliable. I'm sure she would have called us. But that's not what's bothering me. It's something else. I'll have to sleep on it."

"You know, finding Betty Kernan is not important anymore. I mean, we got Mangan."

"You're right, it doesn't matter anymore. I think what's bothering me may have something to do with Donaldson, the one Mangan whacked."

"Yeah, the big question being why?"

"Yeah, Spider. Why order a hit on a guy who had paid his money, served his time, and was enjoying the good life?"

"Until maybe he found out he had terminal cancer?"

"You think he wanted his dough back from the Summerlin Institute?"

"Maybe. And if they said no, maybe he threatened to rat on them."

"So they whacked him to shut him up permanently?"

"Maybe, or maybe they whacked him as a preventive measure, *before* he found out he was terminal."

Now the thing was really banging around inside my head and when the guy sitting in back of me violently coughed, it came bursting out, like the cartoon light bulb flashing brightly. "That's it! Howard Sunshine!"

"What about him?"

"He was coughing up a storm when we interviewed him, remember? Maybe he's sick. Maybe he's dying in jail. Maybe when we see him again we tell him about Evan Donaldson being whacked because he too was sick. We tell him he's next unless he plays ball with us."

"And what do we offer him to get him to play ball?"

"A pardon and immediate treatment at whatever hospital is the top-notch one in the country for treating whatever he has."

"And who is going to pull that off?"

"Superman, of course."

"I looked over my seat across the aisle, to one row back where Mike Havlek was deeply engrossed in the research material. I said, "Hey, Mike. You'll do that for us, won't you?"

Knowing us well by now, Mike grinned and said, "Sure Danny, no problem."

* * *

Two days later we had all read the material provided by the FBI's Research Unit and were all sitting around a conference table at FBI Headquarters in Manhattan, sipping coffee and waiting for Allison Havlek to connect on the speakerphone.

We had accomplished a couple of things since we got back to New York besides reading mountains of scientific material. We had Evelyn Holmgren flown up by a couple of Columbus, Ohio FBI Agents, and she successfully retrieved the money from the safe-deposit box in Brooklyn without incident.

When she asked what was going to happen to the money Mike had said, "Are your children with your parents?"

"Yes."

"Well, my wife is over six months pregnant, so why don't you and I take the dough, and fly to the French Riviera, and see if we can spend it all in a week."

This was certainly so uncharacteristic of the normally serious, straight-arrow FBI agent, that we all reacted with open-mouthed silence.

"C'mon, you guys," he said as the color rose in his cheeks. "I'm joking here."

Evelyn Holmgren evidently had a sense of humor. She grabbed Mike by the arm and whispered, "Only a week, Superman?"

We burst out laughing and Mike, now blushing brightly said, "Okay, okay. The money will go back to the firm from where it was stolen. If the firm is not still in business, it will go to the Victim's Compensation Fund."

After saying good-bye and thanking Mrs. Holmgren for her cooperation, we left her with the two Ohio agents for her return trip home. Spider and I also made Mike aware of our conversation on the plane concerning Howard Sunshine and he said, "If he tells us substantial, credible information about the Summerlin Institute, I would not be averse to granting the deal."

Sometimes I really liked Mike when he was serious and spoke in FBI-ease, especially when I got what I wanted from him.

And, ironically, we weren't back in the Nassau Homicide office for more than two hours when the phone rang, and it was none other than Mrs. Aronoff informing me she had received a request to forward the Kernan children's school records. That destination would be made available to us upon serving her with the necessary subpoena. I said, "Would this request coincide with the start of a new school semester?"

"Yes," she said.

"Good. Thank you very much, Mrs. Aronoff. We'll get that subpoena to you eventually. The importance of speaking with Mrs. Kernan has diminished somewhat as we progressed on this case."

"Oh, how is that working out? That wasn't an accidental shooting at all on the Southern State Parkway, was it?"

"You'll have to serve me with a subpoena for me to divulge that information, Mrs. Aronoff."

She chuckled and said, "Touché, Detective Boyland."

"I'll give you all the gory details when I drop the subpoena off, okay?"

"I can't wait."

When I disconnected, I looked around the squad room with trepidation, but Doctor Death, the would be crime novelist, was nowhere in sight. I went into Father Finn's office, where he was engrossed in reading the material I had given him and said, "Where's Bernie, Sarge?"

"On a week's vacation to some warm tropical island."

"By himself?"

"With a *honey*, so he told us."

"What woman would go with Bernie – anywhere?"

"C'mon, Danny, for every male, evil-smelling gorilla out there, there's an equally evil-smelling female gorilla. You know that."

"Yeah, Boss, I guess you're right."

* * *

So now the seven of us, having diligently read all the research material, heard Allison pick up the phone and say hello.

"Hi, sweetheart," Mike said. "How are you doing?"

"Getting bigger by the minute."

"Stop eating pizza," Spider said.

"I wish that was the problem. I'm eating practically nothing. Who's all there?"

"Danny, Spider, Vince Genova, Tara, Francis Finn, and Pete Veltri," Mike said.

"Good, do you all mind if I speak first?"

"Not at all, you are a Pulitzer Prize winning investigative reporter, aren't you?"

"And I definitely smell another Pulitzer with this story. If half of this stuff is true, and if this Summerlin Institute has accomplished half of that half, we really have something here."

"Please give us your thoughts," Vince said. "Take your time, the FBI's paying for this call."

"Okay, the keys to longevity and a long, healthy, productive life are many and complex. Do we all agree on that?"

They all said, "Yes."

"But there are some basics that have to be followed before we get to the complex, esoteric stuff. For instance, a common-sense diet and exercise regimen with moderation being the key. A limit on alcohol consumption. No cigarettes at all, but maybe an occasional cigar. Maintaining a normal weight. Wearing your seat belt. Avoiding accidents. An active social life. Sound nutrition with the recommended dosages of vitamins and minerals. This lifestyle is conducive for a longer life because it serves to prevent accidents and diseases that will kill us – cancer, heart disease, stroke, diabetes, dementia, and Alzheimer's."

"But that doesn't work all the time for everyone," Spider said. "I mean we all have to eventually die from *something*."

"Yes, but it might get you into your eighties and nineties, perhaps to a hundred."

"Unless you're genetically disposed to those diseases, right?" Pete asked.

"Right, the genetic fly in the ointment. I'm glad to see you have read this stuff, too. But let's save that genetic stuff for later. Putting disease aside, what causes aging?"

"Invisible rays," I said. "The sun, ultraviolet rays, X-rays, cosmic rays, neutrinos, microwaves – and who the hell knows what else is bombarding our bodies."

"Correct, but it is what these rays do to our cells that cause aging. The three causes of aging are inflammation, free radicals and cell deterioration. And it's not only rays that cause aging, it's environmental toxins, pesticides and who knows what else we eat and drink."

"But what about those few people who make it past a hundred and ten?" Finn asked. "The so-called super-centenarians."

"Yeah," Mike said "and the ironic part is most of them hadn't lived a healthy lifestyle at all. I mean, one old guy attributed his advanced age to drinking a half-pint of bourbon every day."

"And another to scarfing down bacon and eggs most days of his life," Vince said.

And how about the 114 year-old lady who smoked a pack and a half of unfiltered cigarettes for almost a hundred years?" I asked

"Correct," Allison said, "and those folks are the key. What allows them to live to reach 120 years old, which seems to be, and has always been, the maximum age we can prove any human being ever attained, *despite* all their bad habits?"

"They must have some inner protection that prevents them from getting all the routine diseases." Pete said.

"Why do they die at all? Why is 120 years our apparent limit?"

"I don't think I read anything in all that pile that answered that question," I said.

"You didn't, Danny, because it wasn't there. So I did some additional research on the good old internet."

"Sometimes I think you're a better investigator than we are," Mike said.

"Sometimes? I got a Pulitzer. What do you have?"

"I have you, my love, braggart that you are."

"And what of interest to us did you find on the internet?" Tara asked.

"The answer is in our cells. And within our cells are our DNA and our genetic footprint. That's what we have to protect us and prevent our genes from mutating in a bad way, causing disease. However, despite never contracting any fatal disease, the one disease that kills us all is old age."

"Are you saying aging *itself* is a disease?"

"Yes, a disease that has no cure, nor any prevention."

"So maybe," Vince said, "we should feed our cells something to encourage them to stay healthy and mutate in a *good* way."

"Ah, yes, a magic bullet, like the so-called Methuselah gene," Allison said. "And I think that's what the Summerlin Institute is developing."

"Or maybe has already developed," Spider said.

"They sure discovered something to make those people look years younger," Pete said. "That's for damn sure."

"Not to throw a wet towel over this interesting discussion," Vince said, "but what is the crime here? Why should we investigate the Summerlin Institute?"

"Are you kidding?" I asked. "We got a trail of dead bodies here."

"And the Summerlin Institute killed them?"

"No, Jordan Bigelow had them killed, and Bigelow is a member of the Institute," Spider said.

"Did Bigelow admit that to you?" Pete asked.

"No, you know we didn't contact him yet. We don't even know where he is."

"Maybe you hotshots, including Superman here, ought to find him and ask him," Father Finn said with a smile. "How long are you going to hang around reading this scientific bullshit?"

We all had to chuckle at Finn's jibe. Mike said, "You don't have to break our chops, Sarge. We already have the fire in our bellies. We're going to crack this thing wide-open. Me, and Batman, and Robin."

"God save us from the ravings of these youngsters," Vince said.

"Better be nice to us, you old bastards," I said. "When we take the Summerlin Institute down, we won't give you a swig from the fountain of youth. And you three senior citizens look like you could use it."

"You know, I could get mad at you for that wiseass comment," Pete said, "but I grant you that Vince, Francis, and I, might need a few shots of that elixir. Supervising guys like you and Spider is enough to make any man old."

"So what's the plan of action?" Vince asked.

"First, we find and talk to Jordan Bigelow," I said.

"Then we re-interview the ten remaining big shot embezzlers – with special attention to Mr. Howard Sunshine – who we believe are members of the Summerlin Institute," Mike said.

"Then we pay a personal visit to the Summerlin Institute," Spider said.

"And who will you talk to there?" Allison asked.

"Uh, we don't know yet," I said. "I..."

"Have any of you done any research on the place yet?"

The three of us sat in silence avoiding answering Allison's pointed question. I could envision her shaking her head as she said, "Jeez! Well, thankfully, I have. Shall I proceed?"

"Yes, dear," Mike said.

"As you might expect, there is little information publicly available on it – I mean *very* little. Basically, it says the Summerlin Institute is a privately funded research institution devoted to health and longevity by exploring all scientific disciplines and their application to human disease prevention."

"Kind of vague," Tara said. "Any contact information?"

"Yes, a Victoria Bennett. Here's the phone number."

"What's her title?" Mike asked.

"Doesn't say."

"Anything else on Summerlin?" Vince asked.

"Nada. Are we done here?"

"Getting hungry, Allison?" I asked.

"No, wiseguy. If you have to know, I have to pee – badly."

"Well, let's not stop you from that," Mike said. "Talk to you later."

"Get your spare asses going and solve this case. I want the story."

With that statement, Allison disconnected and Pete said, "I see Allison has not changed one bit since you snagged her out of Long Island, Mike."

"If anything, she's tougher."

"And smarter than a lot of so-called investigators in this room," Tara said.

"Hey, now wait a minute," I said.

"Talk to me when you three got Bigelow in cuffs. I gotta get back to the office."

"Talk about tough broads," Vince said, shaking his head. "Thank god they're on our side."

Chapter 23

Where the hell was Jordan Bigelow? Spider had called the LV Betterment Group and was told Bigelow was out of town on business, and it was uncertain when he would return to the office. We were back in D.C. and Monaghan was still in our local lock-up awaiting placement in Witsec, so I went over to see him. "Bradley," I said, "it's Thursday, and Mr. Big is not back in Vegas yet. Where the hell is he?"

"Like I said, he usually spends three days at Summerlin and once in a while stays in the city for a couple of days. Usually he's back by now. Have you checked the airline to see if his return ticket is still open?"

"Yes, and it is. Should we be concerned?"

"Yeah, but I'd give him a few more days."

"And if he doesn't show up somewhere by then?"

"They whacked him."

"Like you thought he was going to whack you?"

"Yeah. Listen Boyland, he was out there at Summerlin when the shit hit the fan. My guess is he's dead and buried deep."

"Isn't Summerlin a medical research place? Would they have the means, and the balls, to cap a mob leader?"

"When there's a lot of dough involved killers can be bought, and all you gotta do is point out the target. Doesn't matter who it is. You know that."

"Yeah, I guess I do. Thanks."

It was now on to the second phase, the interviews. To speed things up, and leaving Sunshine for last, we divided the nine embezzlers into three groups of three, clumped as geographically close to each other as possible, and me, Spider and Mike hit the road in different directions. It took us over a week to locate and interview, or attempt to interview, them all. Of the nine, five refused to be interviewed again, claiming they told the first interviewers all they knew. Those five were now out of prison and referred us to their attorneys. The remaining one on the outside, and the three still in jail, consented to the second interview, but politely and pleasantly, told us absolutely nothing new at all. Despite our best efforts, we had no leverage on any of them, and they knew it.

They had all denied any knowledge of the Summerlin Institute or any special health programs, but dammit, they all looked happy, healthy, and much younger than their actual ages.

Jordan Bigelow still had not returned to Las Vegas. The receptionist hemmed and hawed and stammered on about an unexpected business trip of undetermined length to some undetermined country overseas. That left our one last hope, Howard Sunshine, to spill his guts to us about the inner workings of the mysterious Summerlin Institute, and allow us to advance this mysterious investigation.

* * *

Two days later, Spider and I were back at the Allenwood Low Security prison and first spoke to Warden Bennington. After informing him of our desire to re-interview Howard Sunshine I said, "We noticed when we were here several weeks ago Mr. Sunshine was coughing a lot. Is he ill?"

"Yes. We treated him for his cough, but the medicines did not work, so we ordered a chest X-ray for him."

"Any bad news?"

"Spots on both lungs. We are going to transport him to a medical facility for a biopsy in a few days."

"Poor guy," Spider said, "and if I remember correctly, he was not a smoker."

"No, he told us he never had a cigarette in his entire life. Claimed he never used tobacco in any form."

"Bad break," I said, "but things like that happen."

The warden called to have Howard brought to an interview room and a few minutes later we walked in. Howard had changed – drastically – since we last visited him. A gray pallor had replaced his healthy, fair-skinned complexion. He looked drawn and thinner; worried and *older*. I immediately brought his changed condition up saying, "My god, Howard, what happened?"

"What do you mean?"

"You look awful. Are you sick?"

"Some lung problem," he said, raising his fist to his mouth and coughing in it.

"Then we'll get right to the point," Spider said, laying a full-faced picture of an alive, healthy-looking Evan Donaldson on the table in front of him. "Recognize him?"

"No, who is he?"

"His name is…was, Evan Donaldson. He was a member of the Summerlin Institute." Spider placed a second photo of Donaldson from the crime scene showing the two bullet holes in the back of his head. "This is him, too."

"Someone shot him?"

"Yeah, but they wasted two bullets. He had terminal cancer. The ME said he would have lasted only three more months."

"Obviously the killer didn't know that."

"On the contrary," I said. "We think he was murdered *because* he had the cancer."

"I don't understand that at all."

"We believe the Summerlin Institute had him killed to keep him from talking about what goes on there. We believe he wanted some, or all, of his membership fee back as it was now obvious he wasn't going to live to be 150 years old."

"What has this got to do with me?"

"If your biopsy comes back positive, Summerlin is not going to help you. You'll be on your own and might well end up dead like Donaldson."

I didn't know if Sunshine knew I was taking a stab in the dark with what I said. He sat there quietly, head down, mulling it over. I glanced over at Spider, who put his hand on top of Howard's and said, "Here's the deal. We get the rest of your sentence commuted, and we treat you at the best hospital in the country. Assuming you recover, we put you in Witsec."

Howard looked up and said, "And what do I have to do for that generous offer?"

"Tell us everything you know about the Summerlin Institute, and maybe act as our man on the inside when you go back for you quarterly treatment."

"You seem to know some things about Summerlin already."

"But not as much as you."

"I'm getting the biopsy in a few days. I'll call you after I get the results."

"Okay," I said handing him my card. "Despite what you did to get in here, you seem like a decent guy. I hope your biopsy comes out negative."

"But then I would have no reason to accept your offer, would I?"

"No, but then you don't have cancer, or some other horrible disease, which I wouldn't wish on you. We'll find another way to investigate Summerlin."

"I appreciate that, Detective. I'll call you one way or the other."

As we drove away I said to Spider, "Strange, isn't it, just like Mike Mackey with the lung cancer. Remember him?"

"I sure do. His testimony put Sonny Slick on Death Row."

"I wonder if Howard will be just as valuable if he ends up positive for it, but like I told him, I don't wish that goddamn disease on anyone."

"Me neither, and I'd be much happier with healthy witnesses from now on."

* * *

Back in Washington we had nothing to do but wait for Howard Sunshine to get his biopsy results and call us. "What are our options now?" Mike asked.

"None immediately come to mind Spider said, "other than a personal visit to Summerlin to see what we can see."

Then I had a thought – some things to occupy us while we played the waiting game with Sunshine. "Mike, let me call my son and see if they can come up to Quantico this weekend for the tour I promised them."

"Sure. I'll set it up if they can make it, and I'll personally escort them with you."

"Why don't you spend the weekend with Allison instead? And Spider, you should go home to see your wife and kids. We all need a break."

They both agreed and I picked up the phone and called my father-in-law's home in Roanoke. Doris answered and I said, "I know it's Thursday and it's short notice, but can you and Bill and the kids come up to Quantico this weekend for that tour we discussed?"

"Let me check with everyone, and I'll call you back. I don't think there's anything big planned so far."

She got back in five minutes and it was a go. They would come up late Friday and stay in a nearby motel. She said they were all excited about the visit.

I dropped Spider at Reagan Airport Friday afternoon and made reservations for dinner at an Italian restaurant near the Ramada Inn where my in-laws and kids would be staying and then went back to the office until they arrived. Mike told me he had arranged everything and two agents would meet us here Saturday morning and host us all for the entire day.

"Terrific, Mike, now get out of here and go home to Allison, and don't come back until Monday morning."

"Okay, but I know I won't be able to turn off my mind about this case."

"Me neither, but I'm sure going to try."

* * *

Dinner at Sorrento's was enjoyed by all and there was no tension palpable between me and my in-laws. Maybe the crack in the ice that occurred on Christmas would develop into a full-fledged thaw. I picked them up early the next morning and drove us all the to the Quantico site where we were met by two smiling agents – Gina Santos and Carl Malone – who gave us all visitor's badges and we began the tour.

Gina and Carl seemed to enjoy their escort duties despite being constantly peppered with questions by Patrick and Kelly. The agents had everyone except me finger-printed and gave them the cards for souvenirs, and we spent a couple of hours in the FBI Laboratory followed by observations in classrooms where new agent training was underway. But, after lunch in the cafeteria, the highlight of the day was the pistol range where, much to my surprise, they allowed the children to fire a few rounds each from a variety of handguns after the standard safety lecture.

Bill and Doris had somewhat reluctantly agreed to allow the kids to shoot and, much more surprisingly, fired a few rounds themselves when prompted by the agents. Bill's paper target had the most holes in it, and when I commented on his marksmanship, he said, "I was pretty good with the M-16 when I was in Vietnam, and I shot a few pistols, too."

"I didn't know you were in the war, Gramps," Patrick said. "Did you kill any Viet Cong?"

"I don't want to talk about that now, Pat. Okay?"

"Sure," he said. "Maybe some other time."

The day wound down with more sightseeing, a drive to the Marine Corps Base across the interstate, and a visit to the PX, where we bought the kids some mementos of their visit. I got them back to their motel by five and we all went out for dinner at a Japanese Hibachi restaurant, where the chef entertained us with his culinary tricks including popping a piece of shrimp right into Kelly's open mouth.

Patrick began the questioning by saying, "Okay, Dad, tell us about your case. All solved?"

"Yes and no. Here's where we are...."

"So," Bill said, "you feel the missing guy from Las Vegas was the one who ordered the murders of the people in the Witsec program?"

"Yes, we do."

"Why did he want them killed?" Doris asked.

"We think to either show some big shots he had the muscle to accomplish it, or as a favor, or for payment of his continuing membership dues in an exclusive club."

"What club would want a murderer as a member?" Patrick asked.

"Indeed, and that's what we're trying to find out. So far, it's a mystery."

"Do you know the name of this club and where it is?" Bill asked.

"Yes, but that information has to stay with me and my partners for now."

"Until you figure out how to infiltrate it, right?" Patrick asked.

"Right."

"Send some Black-Ops guys in there. They'll get it done."

"How about Seal Team Six?" I said with a laugh.

"Fly some drones over it with bombs," Kelly said.

"Hey! What kind of stuff are you two watching?"

"Dad," Kelly said in an exasperating tone of voice, "this stuff is on all the video games."

Bill shook his head and said, "All these kids with this violent material. I refuse to buy it, but their friends have it all."

"Times change, Pop. No more running around the streets with cap guns."

"What's a cap gun?" Kelly asked.

"Ancient history," I said.

After I dropped them off at the Ramada and we all said our good-byes, I drove back alone to my motel thinking about what a great day we all had, but also thinking about Black-Ops. The FBI had to have a Black-Ops group, didn't they?

Chapter 24

With nothing to do on Sunday and the kids heading back home, I decided to stroll around Washington and take in a couple of the city's fabulous museums. I called Tara after breakfast and filled her in on the situation with Sunshine. She said, "I guess the investigation is at a standstill until he makes his decision?"

"Seems that way. Any advice for us?"

"Can't offer any, I'm afraid. What's your goal here with Summerlin?"

"We all know someone there – their CEO, or President – invited Jordan Bigelow to join their longevity program to utilize his talents as a hit man. They used him successfully until his recent big screw up. Now they have no use for him, so they had him whacked. They are the murderers who called the shots on all the guys in Witsec, and on Evan Donaldson."

"A lot of supposition there. How are you going to prove it?"

"First, we'll have to see what Howard Sunshine can provide, and go from there."

"You'll call me if he spills the beans, right?"

"Of course, we all value your input, my dear. Talk to you later."

* * *

The call from Howard Sunshine came on Tuesday. Mike and Spider stared at me as Howard began speaking. His first words were, "It's definitely cancer, and I need immediate treatment."

"I'm sorry to hear that, Howard. We can make the arrangements we discussed, if you want to proceed."

"Yes, I want out of here. I want to go to Memorial in Manhattan."

"So, we have our deal?"

"Yes."

"I'll get on it right away. See you soon."

Mike Havlek picked up his phone and dialed AUSA Christine Silvera, who he had previously notified of the situation, and she promised quick action. Two days later we were all on the way to Allenwood to meet with Sunshine and his attorney to finalize and sign our agreement. And Christine brought with her a commutation of sentence agreement – for exigent medical reasons – signed by a Federal judge.

After three hours of negotiations all the kinks were ironed out, and the deal was signed. Howard's lawyer left and Howard told us all he knew about the Summerlin Institute, which to our great disappointment, was not much at all. He had been invited to join fifteen years ago, seemingly out of the blue, by a man he met at his country club. The man, who gave his name as Alan Gerard, explained the Summerlin Institute was past its beginning stages and needed a big cash infusion to ramp up its research into longevity. He said they were only approaching the elite members of society to join.

"And the price of your entry was fifty million?" I asked.

"Yes, but I was about ten short at the time."

"So you embezzled the rest?"

"Yes, but to avoid detection, I did it a little at a time. The Institute accepted half up front, with my promise of payment of the rest over the next two years."

"And you began their treatments right away?" Mike asked.

"Yes, until I got caught. Until Jerry Harrison got caught, and ratted us out."

"And Jerry, a/k/a Jonathan Holmgren, got whacked. But you said *us*?"

"Several of us at the firm went down. I had to bring some others in on my embezzlement scheme and pay them off, including Jerry, because suspicions were increasing and pointing in my direction. And I had gotten greedy."

"You stole more than the ten million you needed?" Spider asked.

"Much more, to support my lifestyle, and because all I had went to Summerlin."

"Was it all worth it?"

"Yeah, until I got fucking cancer."

"Now this is important, Howard. Did this Alan Gerard, or any other member of the Institute, tell you they would kill Jerry Harrison for you?"

"Not directly. I never saw Alan Gerard again after those initial meetings to finalize my membership. But one day, when I was at my three-day treatment protocol, and out on bail after my conviction awaiting sentencing, a guy in a business suit stopped me in the hall and said, "We'll try to take care of you while you are in prison, and we'll definitely take care of the guy who put you there.""

We paused our questioning while Howard provided us with descriptions of Alan Gerard and the unnamed man in the suit. Mike asked, "How could you keep up your protocols while you were here?"

"Not very well, I'm afraid. They send me the nutritional supplements – vitamins, minerals and whatever else – and I take them every day. I also do my fitness exercises and watch what I eat according to their guidelines."

"But you still got sick," I said, "and if truth be told Howard, you don't look as young as you did when we first met you."

"It's the infusions into the bloodstream I get when on the premises. That's the key to the program. The rest is merely maintenance."

"And what is in these infusions?" Mike asked.

"The fountain of youth. The stuff that dreams are made of, as Bogart once said in the *Maltese Falcon*."

"Can you be a little more specific?" I asked.

"On day one, I get infused with three bags of solutions that contain ingredients to prevent all forms of the big killer diseases – cancer, heart disease, diabetes, and dementia."

"Which didn't work in your case."

"Because I haven't had an infusion in over a year. You must get that treatment four times a year for it to continue its effectiveness."

"Continue," Mike said. "What happens on day two?"

"Three more bags of liquid pumped into my veins. These contain cell rejuvenators and chemicals to wash out senile and senescent cells. It also contains anti-inflammatories, glycation reducers, and a bunch of other stuff with names I can't pronounce."

"And on the last day?"

"On day three we get the biggie – three more bags of liquid that contain genetic modifiers which target those genes which control aging and change my DNA structure by supplementing it with longevity inducing genes."

"The Methuselah gene," I said. "According to the Bible, he lived to be 969 years old."

"They have used that term, but the immediate goal is 150 years – 150 *good* years."

"Do you feel they are reaching that goal?"

"I can't tell you that, but I know I looked, and felt, twenty years younger before I got in here."

"Have you ever heard of Jordan Bigelow?"

"No, who is he?"

"Here's his picture," Spider said, placing the photo on the table in front of Howard.

"He doesn't look familiar...."

"He's a member of Summerlin," I said. "How old does he look?"

"About forty-five."

"He's seventy-five," Mike said, "and he's the head of a company that is a front for the Las Vegas Mob. He's the guy who carried out the hit on Jerry Harrison and many others."

"Personally?"

"No, through his underlings, but he directed the hits on behalf of Summerlin."

"So you caught him?"

"He's disappeared. His outfit screwed up their last batch of hits and we think the Summerlin brass had him whacked. That's one of the things we want you to find out when you get back in there."

"If I survive," Howard said.

"Try to be optimistic, Howard. Let's get some lunch, and then Danny and Spider will drive you to the hospital in New York. They are awaiting your arrival."

* * *

We had driven to Allenwood in separate cars. Mike and Christine headed back to D.C., and Spider and I walked out the front gate with Howard into the icy, February air. He breathed deeply and said, "Thanks for getting me out of there. I know it's low security, but it's still a jail."

I knew the feeling, of course, but kept my experience at Wallkill to myself. I said, "You're welcome. Let's hope you rapidly recover and get back to Summerlin. Is your wife in the loop?"

"Yes, Arlene and I have been on the phone a lot. She's flying to New York as we speak. She'll meet us at the hospital."

"Howard, I have a disturbing thought," Spider said. "Assuming Summerlin employs top notch doctors and researchers, some of them may work at Memorial, too. If you are recognized, tell the truth. You were released early to get treatment, and you can't wait to resume your protocols at Summerlin."

"Good thinking, partner," I said as I drove east on Interstate 80.

We made it to the George Washington Bridge at the start of the rush hour and worked our way down the east side to the hospital. We parked in their garage and escorted Howard inside to Admissions. His wife had not yet arrived, so we hung around with him. I said, "Howard, how does Arlene feel about you looking younger while she ages normally?"

"That's one of the reasons I continued to steal from my company – to get Arlene into the program."

"Summerlin allows that?"

"They encourage it. A lot of spouses are in the program from what I understand."

"I can see why," Spider said. "To promote marital happiness. Some women, men too I guess, would get upset with a younger-looking spouse out and about."

As we were about to leave, Arlene Sunshine walked in, suitcase in hand. We stood by as they hugged and kissed, and after Howard introduced us, we took our leave. I said, "Keep in touch and good luck. We will all be praying for you."

"That's very kind of you," Arlene said. "Thank you for getting him released and into the hospital."

Back in the car Spider said, "Home, James, we have to plan our visit to Summerlin."

* * *

The next morning we were back at Nassau Homicide in Pete Veltri's office with Father Finn. Connected on the speakerphone were Mike, Allison, Tara and Vince Genova. Spider and I brought everyone up-to-date and solicited opinions on our approach to Summerlin. Tara said, "Are you going to call the contact person for an appointment, or will you drive up to the gate cold and try to schmooze your way in?"

"That's what we want your opinions for," Spider said.

"If you call for an appointment, you lose the element of surprise," Mike said.

"But on the other hand, it reduces the suspicion involved with a visit from the police," Finn said.

"If you called this Victoria, what would you say?" Vince asked.

"We are investigating a missing person and think Summerlin may be of assistance," Spider said.

"That would raise too many questions in her mind, and she would start asking them," Pete said. "Hit her cold, in person, and you can observe her reactions."

We kicked it around a bit more and decided Pete and Mike were right – go with a face-to-face approach with no prior warning. I said, "That's assuming they open the gate and let us in."

"If they don't," Allison said, "call Emergency Services and have them knock it down."

"Strong words from a mommy-to-be. How are you feeling, by the way?"

"Tired and cranky, Danny. Tomorrow's my last day at work. I gotta go and pee. Keep me informed."

After she disconnected Mike said, "I guess I'm in for a tough few weeks. She's not happy when she's not digging for a story."

"Grin and bear it," Tara said. "Be super nice to her, and do not comment on her appearance or attitude."

"Good advice, and I will try. Are we done here?"

We were, and I looked at my watch as we left the office. "Ready for a ride to the Gold Coast, Spider?"

"Ready as I'll ever be. Let's go."

As I reached for my coat, I spotted Doctor Death heading our way. "Hey Danny, wait a second!" he shouted. As he approached, something about him seemed different. He was smiling, not frowning, as was his usual demeanor. But that wasn't it. He looked…clean! And he was not preceded by his usual foul body smells. In fact, a pleasant odor of expensive cologne, maybe Georgio Armani, came my way as he approached. But best of all, he had no manuscript papers in his big mitt.

"What's up, Bernie?"

"I want to let you know I put that novel of mine on the back burner."

"Oh, why?" I asked as a wave of relief washed over me.

"Melanie thinks it's good, but a bit over the top. She wants to help me write a romance novel instead. We could put *some* crime stuff in it she said."

"Uh, Melanie?"

"Oh, yeah, my new sweetheart. I met her at Mulvaney's a few weeks ago and we just came back from St. Maarten."

"You only knew her a couple of weeks and already you're going away together?"

Bernie actually blushed and said, "I guess it was love at first sight. And I suggested St. Maarten because of the way you described it in your journal."

"You told your sweetheart about me and Niki?"

"Yeah, and we tried to find the spot where that bitch buried you alive, but it was all grown over."

"I'm happy for you, Bernie, but me and Spider gotta go. And I'm happy for you and Melanie."

"Me, too," Spider said, finding his voice.

"Thanks guys," he said, beaming and walking away.

"Can you fucking believe that, Spider?"

"Barely. Miracles do happen, I guess. I mean, he didn't smell at all."

"Yes, he did. He smelled *good*."

"There's a downside to this, Danny. What do we do when we need *Gigantus Bernus Horribilis* to scare the shit out of some dirt bag?"

"Or maybe not a genuine dirt bag, but some front-desk person who adamantly refuses to tell us what we want to know?"

"Like you think Victoria Bennett won't?"

"Let's go find out, partner."

Chapter 25

It was a typical February day on Long Island – cold, cloudy, dreary, damp, but no threat of snow in the air. We drove north on Port Washington Blvd. and crossed into Sound View Point, where the road's name changed to Main Village Road. Spider pulled the car into a parking space at Village Hall on Tibbits Lane, which housed the police department and all other municipal offices. Years ago, when the Nassau County Police Department merged with the New York City Police Department to form the NYMPD, most of the village departments dissolved themselves and joined the NYMPD – the cost savings to the taxpayers was too much to pass up – and only a few wealthy village departments chose to stay independent. Sound View Point was one of those villages, and they employed twenty officers to patrol five-and-a-half square miles of territory with a population of 4,000 persons. Not bad if you could afford it, and the Sound View Point residents could certainly afford it.

We entered the police department and were greeted by the desk officer, a pleasant-looking sergeant in his mid-thirties, who recognized us as fellow cops. "What brings you two dicks up to our fair village?" he asked. "Oh, I'm Jim Kendrick, by the way."

"Pleased to meet you, Jim" I said, and Spider and I shook hands with him. "We heard you had *two* barking dogs bothering the residents last night, a major felony I understand, and we're here to investigate on your behalf."

He laughed and said, "Yeah, they really sounded vicious. Thanks for coming up."

We could kid around, but these village cops had the exact same training as all NYMPD cops received, and were equally as competent. And although their activity was mostly limited to minor crimes, they could get ambushed and shot just as easily as if they were on patrol on Pitkin Avenue in Brooklyn. I said, "Sarge, tell us all about the Summerlin Institute."

"Sure, you got something going on up there?"

"Maybe. We're from Homicide and involved in a weird caper. One of our suspects, a guy named Jordan Bigelow, is now among the missing. The last we knew of him he flew into JFK over a week ago, and was supposed to stay at Summerlin for a few days. But as of today, he hasn't returned to Las Vegas."

"And you're on your way up there to ask a few questions?"

"Yes," Spider said, "we have the name of a Victoria Bennet as a contact person."

"Ah, yes. Vicky Bennet. Pleasant lady, and easy on the eyes. She's the PR person who shows people around."

"You've been up there?"

"Sure, many times. Mostly on aided cases. You'd be surprised how many people fall off treadmills."

"So they have exercise facilities?"

"Oh, yeah, all top of the line equipment, but the place is not only an exercise facility, it's basically a research institute."

"For disease prevention and longevity research?" I asked.

"Yes, a lot of high-powered scientists work there."

"Do they live there?"

"Some, but most commute from the city. And most of them don't drive out. They take the Long Island Rail Road to its last stop in Port Washington and take a taxi the rest of the way."

"And all those taxis and car services have to go up Main Village Road, right?"

"Right."

"Too bad you don't record the plate numbers of those vehicles," Spider said.

"Who says we don't?"

"You're kidding!"

"Not too many people know about it, you understand."

"We sure do. How long do you keep the recordings?"

"Ninety days, so if you know the date and approximate time a car driving Bigelow came through, you might have a nice lead to follow up on."

Sergeant Kendrick showed us into a back office and directed a police officer to assist us in locating the vehicles that passed through on the Friday in question. Assuming Bigelow's flight landed on or near schedule, and adding thirty minutes for luggage pick-up, the car service should have passed the video camera between three and four in the afternoon. I said, "Officer, could you run the recording from two to five p.m. for us?"

He fiddled with some knobs and switches and said, "Here you go. Tell me when you want me to stop it, or slow it down."

At 3:27 a marked taxi passed, and when the officer slowed the recording down, I copied the plate number and time in my notebook. The officer said, "That cab is Station Taxi from Port Washington. I doubt he went into JFK, but it's a possibility."

The next vehicle, passing by at 4:32, was a black stretch limo. I noted the plate number and we continued to watch. No others passed. Spider said, "I'm guessing the limo gotta be Bigelow. I'm surprised there were only two cars going up there."

"A lot of people come by chopper," the officer said.

"They have their own helipad up there?"

"Yeah, and it gets a lot of use. The choppers fly out of Manhattan up the East River, make a right turn and set it down right at Summerlin."

"Don't the villagers complain about the noise?" Spider asked.

"No, there is none. The entire flight pattern is over water, and Summerlin's property goes right up to Long Island Sound where the helipad is located. A jitney takes the people through a road cut into the woods right to the front door."

"Maybe Bigelow came that way," I said. "He could certainly afford it."

"Want me to run those plates for you?"

"Sure, thanks. We'll be out front with Sergeant Kendrick."

Five minutes later the officer came out with the information, and after Spider and I looked it over Kendrick said, "Hit pay dirt?"

"Maybe," I said, "but your officer also told us about the helipad."

"Yeah, your guy could have come in that way."

I looked at the information on the limo and went over to a phone and dialed their number in Queens. A woman's voice said, "Kew Forest Limo. How may I help you?"

I identified myself and asked her if she would check the logs for the day in question. She said, "I can't do that, sir. Not over the phone. I really don't know who I'm speaking with."

"I understand, and I agree with you. If we come over there in person, will you show us, or do we need a subpoena?"

"If you come into the office with a proper I.D., you can see our logs," she said.

"Terrific. We'll be there tomorrow. At your main office on Queens Blvd.?"

"That's the one."

We thanked Sergeant Kendrick for his assistance and headed up to Summerlin.

* * *

The fifteen-minute drive took us through some beautifully wooded areas interspersed with huge private homes set far back from the main road. The land we were on was surrounded by water on three sides, and I guessed all those residences had a great view of the Sound, Manhattan, or both, plus a dock for a large boat. The main road made a left turn and now ran parallel to the Sound, and on our right a rustic stone fence came into view, which we followed to an opening. The opening was secured by a black steel fence and an intercom was mounted on a stone post in front of it. Spider pushed the button and when a man's voice said, "Please state your name and appointment time," he said, "Detectives Webb and Boyland, NYMPD, to see Victoria Bennet."

There was a few second hesitation before the voice said, "Do you have an appointment with Miss Bennet?"

"No."

"Please hold."

Thirty seconds later a woman's voice said, "This is Miss Bennet. How may I help you?"

"We're investigating a missing person's case," Spider said, "and we were hoping you might assist us."

"Well, I don't know if I can, but come in and park by the front door. I'll meet you there."

We drove through the open gate, and after what seemed to be a mile of perfectly- edged, winding gravel driveway, the house rose into our view. I had half expected to see a Transylvania-like castle with scary stone towers and huge oak doors, but Summerlin was not scary at all – Summerlin was majestic. Constructed of stone and granite with marble inlays, the central portion rose six stories into the gloomy sky. A wing angled out on either side, each one story lower than the main middle structure, but each at least fifty yards longer than it. Both Spider and I had involuntarily sucked in our breath as the view of the magnificent mansion hit us full on. I released my breath and said, "Wow!"

"Wow, indeed!" Spider said.

* * *

Spider and I, with the assistance of everyone else involved in the case, had meticulously planned our tactics for this interview, but we both knew those tactics could, and would change, depending on the answers as we went along. Vicki Bennet, as she introduced herself, was an attractive brunette, in her mid-thirties, dressed in conservative business attire with modest heels on her expensive looking shoes. We introduced ourselves, showing our shields and I.D.'s, which she scrutinized rather closely. She said, "Follow me to my office and I'll get coffee for us, if that's okay?"

"Thank you, that will definitely be okay," I said. "My body is craving its mid-morning caffeine fix."

We arrived in her well-appointed office and I noticed her name was on the door, but no title to go along with it. She sat behind her desk and motioned for

Spider and I to sit on the two chairs in front of her desk. She said, "You have me intrigued, Detectives. How may I assist you?"

"Is Jordan Bigelow a member here?" I asked, showing her his photo.

Without batting an eye, or twitching a muscle she said, "I am not at liberty to confirm or deny the membership status of anyone. That is confidential information."

Perfectly rehearsed, I thought. "Why would that be confidential? Isn't Summerlin a research institute for disease prevention and longevity?"

"Yes it is, and our members' medical information is strictly protected. I'm sure you know that, as a matter of law."

"Of course we do," Spider said, "but we don't want Jordan Bigelow's medical records. We want Jordan Bigelow himself."

"May I ask why?"

"He's a suspect in a murder case we're working on."

"Murder? How awful! Who did he kill?"

"More than one," I said.

Vicki looked genuinely shocked, and after a few seconds responded, "I wish I could help you, but as I said before…"

"Yeah, yeah, I know, the confidential stuff, but we already know the answer to our question. Jordan Bigelow is a long- time member here, or maybe I should say *was* a member here…"

"Then why did you ask me?" she said, sounding a bit perturbed.

I took a shot and said, "You're a lawyer, right?"

"Uh, yes…"

"And good lawyers never ask a question they don't know the answer to, especially when they have someone on the witness stand. We try to emulate good lawyers in our approach."

"Please get to the point."

"Fine, we will," Spider said. "Jordan Bigelow arrived here in a limo last Friday at 5:00 p.m. for his quarterly three-day treatment protocol, and no one has seen him since."

Taken aback at this piece of knowledge Spider had thrown out she said, "I don't know…"

"Stop!" I said, raising my hand and deliberately raising my voice. "Is this place like the *Hotel California?* You can always check in, but never check out?"

"I believe the line was you can always check out, but you can never leave, partner."

"Whatever the hell it is, Spider, Jordan Bigelow checked in, and never left here. Where the hell is he, Vicki? Or his body?"

Taking a moment to compose herself after my verbal attack she said, "I believe this interview is over. I have nothing more to say to you two. Please leave now."

"Not quite yet, Vicki," Spider said withdrawing his other I.D. case. "We are deputized as Federal Agents, and we work with the FBI with full Federal powers and authority. Do you know what that means?"

Bennet did not respond, but glared at us until I said, "It means we can bring a thousand agents in here to tear this place apart. It means we can have the IRS scrutinize every aspect of this operation. It means we can, and will, destroy the Summerlin Research Institute unless we get your cooperation."

She put her head in her hands and broke into sobs, "You are terrible people!"

"No, we are not," Spider said, "and more importantly *you* are not, Miss Bennet. We are convinced of that."

This was our move, our shot at getting somewhere on this crazy case. I said, "Miss Bennet, calm down. We believe you are a good person, and not fully aware of what is going on here."

She looked up and said, "But these are good people here, doing good things…"

"Like they did for you, right?"

"What do you mean?"

"How old are you, Vicki?"

"That's not a proper question to ask a woman."

"I'd guess thirty-five, maybe thirty-seven at the most."

"I'll take that," she said with a hint of a smile, and now apparently fully composed.

"But we all know you are fifty-six," Spider said. "Can't hide from a Google search nowadays."

"Vicki," I said, "we have encountered eleven members of Summerlin during our investigation. They all look at least twenty years younger…"

"Why is that a bad thing?'

"It's not, on its face. Do you know how much they paid for their membership here?"

"That's confidential…"

"Do you know?"

"No."

"Fifty million dollars each in the start-up phase, and now it's a hundred million."

She put her hand up to her mouth in shock.

"Vicki," Spider said, "something bad is going on here at Summerlin, and we believe you don't know what it is. We believe you were told to expect an appearance by law enforcement, and you were coached as to what to say concerning Jordan Bigelow."

"Which was to tell us absolutely nothing," I said. "And you dutifully followed your instructions, but I'm sure you wondered why they wanted you to stonewall us, didn't you?"

"I…I…"

"Listen, Vicki, we don't want to endanger you in any way, but we definitely need your help."

"I'm afraid to do that. I don't know what would happen to me."

We had her now. I pushed on. "Vicki, we don't want anything to happen to you either, but we guarantee no one will ever know."

"What do you want?"

"The membership list," Spider said, pointing to the PC on her desk. Can you print it out for us now?"

"No, I do not have access to it."

"Who does?"

"Only the Chairman, Mr. Baxter."

"And it's on the PC in his office?"

"Yes, and I'm sure it's password protected."

"I'm sure it is," I said, "and let us be honest. We strongly suspect something criminal is going on here, and a look at who the members are may help us confirm that."

"Or," Spider said, "there may be nothing nefarious going on, and we can close our investigation and go on vacation."

"Do you think printouts may exist of the sign-in and sign-out sheets?" I asked.

"I've never seen one," she said, a bit evasively

Realizing we better cut this off now I said, "Here are our business cards. Tell your chairman two cops were looking for Jordan Bigelow on a routine missing person's case, and you told us exactly what he directed you to tell us. Tell him we looked satisfied, and left right away. That shouldn't arouse his suspicions."

"And thank you for listening to us," Spider said. "I'm sorry we had to upset you, but there are a lot of dead people whose relatives are looking for answers."

"I understand."

"And if you accidentally happen to come across a copy of that membership list, drop it in the mail to me. My address is on the card."

"Sure," she said as she walked us out.

"I mean it can't be too big. A hundred names, or so?"

"How about four hundred and seventeen?"

"What?" we both said.

"I've heard that number mentioned by the board members more than once."

"But no individual names?" I asked.

"No names."

"Thank you, Miss Bennet. Until we meet again."

"I certainly hope not," she said, turning away and walking back into the building.

Chapter 26

The next day Spider and I drove into Queens and showed our I.D.'s to the receptionist at the Kew Forest Limousine Service. She said, "Glad to meet you, Detectives. I dug out the logs for that Friday. They're on the table in the kitchen. Right through that door on the left."

"Thank you, Miss...?" I said, pleased at her helpfulness.

"Call me Betty Ann. Help yourselves to coffee while you're in there. Gotta run, damn phone's ringing again."

The handwritten logs revealed driver Willy Nuzzo picked up a Justin Bernard at JFK Airport at 3:45 p.m., and dropped him off at the Summerlin Institute at 4:46 p.m.

"That's got to be Bigelow," Spider said. "Note the same initials, like the Witsec people."

When Betty Ann got off the phone I asked her about Bernard, and she said he was a regular customer, usually four or five times a year. She popped his name into her PC and gave us the dates he used the service going back a year. "You can check the log books for the details," she said, turning to pick up the phone.

There were three more trips to Summerlin going back the full year, and on the middle one, Justin Bernard had been picked up at Summerlin and driven to Manhattan, and picked up there three days later and driven to JFK. But on this last trip, the records did not indicate he was ever picked up at Summerlin for the return to JFK, or anywhere else. Spider said, "Guess Bigelow's still there, huh?"

"Yeah, partner, but I doubt he is still among the living."

"Fish food?"

"Oh, yeah. Let's verify these entries with Betty Ann to make sure we didn't miss anything."

Betty Ann confirmed there was no record of Bernard being picked up at Summerlin for his return to JFK, or any other location. "That's odd," she said. "Maybe he's still there?"

"Maybe, and thank you so much for your help."

"And for the coffee," Spider said.

"You're welcome. Gee, I hope Mr. Bernard is okay. The drivers love to get the job with him."

"Big tipper?"

"So I understand. And supposedly a nice guy, too."

* * *

Another conference call and another period of inaction. Howard Sunshine began his radiation treatments and chemo as an in-patient. He would be evaluated after four weeks. After one week, with no word from Victoria Bennet, Spider and I decided to visit Betty Kernan and tie up that loose end. We got the required subpoena and delivered it to Mrs. Aronoff at the school. She provided a printout of the information for us and, as she handed it over she said, "So what can you tell me?"

We told her how Jonathan Holmgren was not accidentally shot, but intentionally murdered by a hired hit-man who did the job to pay off his gambling debts.

"I *knew* it. I smelled something fishy with that whole thing. What was the killer's name?"

"You know that, Mrs. Aronoff. Kevin Kernan."

"Was that his real name?"

"Yes."

"I didn't see anything in the papers, or on TV, about a trial or anything."

"And you never will," Spider said. "Kevin was killed in jail after he was there only a few months."

Mrs. Aronoff put her hand to her mouth and whispered through it. "A mob hit?"

"We think so. We never found out who hired Kevin, or why," I lied. "And I guess we may never will."

"Unless Mrs. Kernan tells you when you confront her."

"We believe Betty Kernan had absolutely no knowledge of her husband's gambling problems," Spider said, "but we will go find that out. And thank you for all your assistance."

"I was happy to help, and please call me if it turns out she was involved."

"Oh, we will," I said as I picked up the printout. We hustled out of the office before we had to field any more questions from the helpful, but overly inquisitive, Mrs. Aronoff.

"Pete's not going to be too happy about us flying all the way out to California to interview Betty Kernan," Spider said when I read the location of the school was in San Diego.

"He shouldn't mind, the Feds are paying. And maybe we'll rent a car and drive over to Vegas and pay a visit to the LV Betterment Group while we're out that way."

"Good idea. We need a break. Maybe get some gambling in, maybe a girlie show or two, and some great food."

"And our wives don't have to know about our boy's night out, right?"

"Right, partner, and we shouldn't feel guilty at all."

"No, we shouldn't," I said, feeling guilty already.

* * *

Our trip out West was basically a waste of the taxpayer's money. Betty Kernan, although surprised to see us, verified our assumptions. She had been married to Kevin for two years, and basically hooked up with him because she needed a father for her two children, and he seemed like a nice guy. Her first husband was a drinker and had been killed in a one-car, one-tree accident early one morning as he drove home, totally drunk, from one of his hangouts. In marrying Kevin, she hadn't known she was trading one addiction for another. We wished her well and drove on to Las Vegas.

The LV Betterment Group no longer occupied any part of the building that once housed them. Gone was the flashy receptionist, and no one knew where they had re-located. We presumed, with the absence of their leader and consigliere, the Las Vegas Mob had re-grouped somewhere else while they decided on new leadership.

Back in New York, we let everyone know our meager results, and no one had any suggestions how to proceed with the investigation. We were temporarily at a dead end, waiting for Howard Sunshine to get well enough to get back inside the Summerlin Institute, or for Victoria Bennet to have a change of heart and provide us some pertinent information. Neither instance seemed promising, and with Jordan Bigelow presumed dead, how were we ever going to find out who ordered him to have those witnesses killed? How would we ever find, and arrest, the masterminds at Summerlin?

*　*　*

Victoria Bennet had a lot to think about after her disquieting visit from Detectives Boyland and Webb. The most obvious being she had seen Justin Bernard, who the detectives had called Jordan Bigelow from the photo, arrive on Friday afternoon, but never saw him leave, as she saw everyone arrive and leave. And she knew their names because she signed them in, and signed them out, contrary to what she told the detectives. But those names, she suspected – and in some cases knew for sure – were not their real names. Stan Jackson, for example, was in fact the majority leader of the Republican Party in the U.S. Senate. His real name was Martin Haywood, and she had seen him on TV many times. And there were other VIP's whose names she knew for certain were phonies – senators, congressmen, governors, and two U.S. Supreme Court Justices. Yes, Vicki Bennet knew a lot more than she had offered up to those two snoops.

The day after the visit, Vicki knocked on Randall Baxter's office door. "It's Vicki," she responded to Baxter's, "Yes?"

"Come right in," he said.

"You were correct, sir. Yesterday, when you were not here, two detectives came around looking for Mr. Bernard, although they referred to him as Jordan Bigelow."

An obvious look of concern crossed Baxter's face and he said, "And what did you tell them?"

"I told them nothing. I told them this is a private research institute, and the names of our members are held in the strictest confidence."

"And are you certain that satisfied their curiosity?"

"It seemed to, but I'm not sure."

"Did they say why they were interested in speaking with Mr. Bernard?"

"Yes, they said he is missing, and they are investigating his possible whereabouts."

"Well done, Miss Bennet, but if they, or any other law enforcement people come back, you are not to let them in, and you will notify me right away."

"Yes, sir, but if you're not on premises?"

"Call me on my cell phone immediately."

"Yes, sir. We do great work here and I'll be damned...er...excuse me...I'll be darned if they'll get past me without a warrant."

"I'm happy you work for us, Victoria, and I'm happy to see our treatments have benefited you so well. You look absolutely radiant today, and more so when you use profanity."

"Oh, sir, I am so sorry..."

"I'm only kidding with you. Those two deserved your condemnation. Keep up the good work."

"Thank you, sir. Will there be anything else?"

"No, Miss Bennet, that will be all."

As she left Baxter's office, she was glad she hadn't told him all the questions – and the nature of those questions –the detectives had posed. For the first time in her five-year employment at Summerlin, she had detected something strange, something out of sorts, with the jovial Chairman. Something sinister. And he never mentioned the Bernard/Bigelow discrepancy.

Although she was pleased she hadn't divulged any information to Boyland and Webb, she now wondered if she should have told them more. Victoria Bennet found herself in a difficult position – between a rock and a hard place as the old cliché went – and she didn't know what to do. So she did nothing.

* * *

A few weeks went by and Howard Sunshine's treatments had worked as hoped for and sent the cancer into remission. A better looking and mentally uplifted man left MSK Hospital with his wife for two weeks rest at home. He would call Summerlin from there and schedule his visit. Howard was as anxious as they all were for his return. He truly felt a resumption of his treatments at Summerlin would wipe out any remaining trace of cancer in his body, and Mike, Danny and Spider hoped Howard would provide them with sufficient information to obtain a warrant to search the premises and Baxter's computer.

Two days before his scheduled visit to Summerlin, Howard Sunshine was briefed by me, Spider and Mike Havlek, who had flow up from D.C., leaving his eight-month pregnant wife behind.

"First, let me ask you if any doctors or staff personnel at MSK recognized you and spoke to you?"

"No, Detective Boyland, but I think I recognized a couple of the doctors."

"Are you sure they didn't recognize you?" Mike asked.

"Well, one looked at me kind of funny, like maybe he did recognize me, but he didn't say anything."

I knew I didn't like the sound of that, and I knew Spider and Mike didn't either, but none of us said anything. I said, "Howard, it's important for you to note everything on this next visit. From the moment the taxi drops you off at the gate to the moment it picks you up when you leave."

"Like who greets you when you arrive, the names of the doctors who treat you, and the names of any staff that assist the doctors," Spider said.

"And most importantly, the names and descriptions of any other patients that are there for treatment," Mike said.

"I can give you most of that information now. The routine never changes."

"What do you mean?" I asked, wondering why he hadn't told us this before.

"I walk in and get greeted by Vicki and she writes something on a pad. Then an attendant comes to get me. His nameplate says General Staff. He takes me to the locker room to change and another general staff guy takes me to the first treatment room. The doctor in charge has a nameplate which reads Nutrition Chief, and the others who help him have Nutrition Staff on their nameplates."

"And is this the same for your other two days as well?" Mike asked.

"Yes, and they never call each other by names, as far as I can remember."

"But when you're done for the day, don't you mingle with the staff?"

"No, never. After the day's treatment, I get escorted straight to my room and eat my dinner alone. I order it sometime during the afternoon. Each room is a small suite with a small refrigerator and a microwave."

"Then what do you do?"

"Watch a little TV and go to sleep. Believe me, those infusions knock the hell out of you."

"Are you saying you've never run across any other members of the Institute?"

"Never."

You can imagine how shot down we were upon hearing this from Howard. I was a bit annoyed with him and snapped, "How the fuck come you never told us all this before?"

Nonplussed, he replied, "Because you never fucking asked me."

And Howard Sunshine was one hundred percent abso-fucking-lutely correct. Ace investigators Danny Boyland and Spider Webb had never asked him. I said, "Okay, Howard, I'm sorry for snapping at you. Maybe things will be different this time. Stay observant and try to pick up some names for us."

"Sure."

"Listen," Mike said, "we want to take you down to FBI Headquarters and have a doctor implant a microchip in you. Under your armpit hair. It doesn't hurt much."

A look of alarm came into Howard's eyes and he said, "Why?"

"Let me be frank and honest with you. Your life could be in danger if they suspect you're working with us."

"So the chip will help you locate my body if they kill me?"

"Yeah," Spider said, "and help us locate your *alive* body if they force you to stay there against your will."

"How could they possibly know I'm, uh…undercover?"

"Suppose one of those doctors at the hospital did recognize you, and passed that up the chain of command?" I said.

"I don't get this whole cloak and dagger thing. I mean, what ulterior motives are you implying here? What do you think is *really* going on at Summerlin?"

"We have no idea, which is why we need your help."

"Or maybe you're wrong. Maybe Summerlin is what it appears to be – a research institute that extends people's lives for the right price."

"What about Evan Donaldson and the dead Witsec people?" Mike asked. "What about Jonathan Holmgren a/k/a Jerry Harrison?"

"You can't say Summerlin is responsible for those deaths."

"That's why – again – we need your help, to prove or disprove our supposition. And if you want to back out and not go back there, we'll understand."

"Back out? Are you crazy? I paid millions and I'm gonna get my money's worth. They're not gonna kill me. Maybe you guys are watching too much TV."

Howard Sunshine was a much different man than the hacking, coughing, depressed one we spoke to in Allenwood. Amazing what can happen to a guy when he's told his cancer is in remission and he can resume the treatments that will allow him to live a healthy life for next hundred years.

But upon reflection, I realized that wasn't so amazing a reaction after all. Howard Sunshine had unexpectedly been given a brand new lease on life. Unfortunately, as things later developed, Howard would never make it to a 150 years old. More unfortunately, Howard wouldn't make it to his next birthday.

Chapter 27

We had the microchip implanted and Howard Sunshine went to the Summerlin Institute as planned. After his three-day stay, the taxi took him back to the Port Washington railroad station where Spider and I picked him up in our police car. Spider drove, and I interrogated him on the ride to the airport for his flight back home.

The interview was short. Nothing had changed one bit since his last visit. The only thing he noticed was Vicki Bennet looked a lot younger and a lot more attractive. "Oh, yeah," he said, "and they have made strides in their protocols. On my next visit, I have to be there only two days, and the overall bags of infusions will be reduced from nine to five. Their next goal is to do the treatments on an out-patient basis in a couple of years."

"Anything else?"

"Nothing. Everyone was friendly, and everything seemed normal. I don't think anything evil is going on there."

We dropped Howard at La Guardia and wished him well. Another promising lead gone nowhere. Maybe we had only *wished* Howard Sunshine would be a promising lead, because we didn't have many leads at all. Maybe Vicki, but she hadn't called, and as the days went by, she probably never would.

"Spider, let's call Mike as soon as we get back to the office."

"Wasn't that the plan? He does want to know what Howard Sunshine had to say, right?"

"Right, but I have an idea to bounce off him."

"Oh?"

"Yeah, Black-Ops."

Spider laughed and said, "Black-Ops? You *got* Black-Ops, partner. You got *me*."

"You're not black, you're brown. And a medium-brown to boot. I mean *real* Black-Ops, and I don't mean their skin color. I mean Navy Seals, Marine Recon guys…"

"Give me a break. I think you need a drink – or a shrink."

"Let's see what Mike has to say, wiseguy."

* * *

"Where the hell did you come up with this crazy idea?" Mike Havlek said when I broached it.

"Patrick, my son. When they came to Washington to tour the FBI facilities, he said something like, when all else fails you still got Black-Ops. And you do, right Mike? The FBI got everything. Don't bullshit us."

"If we do, which I won't admit to anyone, what would you have them do?"

"Break into Randall Baxter's office, crack his password, and copy all his files."

Pete Veltri and Father Finn, who were in the conference room with me and Spider, looked at me and rolled their eyes. Mike hadn't answered so I said, "What? What's wrong with that?"

"What's wrong? Everything. We are law enforcement, not burglars. We don't commit crimes, we solve them…"

"Well, we ain't solving this one too well, are we?" I asked, hoping my sarcasm came through loud and clear.

"The answer is no. We simply have to continue our investigation and develop sufficient information to convince a magistrate to sign a warrant for that material."

"And tell me, oh Superman, how are we to do that?"

There was silence from Mike, so I said, "Pete, Francis, any help from you two ace supervisors for your ace investigators? Please?"

"Let's all step back and think it over," Pete said. "Two days okay with everybody?"

"Sure," I said. So did the others. "Let me bounce it off Tara. And Mike, talk to Allison. Oh, how's she doing?"

"Doing fine. Three weeks to go. Talk to you all in a couple days."

The dejection in Mike's voice was apparent and matched all our moods. We shuffled out of the conference room and back to our desks. I pulled out the case file and started to review it, but I knew no answers were in there. This case needed some proactive action – or a lucky break. I recalled my time on the Joint Terrorist Task Force working with NYMPD Detective Nick Faliani. When things were at their gloomiest, and the investigation was at an apparent dead end, Nick would always say, in his classic New York voice, "What we need is a fucking lucky break!"

Right on, Nick. Right on.

* * *

Tara had nothing to offer, and when we reconvened two days later and got Mike on the phone, we were all hoping he or Allison had a flash of inspiration to guide us on a new path. We did not get that, but what we did get left us shocked and speechless. Mike said, "I just got off the phone with my boss, Assistant Director Jay Carlston. We're off the case. Our group has been disbanded."

When we found our tongues, I was the first to break the silence. I said, "I'll try to remain calm, Mike. Why?"

"Carlston said his review of the case revealed it had nowhere else to go because it was over. There's no doubt Jordan Bigelow and his mob carried out the killings, so therefore case closed."

"But what about this missing Bigelow and the *real* people behind the murders?" Pete Veltri asked.

"Pure speculation. And who cares if a mob boss is missing or dead. They knock each other off all the time. Those were Carlston's words, not mine."

"Somebody got to him," Spider said.

"Or maybe Director Kobak ordered it," Mike said.

"I get the idea you might want me to call him?" I said.

"You know him better than I do. Oh, and please send me back our Federal I.D.'s and shields."

"Your idea to do that?" Spider asked.

"No, Carlston's orders. Send them FedEx overnight, okay?"

"Sure, Mike," I said. "It's been great working with you again. But this case has been a big disappointment."

"I know. Let me know what the Director has to say – if anything."

As soon as we disconnected with Mike, I dialed Walt Kobak's office in Washington. His secretary, Wendy Mays, immediately recognized me and after a brief chat, she put me on hold. Thirty seconds later she came back on the line and said, "I'm sorry, Danny, but the Director cannot speak with you now. What's the best number to get back to you?"

I gave her the squad's number and my cell number, both of which I was certain Walt had. This was the first time in our long relationship Walt had refused to take a call from me.

Uh, oh.

* * *

Spider and I dutifully sent our Federal credentials back to Mike, and the next day when eleven a.m. rolled around and I hadn't heard from Kobak, I called his office once again. "Oh, hi Danny," Wendy said when I identified myself.

"Did you give him my message?"

"Uh, yes, right after you called yesterday."

"Is he in now?"

"Uh, yes, but he's not taking any calls."

"You mean he's not taking *my* calls, don't you?"

"Uh, yes," she whispered. "What's the matter?"

"That's what I was going to ask you. This is not like Walt Kobak to ignore an old friend."

"I'll tell him you called again," she said. "That's all I can do."

I scrolled through my phone contacts and dialed former NYMPD Police Commissioner Harry Cassidy, who was officially retired from law enforcement and living in the wilds of Wyoming, but contemplating a run for county sheriff. He was happy to hear from me, and we chatted a bit and caught each other up in our lives since we last worked together on the Romen Society caper. Then I got to the point. "Harry, I need a favor. I need you to call Walt Kobak for me."

"And you can't call him yourself because …?"

"Because he won't take my calls, but I'm sure he'll take yours. Here's my story…"

"I'll call him right away, but I think I know the reason he doesn't want to speak with you."

"Oh?"

"He doesn't want to lie to you. From what you told me, Walt ordered Carlston to have Havlek close the case. But I bet he didn't do it on his own. I bet *he* was ordered to as well."

"From the Attorney General?"

"That's his boss, isn't it?"

"And the AG's boss is the president…"

"Yes, POTUS himself. Talk to you later."

Less than an hour latter Harry got back to me and said, "I was right, Danny. Walt is as upset as you are, but he cannot talk about this case with you at all."

"I got it. Man, this thing goes up to high places, doesn't it?"

"Guess so. And Walt feels terrible about blowing you off, if that's any comfort."

"Sure, I can live with that. I'm not sitting in his seat, so I won't criticize him. He'll always be a friend."

"Hang in there, Danny. There'll be more cases down the road."

"Thanks, Harry, and thanks for calling Walt."

I passed the information on to Spider and we went in to speak with Veltri and Finn. When we finished Pete said, "So I guess that's it. Case closed, and you two are back working for me now."

"About time," Father Finn said. "Spider, you're catching cases tomorrow and you the day after, Danny Boy."

Maybe our bosses thought this case was closed, but I didn't, and I know my partner didn't. "Spider, we're not done with the Summerlin Institute, are we?" I whispered as we walked out of Veltri's office.

"No fucking way, partner. The Feds may be done, and Finn and Veltri think we're done, but I ain't letting go."

"Me neither and I got some ideas."

* * *

Because we were catching cases the next two days, we couldn't put my ideas into action, but fortunately we caught nothing major that would require extensive follow-up investigation. We only rolled on two ground ball cases – a hit-and-run where the perp gave up an hour later, and a shooting which turned out to be accidental. The next day we were free and headed out the door right after coffee. "Where are you two prima donnas going?" Father Finn asked, eyeing us suspiciously as we put our coats on.

"Tying up a few loose ends on those two cases we caught," Spider said.

"Stay away from Summerlin."

"Why would we go back there? That case is closed."

"Make sure it stays that way," he said, grabbing his coffee mug and heading back to his office.

"Tough guy to fool," Spider said. "We better be careful. Where to first?"

"Sound View Point PD. They keep those recordings of plate numbers for three months. Let's get them all and run the plates. Maybe we'll find a few more members' names."

"Real names or phonies?"

"Probably phonies, but we gotta try."

There was a different sergeant on the desk, and he was as friendly as Sergeant Kendrick had been. But when we asked for a review of the recordings, his face turned into a frown and he said, "We don't do that anymore."

"How come?"

"The Chief said he got a few complaints and a threat from the ACLU, so he pulled the plug on the project."

"How long ago?"

"Not long. About a week."

"So you still have a dozen weeks we can review, right?"

"No, the Chief pulled the DVD and took it with him into his office."

"Is he in?" I asked

"No, he's at some State Police Chief's convention up in Albany."

"Okay, Sarge, thanks anyway."

"Anything or anyone in particular you guys were looking for?"

"No, just fishing around."

As we drove away, I had an uneasy feeling about this sudden stoppage of surveillance, but it passed away. I didn't mention it to Spider, and if he had any similar suspicions, he didn't mention them to me either.

"Have any other ideas?" Spider asked.

"You mean other than confronting Vicki?"

"Yeah."

"We could take a ride into the Manhattan heliports and see if we can check out their logs for flights to Summerlin."

"Maybe we should call them first and see if we need a subpoena. The FAA is a Federal agency and may not be too cooperative to us locals."

"We could ask Mike..."

"Who is officially off the case," Spider said.

"Shit! We might as well go back to the office."

* * *

As we began to busy ourselves with paperwork, Spider looked over at me and said, "I got a super contact in the Computer Crimes Section. Maybe he can give us some advice on Baxter's PC."

"You mean like get him to do a Black-Ops caper and break into his office?"

"I don't think he would do that."

"No, but I would. We could take him with us."

"Think about what you're saying, Danny. Breaking and entering and grand larceny. Are you prepared to do twenty years back up in Wallkill?"

Spider called his friend, Detective Roland Savini, and spoke with him for a good length of time. When he hung up, he said, "Let's go out in the hall where we can talk."

"So what can your buddy do for us?"

"First, Rollie and I came on the Job together. I can tell him anything, and it stays between us."

"Okay."

"When I told him what we needed and how you proposed to get it, he burst out laughing and said, 'Tell that dumb partner of yours to join the rest of us in the 21st century.'"

"I don't get it."

"We don't have to physically break into the computer's location. He said he can hack into it on-line – right from where he is sitting."

"You're kidding!"

"No. He said when the Chinese broke into the government's computer, they didn't parachute a dozen Chinamen over in the middle of the night. They hacked into if from Beijing."

"But he still needs the password."

"That's the easy way in, but he could bull his way through the encryption levels if they are not too sophisticated."

"What does he need to get going?"

"He'd like to try the easy way and find the password. He wants all Baxter's personal information – and his family's – that we can get."

"Like birthdates, anniversary dates?"

"Yeah, and any nicknames and pets names."

"Maybe Vicki can help us. What do you say we ask her later?"

* * *

We signed off duty a little after four p.m. and headed over to Mulvaney's for an early dinner. We had called our wives before we left and told them we had to work late. There was no problem with Marla, Spider's lovely wife, but Tara, ever the suspicious detective, gave me the third degree. "You have nothing big going on there that should cause you to work overtime," she said.

I told her I was cheating on her, that I found another woman – a white woman – who promised not to bug the hell out of me with twenty questions. She burst out laughing and said, "You lying piece of white trash. You ain't cheating, you're working on that Summerlin caper, aren't you?"

"Yeah, but you don't know that."

"You be careful, Danny. I don't like anything about that case. I almost wish you *were* cheating instead of poking around that hornet's nest."

"I won't be long. An hour or two at most."

Another off-hand comment of mine that proved to be way off the mark. Tara's worried tone, the Sound View Point Chief pulling the license plate project, Kobak being ordered to drop the case – all these things should have triggered loud alarm bells in our heads – but no, we two hotshots ignored them all and plunged ahead, convinced of the holiness of our crusade.

And our bullheadedness, in so doing, almost cost us our lives.

Chapter 28

In the old days, we would have sat surreptitiously in our car outside the gates of the Summerlin Institute and followed Victoria Bennet to her home. But today, the computerized databases gave us all that information in a matter of seconds. Age, date of birth, make and model of car, plate number, home address and phone number, business address and phone number. Cell phone numbers. Spouse and children. You name it, we could find it. It was wonderful – and it was scary. Nothing was private anymore, and if we could find out all this about Vicki, some asshole I locked up could find out all this information about *me* when he got out of the slammer.

Armed with Vicki's info, Spider and I left Mulvaney's a little after five and drove to the north shore city of Glen Cove, where she resided on School Street in an upscale residential building within the city limits. We figured to arrive there about the same time she would after her ride home from Summerlin, assuming she left work around five p.m. We parked on a side street, which gave us a view of the underground garage entrance to her building, and not ten minutes later her newly-leased Volvo pulled in. We gave her another ten minutes to get settled in and rang the bell to her apartment, 6B, wondering what type of reception we would get, or if she would even let us in.

She had no doubt peered through the peephole on the door and she opened it, but it was still on the chain. She looked past us, and satisfying herself there was no one else there except Spider and me, she slipped the chain and said, "Come in."

"Thanks for seeing us without a call ahead," I said.

"I was wondering when you would come after me again. I almost called you – several times – but couldn't work up the nerve."

"What's bothering you?" Spider asked.

"A few things. Things you put in my head the first time we spoke. Things Mr. Baxter said, or didn't say, when I told him of your visit."

"Did he seem concerned?"

"Extremely, and when I mentioned Justin Bernard, and how you referred to him as Jordan Bigelow, he made no attempt to explain it."

"We think most of the members of Summerlin use aliases to avoid detection," Spider said. "At least the ones in the public eye."

"Like Martin Hayward uses Stan Jackson?"

"Martin Hayward, as the big guy in the US Senate?"

"One and the same."

"Can you remember any other VIP's that are members of Summerlin?" I asked.

"Do you have a notepad? I can give you several dozen."

"Before you do, can you give us some personal details about Randall Baxter and his family. Our computer research didn't give us much about him."

We scribbled furiously as Vicki gave us his two children's names and dates of birth and the same for his wife, Flora. She said, "I'm the one who has to remember all this for him. I even shop for their gifts occasionally."

"How long have you worked at Summerlin?" I asked, more to give my head a rest than to elicit that information.

"Almost seven years. Oh, I've been rude. How about a drink? I have beer and soda, and coffee, of course. Oh, and a bottle of white wine."

Spider and I both opted for coffee and had a chance to relax while she went to prepare it. We weren't sure why Vicki decided to open up, but we sure as hell wouldn't ask her, or stop the flow. When she returned she said, "It will be ready in a few minutes."

"Vicki, can you tell us about the other board members?" I asked as she sat down.

"Sure, there are six others beside Mr. Baxter. Three are medical doctors and two administrators. The doctors head up the main departments of nutrition, medicine and genetics, and the administrators head up personnel and finance. The sixth one shows up only once in a while for a scheduled board meeting, and I don't know his function."

We recorded their names and a brief description of each, and spent the next forty-five minutes writing down member's names and possible aliases. We took a break for more coffee and I said, "Vicki, you have a remarkable memory."

"I didn't always. I believe the treatments have helped my mental capacity, as well as my physical well-being."

After over two hours with Victoria Bennet, we wrapped it up. "Any final thoughts for us, Vicki?" Spider asked.

"I don't know if I did the right thing in telling you all this, but deep down I hope it helps your investigation, and your conclusions are positive."

"Maybe they will be," I said, "but there's that sticky little situation of the missing Jordan Bigelow known to you as Justin Bernard, isn't there?"

"Yes, that troubles me – a lot."

There's also the matter of Evan Donaldson and the many Witsec murders, I wanted to say, but held my tongue.

We thanked Vicki profusely and said we'd call her with our progress. We also advised her not to get too inquisitive at Summerlin, but to remain observant. I said to Spider as we left the building, "Not a bad night's work, eh partner?"

"Not at all. What's next?"

"Tomorrow, you call your buddy in Computer Crimes and give him all the info on Baxter, so he can maybe figure out the password."

"And if he does, and we get the membership list, then what?"

"I haven't figured that out yet. Maybe he'll find some other stuff on that PC, like their mission statement and their plans to take over the world."

"You do watch too many fantasy shows on the tube. Let's go home."

We were about fifty feet from our car when they jumped out at us – four of them, all big guys, dressed in black. Within seconds they had our guns, had our hands cuffed behind our backs, and had gags in our mouths. One guy said, "Around the corner is a nice comfy limo. Slowly now, we're going for a ride."

* * *

They settled us into the back seat and the limo took off. "Listen up," the same guy said. "I'll remove the gags, but it will be best if you don't talk, okay?'

We nodded and he said, "But I gotta blindfold you."

I interpreted this as a good sign. If they were going to whack us, why worry about a blindfold? And we had seen their faces. So they didn't want us to know where they were taking us. But maybe they would whack us there. Spider and I had crossed some invisible line in our investigation. They had stopped Mike Havlek, and now they wanted to stop us.

The limo drove at a moderate speed and I sensed we went over a bridge, maybe the Queensboro, and into the streets of Manhattan. Ten minutes later the limo stopped after moving down a short decline, leading me to guess we were in an underground parking area. We were led from the limo, still blindfolded and handcuffed, and up we went in an elevator, how many floors I couldn't guess. All this time, Spider and I had not spoken a word to each other, but now I said, "Hey partner, if we don't make it out of here, I want you to know it's been a pleasure."

"Yeah, Danny, is sure has."

That's all we said, and the guys with us in the elevator didn't stop us, or say anything themselves. We got out and they walked us down a hall, then a left turn and more walking. We heard a door open and were ushered inside. We heard the door close behind us and I felt someone unlock my cuffs. They left the cuff on my right wrist and pushed me into a chair, and I heard the other cuff click closed around the chair's arm. I assumed they did likewise to Spider. Someone took off my blindfold and I blinked from the sudden change to brightness. Spider sat beside me and both our chairs were facing a desk behind which sat a well-dressed, white-haired man resembling the description of the mysterious sixth board member of Summerlin given to us by Vicki. But for the life of me I couldn't remember his name. He puffed on a cigar and placed it in an ashtray in front of him. He was not smiling. He said, "To put it bluntly gentlemen, you two are getting to be a monumental pain in the ass."

I couldn't help but smile and I said, "You're not the first bad guy to tell me that."

"Don't jump to conclusions about who the bad guys – or the good guys – are," he said. "Agent Havlek was pulled off the case, your group was disbanded, and you two were directed by your bosses to close this case. Yet, here you are, still sticking your noses into places where they don't belong. Why can't you take a hint? Why don't you get the message?"

"Because we are detectives – good ones – Mr. Benton, and we don't give up so easily," Spider said.

The mysterious sixth director - Philip Benton!

"Yes you are. I will concede that, but you two *will* give up now."

"Or you'll kill us?"

"Yes, but only if it becomes necessary."

"You're holding all the cards. Let's hear it."

He smiled for the first time and said, "I knew there was some common-sense inside that thick Irish head of yours, Danny Boy."

This guy knew all about us, but we knew nothing about him. I said, "You know our names, and Spider figured out yours, correct?"

"Call me Phil, and leave it at that."

"And you're a member of Summerlin's board of directors," I stated. "Just what is your function there, Phil?"

He slammed his hand down hard on the desk causing his cigar to fall out of the ashtray. His was livid. "Stop being a fucking wiseguy," he shouted. "Shut the fuck up from now on and listen."

Sensing I had pushed a little bit too hard and with no cards to play I said, "Sorry, Phil. I'll pipe down. It's your show."

"Thank you, *Detective*. Now let's get down to business. Answer a question for me. The national debt is over twenty trillion dollars. What are you two doing about it?"

"Huh?" we both said.

"Nothing, because it's out of your control, and those who have control are also doing nothing. What are you going to do to seal our borders to prevent more terrorists from coming in?"

"I think we're getting your message," I said.

"What are you doing to prevent America from continuing on its path to self-destruction? What are you doing about the escalating dependence on hand-outs by over half of the American population while the filthy rich get filthier rich? What are you doing to break the lobbyists' grip on a do-nothing Congress? The answers, Detectives, are you two are doing nothing, because there is nothing you can do. But we can."

"*We*, meaning the Summerlin Institute?" Spider asked.

"The Summerlin Institute is merely a means to an end. A means to give a certain group of people extended longevity so they may accomplish their goals."

"Which are?"

"To save America. To restore our great nation to its position of leadership. To re-build our infrastructure and provide meaningful jobs so people can get off welfare and be proud to be an American once more."

"Sounds like a campaign speech," Spider said.

"That's the last thing it is. It's a vision which no politician can fulfill. Our political system is inept, broken and corrupt. Democrats and Republicans alike. They are all pompous thieves who think they are royalty."

"But you have politicians among your membership, right?" I asked.

"Did Miss Bennet tell you that tonight, among other things?"

"You know she did. You obviously have her place bugged."

"Indeed, Danny. You *are* a good detective."

"But still a pain in the ass?"

Phil ignored that comment and reached into his desk drawer. He pulled out a binder about a half-inch thick and pushed in over to us. "You want the membership list? Here it is. There are a few congressmen on it – all 535 of them can't be totally corrupt. There are military men, lawyers, and judges on it. There are businessmen, and doctors and professors, and scientists, on this list. And they all have one thing in common – a patriotic love of America – and I bet you two share that belief."

"We sure do, but I bet no ace investigators are on your list," I said. "Are you now offering us a drink from the fountain of youth?"

"I didn't have that in mind, but that could be a possibility down the road – way down the road."

"If we play along?" Spider said. "If we back off?"

"No, I don't wish it to appear I'm bribing you. I want you to back off because you believe in our cause, and because you believe in America."

"So in a nutshell," I said, "your group will have an extended lifespan to implement their vision of a future America."

"Correct, but the ominous way in which you said it implies we may have a sinister purpose."

"Yeah, like a dictatorship."

"Of course, that's not the plan, but I'll agree no one knows what the future will bring. We believe our group is America's last best hope – her *only* hope – for survival into a better future. Now, are you with us – or against us?"

"Listen, Phil," I said, "you make a good case, but I got a few problems…"

"Like a lot of dead bodies?"

"Bingo!" Spider said. "You're asking us to trust you and your group who, to our humble detective's conclusions, are nothing but a bunch of common murderers, the kind we lock up every day."

Strong words from Spider, and I hoped they wouldn't push Phil over the edge into a worse display of anger than we saw before. Phil looked us in the eyes for a few moments and said, "In the beginning we made some bad decisions and some bad choices. Choosing to align ourselves with Jordan Bigelow was the biggest mistake of all. We allowed him to convince us his way – the brutal mob way – would serve us well. It was his idea to have those Witsec people located and *accidentally* killed, just as he had Court Summerlin's children killed. It was his idea to have Evan Donaldson killed when we would have handled it differently."

"But you did kill Bigelow?"

"Yes, we did, and I assure you he was the only one. He had to be stopped. He could have brought us all down if allowed to continue. He was responsible, after all, for your investigation beginning."

"How do we know, and how will America know, this elite group being created at the Summerlin Institute to kindly restore the nation, won't turn into a cabal of despots similar to Hitler's Nazi machine? You killed Bigelow, and you expressed a decidedly cold interest in killing the two us if you have to."

"Point taken, Danny, and I can't answer that question, because I don't know the answer. Human nature is unpredictable. We have to hope for the best."

"Not too reassuring," Spider said. "Now what do you want from us?"

"To go about your lives and careers and forget about us. Drop your unsanctioned investigation. I have to tell you though, when you leave here, I'm going to take a couple of steps to ensure you do cease and desist."

"Like what?"

"We're going to have you transferred. Where do you want to go?"

"What?" I said. "You have the juice to do that?"

"We stopped the FBI investigation, didn't we? Why can't we stop the two hot shot investigators of the Nassau Homicide Squad, too?"

Phil wasn't smiling when he asked that, but I didn't believe this guy, or his group, could reach into the top levels of the NYMPD. I decided to play along. "Queens North Homicide," I said.

"Nice try, Danny Boy, but too close to Summerlin – right across the boro line. Try again."

"Brooklyn North Homicide," I responded, pretending for a moment this guy was for real.

"And you Spider? But not the same place as Danny."

I didn't believe Spider was buying any of this nonsense either, but he also went along and said, "Manhattan South Homicide."

"Do we have an agreement?"

I looked at Spider and we nodded to each other. I mean, what the hell were we supposed to do, say no and get shot in the head? Those four guys were secreted right next door ready to dismember us and dump us in the Sound alongside Jordan Bigelow. "Yeah," I said. "I guess we do."

"Wonderful." Then Phil frowned and said, "I'm afraid Howard Sunshine is not going to make it."

"Why? Are you going to kill him, too?"

"No, no, his cancer will. He insisted on getting his last treatment at Summerlin, as you know. Oh, we discovered the microchip, but that's neither here nor there. The doctors told him although his cancer was in remission, it didn't mean he was cured. And they warned him the solutions they use can sometimes act like pouring gasoline on a fire if you have any disease. But he insisted."

"How long does he have?" Spider asked.

"Two, three months at the most."

"How do you know he won't turn on Summerlin like Donaldson was going to?"

"We're going to put his wife into the program, free of charge. We'll tell him that right after he gets the bad news."

"Is that why you can't take any treatments yourself?"

"Again, very perceptive. I'm not forty years old. I'm seventy-two, and I know I look it. Diabetes and heart disease ruled me out. I take some safe preventative drugs and vitamins. Maybe I'll make it to ninety."

"Not if you keep puffing on those big cigars."

"Everything in moderation. One cigar a day. One scotch a day. Healthy diet. Regular exercise. Maybe it will keep me going."

"Will living to ninety give you enough time to see the salvation of America, assuming the elites stay true to their goal?" I asked.

"I hope so. Oh, you may want to keep this visit between us secret. Let me re-phrase that – I'm *ordering* you to keep your mouths shut, got it?"

The look in his eyes left no doubt in my mind we better play along. I said, "Yeah, Phil, I got it. Who would believe us anyway?"

He turned to Spider and stared. "I got it, too," Spider said.

"And convince your friend Allison Havlek to back off. Keep that nosy reporter out of our business, and fully into motherhood."

"No problem," I said wondering how I could ever quench her curiosity about Summerlin.

He pressed a button and the four goons magically appeared through two doorways. Phil said, "Same procedure for the ride back. Handcuffs and blindfolds."

"Maybe your guys can take the blindfolds off after we get out of Manhattan?" I asked.

Phil laughed out loud and said, "Ah, detectives to the end. Sure, I don't see why not. And you'll get your guns back when you get back to your car."

"Are you planning to do something to Vicki?"

"She's got a big mouth."

"Let me ask a favor, Phil. Leave her be. Spider and I will smooth things out with her and calm all her suspicions."

"How?"

I explained my plan, and after Spider jumped in with a couple of good suggestions I said, "What do you think?"

"Okay, I'll go along – for now. Enjoy Brooklyn, Danny Boy."

Chapter 29

It was almost eleven o'clock by the time the limo dropped us off back at our car in Glen Cove. I noticed the neon glow of a bar down the street and said, "I don't know about you partner, but I need a drink."

"Or two. Stiff ones."

"We better call the wives first."

"Good idea, what do we tell them?"

"That we finished up our work – no need for specifics – and we have to discuss it over a beer or two."

"And we certainly have to do that, don't we?"

"Oh, yeah," I said, taking out my cell phone and dialing Tara.

"Where are you, Danny Boy?"

"With Spider. We just finished up and we're going for a couple beers."

"How did you make out?"

"I'll fill you in later, or tomorrow."

"You sure you're with Spider? You sure you ain't with some white woman. You sure that good-looking Spider Webb ain't chasing some white woman, too. Put that boy on the phone."

I could see Tara smiling and chuckling as she broke my chops. "I can't, he's talking to Marla, but I gotta tell you honey, these white gals we got are nowhere near as good-looking as you and Marla. Got fewer teeth, too."

"Then why are you with them?" she asked continuing to play the game.

"Because you and Marla aren't here, and these cop groupies love to be around two ace detectives to listen to our tales of greatness. Hey, here's Spider," I said, handing him my phone.

"What are you and that low-life husband of mine doing out at this hour when you were supposed to be done in a couple of hours?"

"Working hard, Tara. You know us – only work, church and home."

"Don't give me that bullshit. You better not be eyeing no women out there, Denzel. You better not be cheating on Marla."

"Does she never stop, Danny?" Spider said, handing the phone back to me.

"Good night, Tara. Love you."

"Night, honey," she said. "Love you, too."

We were smiling now thanks to Tara. We needed to smile, and we needed a drink, and we most definitely needed to talk.

* * *

We each had two double scotches on the rocks, and an hour later, we had our story straight. For now, what had happened this night would stay strictly between the two of us, and we'd see how it played out. And we'd definitely stay away from Summerlin if we got transferred or not. Spider and I both believed, whether this group was good or evil, they had the power to whack us whenever they chose. We could deal with that, not that we wanted to be killed, but what if they were to come after our families? And we had a plan to assuage Vicki Bennet approved by Phil himself. We hoped she would buy into it, and that nothing bad would happen to her.

Even with the two doubles in me, I felt stone-cold sober as I drove us home, dropping Spider off about 12:30 a.m. I was home fifteen minutes later. Thankfully, Tara was in bed and I climbed in beside her, kissed her on the cheek, and whispered, "Good night."

I tossed and turned and finally fell asleep by four a.m., and the beeping alarm three hours later did not wake me. Tara let me sleep another twenty minutes then rousted me out of bed, none too gently. "So tell me about your investigation, the one you're not supposed be working on."

"It's over. Spider and I are now convinced there's nothing there."

"Huh? All of a sudden it's over? What changed your mind?"

If you only knew, I thought, but said, "Not now. After work. I gotta get in the shower."

The next morning Spider and I went about our routine office duties. At 11:30, I picked up the phone and called Vicki Bennet, hoping she was still employed at Summerlin, and no harm had been done to her as Phil had promised. She picked up on the third ring and I said, "Hello, Vicky, it's Danny Boyland."

"Oh, I, uh...."

I interrupted her and said, "I wanted to thank you for all your help. We were able to clear up a lot of things. And it seems you were right in the first place – there's nothing bad going on there at all."

"Oh, that's such good news," she said, the relief obvious in her voice.

"Yes," I continued, "the members are all there for purely health and longevity reasons. Detective Webb and I have closed our case and should have no reason to contact you again." I sure hoped Phil was listening, or would listen, to this conversation.

"Oh, but what about Mr. Bernard? Uh, the one you call Bigelow?"

"He's no longer a missing person. We checked the helicopter logs and that's how he left Summerlin. It was a family emergency."

"Oh, that's quite a relief."

"Well, I guess we had a happy ending, so I'll say good-bye. Stay healthy."

"Thank you, Detective. Good-bye."

I wondered if she would notice Jordan Bigelow hadn't shown up for his next visit when three months rolled around. But maybe Phil would figure something out. In fact, I'm sure he would, and I hoped no harm would ever come to her.

Spider and I went out to lunch for pizza and a coke. No alcohol this time. He said, "How did you handle Tara?"

"I put her off until tonight, but I'll essentially tell her we interviewed Vicki, followed up on the information she provided, and found no suspicious activity at all. Just like I told Vicki this morning, except I'll leave out the part about Bigelow."

"What if Tara asks about him?"

"Hey, Pete told us the case was closed, and so it is. Although Bigelow can still be considered a missing person, right?"

"Yeah, and that means the Sound View Point PD and the MP Squad have an open case, not us. Ain't no homicide here, partner. I ain't seen no dead body around these parts. Have you?"

"Nope, no dead body at all. Spider, what did you make of what happened to us last night? I mean, after we had a chance to sleep on it?"

"I don't know. Like, did it really happen? Were we kidnapped and threatened with death? Two New York detectives snatched off the street? Is this *group* for real? Are they the bad guys or the good guys? This is some strange shit we got ourselves into, Danny. Super strange."

"I had the same thoughts and questions, but I resolved them all."

"You did? How?"

"It doesn't matter. It doesn't matter if they are good or bad. You and I can't do a damn thing about it, one way or another. We have to get on with our lives."

"The same way we would do if we hadn't been involved in this case at all, right?"

"Right, we have no choice. What will be, will be."

* * *

It was three o'clock and I was tired. I got a cup of coffee and went back to my desk. Father Finn was standing there, white as a sheet. He said, "The boss wants you and Spider in his office."

Spider was within earshot and he looked at me with raised eyebrows as we both got up and followed Finn into the lieutenant's office. "Shut the door and sit down," Pete said. He was not smiling.

"What's up, Pete?" Spider asked.

"You're getting transferred. You too, Danny."

"Why? What did we do?"

"I don't know, but whatever you did it was something that bent someone's nose – some big shot's nose – the wrong way. I mean you're not getting flopped back into uniform, or sent to some routine precinct squad. You'll still be working homicides, just not here."

"Where are we going?"

"You're going to Brooklyn North and you, Spider, to Manhattan South."

I looked at Spider and we were both thinking the same thing – *Phil had the fucking juice all right.*

"When?"

"Monday morning. You got a day and half to wrap things up."

"That's awfully quick," Spider said. "They had to tell you something, Boss. Give you a reason for blowing us out of here."

"Yes and no. The boro commander called me to tell me about it, but he had no additional information. I'm good friends with the Chief of Detectives, so I called him and he said he had no idea. It came right from the top, he said."

"The PC's office?" I asked, wondering how the *group* got to Charlie Carson.

"Yes, and when he pressed the commissioner for a reason, the chief was more or less told to shut up and cut the order."

"You two mightily pissed somebody off," Father Finn said. "Any ideas?"

"Yeah," I said, "about a thousand of them. Pete, I need a favor. I need a couple weeks off. Put me on vacation starting on Monday."

"I could use a break, too," Spider said.

"You got it. I'll call both your new CO's and tell them you'll report two weeks from Monday. And tomorrow, starting at four o'clock, we're going to throw a transfer party at Mulvaney's for two of the best detectives I ever had work for me."

"I second that," Father Finn said, and damned if there wasn't a tear in the old sergeant's eyes.

* * *

Tara was furious, demanding explanations and reasons, and threatening to make waves. I poured her some wine and said, "Are you finished ranting and raving?"

"Not by a long shot," she said, picking up her glass.

"Listen to me, Tara. What's done is done, and there's no changing that. You've been on this job longer than I have, you ought to know that."

"But…"

"No buts. I'm still working homicides, and if I had to choose my transfer assignment, I would have chosen Brooklyn North. I worked patrol there and detective there. I know a lot of the area."

"But why? Who did you two piss off so much they ran to the PC, or the goddamn Mayor?"

"We don't know, and we'll never find out. So we deal with it and move on."

"It was that Summerlin caper wasn't it? They got Mike Havlek pulled off it, but you and Spider wouldn't let it go, would you? So you two got smacked down. Tell me that ain't so. *I'll* go after them now. I'll…"

"Tara!" I yelled. She stopped talking and looked at me, eyes wide open in surprise. "Tara," I said softly as I took her hands in both of mine. "Tara, forget Summerlin, and forget this case. Don't go near Summerlin. Don't poke around in the case files. Promise me."

Detective First Grade Tara Brown looked into my eyes and she knew. She knew I had things inside me which I could not, and would not, tell her. She was a smart, brave detective and a braver, smarter wife. She nodded and said, "Okay, Danny, I promise. And I love you."

"And I love you, Tara. And I always will."

* * *

Transfer and retirement parties at Mulvaney's were always fun and rowdy, but this one was different. There was gloom and doom in the air from the minute we walked in, and it only got worse as the minutes ticked by. In fact, it was the worst party I ever attended, and Spider and I were the guests of honor, at our own funeral, it seemed.

Everyone was upset over our transfers. Not only were they losing two good friends, they didn't understand why. Only that someone got to some higher-up, and got us smacked. And if it happened to us, it could happen to them, too. There were grumbles and curses, none louder than from Bernie Gallagher. After who knew how many shots of bourbon, Dr. Death reverted to his pre-Melanie form – shouting, spitting, and cursing everyone above the rank of detective, except Finn and Veltri.

He came over to me and Spider and put one huge arm over each of us. We involuntarily held our breath, our normal reaction to Bernie's potent stench, but when we had to breathe again, there was no foul odor. He had maintained his new found cleanliness, but his face was pained and blotchy. He said, "I'm gonna go down to One Police Plaza on Monday morning, and I'm gonna piss on the Chief of Detectives' desk, and then I'm gonna go shit on the PC's desk…"

"Bernie," I said, "thanks, but we don't want you to get in any trouble. You gotta be strong now. You gotta stay here. You gotta be the rock of Nassau Homicide now."

He brightened up and smiled a bit. "Yeah, I guess you're right, Danny. Maybe I'll write a book about the bastards. You could write one, too."

"Good idea," I said, gently removing his arm from my shoulder.

"I need another drink," he mumbled as he stumbled over to the bar.

"I thought he was gonna cry," Spider said.

"Yeah, first Finn, then Bernie. This is fucking depressing. I want to get Tara and get the hell out of here."

"We can't go, partner. We're the guests of honor. But I saw a couple guys ease out the door a minute ago. It won't be much longer. Everyone's as depressed as we are."

Spider was right, and the exodus soon began in earnest. Pete and Father Finn stayed with us until the bitter end, which was only 9:00 p.m., an unheard of closing time for a squad party at Mulvaney's. On the sidewalk, Spider and Marla walked to the left, and Tara and I walked to the right. "Hey, partner," I shouted over my shoulder, "See you in D.C."

"Till then," he said, and I swear the light from the bar caught a glisten of wetness on his cheeks. I turned and wiped my own cheeks, and Tara, good wife that she was, said not a word.

* * *

Tara and I had decided to visit my kids in Virginia and then spend a few days hiking the Virginia Mountains in the warm April air. We would end up in

Washington, where Spider and Marla would join us for the birth of a baby. That is, if Allison cooperated and delivered on time.

Everything went according to plan and Patrick, Kelly and my in-laws seemed to buy into my made-up conclusions about the Summerlin case. The mountain air, exercise and scenery completely rejuvenated me and Tara, and Allison gave birth to a healthy, eight-pound boy to be named Christopher, after her dead father.

Spider and I got Mike Havlek alone for a few minutes and told him of our transfers, but nothing else. He said, "So whoever got to my bosses, got to yours, too."

"Looks that way."

"Allison is furious about what they did to me. Wait until she hears this."

"Mike, don't tell her now. She'll find out sooner or later, and then we'll make up something about routine administrative changes."

"Try to prevent her from digging into Summerlin at all costs," Spider said.

"What's up? You guys are starting to scare me."

"Good," I said. "If you can't convince Allison to leave this alone, call me right away. Spider and I will fly down, and *we'll* convince her."

"What are you two holding back on me?"

"Superman," I said, "we worked through a lot of stuff together. Did we ever betray your trust? Did we ever steer you wrong?"

"No, of course not."

"Then you must trust us now," Spider said. "Do what we asked. Do not let Allison pursue this. Like you, me, and Danny, she must be off this case. No more questions."

Agent Mike Havlek stared at us a moment. "Okay, message received. I trust you two with my life."

"Thank you," I said. "Now go enjoy your new baby."

* * *

Monday morning arrived and I reported to my new assignment in Brooklyn North Homicide. The CO, Detective Lieutenant Joe Weidman, greeted me warmly and said, "Pete Veltri told me all about you. Welcome aboard. Get to know the guys and gals today. Tomorrow you're catching cases, okay?"

"Fine with me."

"Glad you don't need breaking in. We're shorthanded, and Brooklyn is a busy place. A lot of our residents like to murder a lot of our residents."

"And I'll be happy to lock them up, Boss"

The next morning, as I was half way through my first cup of coffee, the squad's second whip came out of his office and shouted, "Boyland! In here!"

I went in and he said, "Pleased to meet you. I'm Sergeant Bob Ripp. You got your first case. Ready?"

"Shoot," I said, taking out my notebook.

"Over in Fort Greene, on South Portland Avenue, we got a dead guy in the master bedroom of one of those fancy, gentrified brownstones. He's in a chair tied up with rope and tape. One bullet hole in his forehead. He's not the owner. In fact, he doesn't live there. In fact, it seems nobody knows who the fuck he is."

"Is that it, Sarge?"

"Yeah, uniform and local squad dicks are there. ME and ADA are on the way. Take McClanahan with you."

"I'm on the way," I said, getting up, my heart racing a bit.

I got in the car with McClanahan behind the wheel as he said he knew the quickest way to get there, which didn't seem quick at all in the sluggish Brooklyn traffic. I ticked off the procedures in my head – crime scene log, photos, evidence search, witnesses, identifications. My pulse quickened. "Can't you drive faster?"

"Danny, the guy is fuckin' dead. He'll wait for us."

One bullet in the head. Taped up. Doesn't live there. A mystery! A whodunit! "Drive faster anyway, Mac," I said, turning toward him.

"Whatever you want, partner. You're the squeal man."

With that he flipped on the grill and dash lights, switched on the siren and punched the accelerator to the floor, blowing a red light and pinning me back in my seat. I felt the adrenalin course through my body. A whodunit!

I couldn't wait to get there.

Chapter 30

As time went by, Spider and I held tightly on to our secret. There seemed no reason to bring anyone else into the bizarre knowledge we two shared. And Phil's fears about Allison had not materialized. When she went back to work three months after giving birth, a mysterious source contacted her and provided her with ongoing pieces of information concerning corruption and dirty tricks in the Internal Revenue Service. This led to a nine-month investigation by her newspaper, with Allison as the lead reporter, keeping her extremely busy as she eyed another journalistic prize.

The four of us went down to Washington for Christopher's first birthday and, with her story wrapped up, Allison brought up the Summerlin Institute once again. I said, "That's old news, Allison. Case closed – forever."

"Baloney, something shady was going on at Summerlin. I'm surprised you and Spider aren't still going up there and rattling a few cages."

I almost said we don't work around there anymore, but remembered we hadn't told her of our transfers. Instead I said, "Give it up, Allison, there's absolutely nothing going on up there, except medical research."

After our visit, Allison went back to work hell-bent on digging into Summerlin when, lo and behold, another super informant contacted her out of the blue promising a wealth of information about corruption in

Congress, particularly between defense contractors, members of the House and Senate, and officials from the Department of Defense. She was off and running again and Summerlin was, thankfully, relegated to a position on her back shelf.

"Some coincidence," Spider said with a wink and nod. "*Two* super informants appear out of nowhere to keep our ace investigative reporter fully occupied."

"Yeah," I said, "amazing, although we both know…"

"There are no fucking coincidences," we both said in unison.

"So Phil, or someone in his group, is behind all this?" Spider asked.

"Most assuredly. Fits right in with their plans. Makes the public more aware of the utter corruption of our political system."

"When do you think they'll make their first move?"

"I haven't a clue."

* * *

Two years after I caught that murder case – my first one in Brooklyn North – which turned out not to be a whodunit after all, but a spat between two gay lovers that had escalated to murder, Lieutenant Weidman called me into his office and said, "I thought you liked it here."

I was taken aback by his statement and said, "Sure I do, what would make you think otherwise?"

He slid over a couple sheets of paper. I put my cheaters on and saw it was a detective division transfer order. The first name on it read, "Boyland, Daniel, from Brooklyn North Homicide to Nassau Homicide." I scanned the list and turned to the second page. The last name listed was, "Webb, Virgil from Manhattan South Homicide to Nassau Homicide." Right below his name was the signature of the Chief of Detectives.

"I don't know what to say, Boss. I certainly didn't know anything about this and didn't request a transfer."

"Looks like whoever sent you here decided to send you back. Whoever it was, he's got a lot of juice. You should try to find out who he is; maybe he can do more for you down the road."

"I wouldn't know where to look," I said, as a picture of the white-haired Phil flashed through my mind.

* * *

Spider and I arrived back at our old squad the following Monday and were welcomed with smiles, cheers, and pats on the back by all. In Pete Veltri's office I said, "Thanks for getting us back, Pete."

"I had nothing to do with it. I tried about a year ago, and was told to never bring it up again."

"Guess something changed," Father Finn said. "And I'm glad it did. Ready to go back to work?"

"We sure are," Spider said.

We left the office and headed for the coffee room only to be intercepted by Bernie Gallagher, who had just arrived for work. I should have said intercepted by the *smell* of Bernie Gallagher, as his foul stench preceded him by a good ten feet. "Danny! Spider! Welcome back! Danny, I need your help. My crime novel..."

"Whoa, wait a minute. What happened to your romance novel? What about Melanie...?"

"That whining bitch is history. She..."

"Bernie," Spider said, "we gotta run out on a caper. Danny will see you later. Let's go partner."

Spider pushed me toward the door, grabbing a set of car keys on the way out, and I whispered, "Thank you, thank you."

"Where to partner," he said as we got into the car.

"You know where, partner."

"Up to East Egg, near the tip?"

"Oh, yeah."

"You sure? After all, we're back here – and still alive."

"We're not going to pry. We're going to say hello to an old friend."

"Assuming she's still employed there."

"Yeah, let's hope so."

Spider drove us past the Sound View Point Village Hall, not stopping at the police department office. Fifteen minutes later, we pulled up to the black wrought iron gate and were shocked to see a large, professional looking FOR SALE OR LEASE sign, with the phone number of a prominent real estate firm which handled only high-end properties.

"I guess Phil figured it was safe to allow us back in the area now that Summerlin has flown the coop," I said

"What do you think happened?"

"Maybe, like the late Howard Sunshine said, they got their procedures simplified so they can now do the treatments on an out-patient basis."

"So instead of this huge facility they can use small regional offices around the country to administer their miracle infusions?"

"Or maybe, Spider, their grand experiment in longevity failed. I mean, it's over two years and nothing seems to have happened. No strange murders, no attempted government takeovers."

"Yeah, maybe that's what happened," he said, but there was doubt in his voice.

We did stop at the police department office on the way out, and Sergeant Kendrick was once again behind the desk. "Hi, guys," he said. "Long time, no see."

"What happened with Summerlin, Sarge?" Spider asked. "We see it's for sale."

"Yeah, they packed up and left about a month ago."

"The whole operation?"

"Yeah, I think they went out West somewhere. A shame, isn't it? Another old Gatsby mansion down the drain. What with the property taxes, it will no doubt stay vacant until it crumbles to dust."

"Well, we'll be on our way. Take care of all those nasty barking dogs for your fine, upstanding residents."

"Sure will," he said with a big grin.

"Hey, Danny, how old are you now?" Spider asked me as we drove away.

"Forty-six. Why?"

"Just thinking, I'm forty-three."

"And…?"

"And Bradley Monaghan said to be eligible for Summerlin, you had to reach fifty years old, disease-free, and in perfect health?"

"Yeah?" I said, wondering where my partner was going with this.

"And when you asked Phil if he was offering us a drink from the fountain of youth he said, 'Maybe?'"

"Yeah...?"

"I think Phil likes us and..."

"So you want to join a gym and start jogging?"

"It wouldn't hurt."

"In case the call comes someday, and Phil offers us a swig?"

"Yeah, just in case."

"And in any event, it would be good for us healthwise, right?"

"Right. What do you say we stop at the Vitamin Shoppe in Mineola and stock up before we head back to the office?"

"Sure, Spider. Why not?"

* * *

Twenty minutes later I turned left on Jericho Turnpike and Spider said, "Isn't the Vitamin Shoppe the other way?"

"Yeah, but Mulvaney's is this way. Let's get a burger and a beer and talk this over a little more."

"Some second thoughts buzzing around your brain?"

"Yeah, a few."

Ten minutes later we were at a booth in the almost empty bar having arrived well before the crush of the lunch crowd. As we sipped our first beer Spider said, "So let's have it. What's bothering you?"

"Tara."

"Tara? Don't tell me you two are having problems?"

"No, not at all. The problem is she's almost four years older than me. She'll be fifty in a couple of months."

"So you're thinking when you reach fifty, and if the benevolent Phil decides to let you partake of the magic potion, Tara will be too old to join you?"

"Yeah, and I wouldn't do it without her. You and Marla, on the other hand, don't have that problem."

"You want to scrap our fitness plans?"

"I do, but you don't have to. I'll tell you this though, if you and me were to start gulping down handfuls of vitamins and minerals, and start pumping iron and running around the street, Tara will smell a rat instantly."

Spider nodded his head. "Yeah, and the questions will start flying. 'What are you two up to now? You two getting all toned and healthy 'cause you running around with younger women…'"

I laughed and said, "I'm not worried about that from her, I'm worried about her connecting the dots to Summerlin."

"Is she that smart?"

"Damn, Spider! You know she is."

"Yeah, but I don't know if I want to do this health thing by myself. It's easier when you have a partner."

"Hey, forget about it. We're in good shape right now."

"We are?"

"Sure, we don't smoke and we always wear our seatbelts. That's two of the seven things recommended to live a long life."

"And what are the other five, Danny?"

"I don't recall."

"Bullshit. It's about eating salads, and no alcohol, and no donuts, and so on. It sure ain't beer and burgers on that list."

"A cheeseburger is a perfect food, and so is our other favorite – pepperoni pizza."

"Give me a break."

"No, seriously, each is a perfect blend of fat, protein and carbs. And the tomato sauce is concentrated vegetables."

"And beer?"

"Pure water, and hops and grains, with a wee bit of alcohol. Even Jesus drank a little wine, you know."

Our burgers arrived and we both took a large bite and washed it down with the cold beer. "Tell me, partner, now how could anything this good be bad for you?"

Spider grunted and took another bite. When he chewed that down he said, "What now?"

"Hunh?"

"With Summerlin. What do we do now?"

I thought about it a moment as I drained my glass of beer. I said, "Nothing, I guess, because I don't think there's anything to be done. What do you think?"

"I agree. I can't think of anything either."

"So we watch, and we wait, and see if anything in the news gives us a hint of things to come."

"Sounds like a plan…uh, Danny?"

"Yeah?"

"No way is Phil ever going to offer us a drink of their longevity potion, is he?"

"No chance at all, but we can dream about it for a little while."

Chapter 31

So we watched and waited, and before we knew it, three years had flown by and the Summerlin Institute, or whatever it had become, buried itself in the back of our minds. Things changed a bit during that time – things *always* change. Sergeant Frances Finn pulled the pin and retired at the age of sixty-six, after forty-two years on the Job. Willy Edwards and his wife Edna came up for the party, and now in their mid-seventies, looked frail and a bit shaky. Now *there* were a couple of decent people who deserved a bit of Summerlin's magic potion, for sure.

My son Patrick was a sophomore at the University of Virginia, and Kelly would graduate from high school this spring. Spider's kids were in their early teens, and some gray strands were showing in his curly, dark hair. I was close to fifty myself and had my own gray hair, in more abundance than Spider's. At Father Finn's retirement party, I knew every active cop there thought about his own retirement someday – it happens all the time – and as I enjoyed a drink and mulled over my twenty-seven years on the Job, Spider said, "Ever think about pulling the pin?"

"Sure, at every one of these rackets. Same as you, I bet."

"Yeah, but I'm not in any position to do it, with the age of my kids."

"Well, I figure to do the thirty-five years to get the three-quarters pension. The kids will be all finished with school, but I'll only be fifty-seven. Maybe I'll go for forty or more, like Father Finn."

"If we continue to work here, or somewhere else, we both have a ways to go. And I still like it here."

"Me, too, but I wish we'd catch a hot one. Things have been way too slow for us a long time."

"Yeah, all the whodunits seem to happen when other guys are catching. But we sure had some doozies in our day, didn't we?"

"We sure did," I said, thinking of the Dragon Lady caper, which was before Spider's time, and also that double murder on the golf course, and the Frankie Chandler case, and of course the multiple murders associated with the Summerlin Institute.

We sipped our drinks in silence when our somewhat morose mood was interrupted by the smell of a strong dose of Old Spice cologne unsuccessfully attempting to mask several unpleasant odors underneath it, followed by a loud plop as Bernie Gallagher sat down next to us. Bernie seemed to be in a happy mood. No doubt he had not yet consumed a sufficient quantity of alcohol to start cursing out his favorite judges, politicians, news anchors, and police brass.

Bernie confided in us he had finished his crime novel awhile ago, and so far no publisher would print it. His happy mood switched drastically as he told us this, so I tried to calm him down and encouraged him to write a factual account of his big cases, something which I had suggested once before, but which he had rejected. Now, with no takers on his novel, he said he would take a shot at it. Unfortunately, I could foresee if those stories ever got published, it would open him up to a slew of libel lawsuits. But I vowed to put up with him, and promised to help his efforts as best I could. After all, he was a friend, a fellow detective, and a guy who always had my back.

* * *

About six months after Finn's party, Tara and I put on the eleven o'clock news and the lead story was the shocking, unexpected death of the Senate Majority Leader, Martin Haywood. I was about to say, *Yeah, alias Stan Jackson when he checked into Summerlin*, but I caught myself up and bit my lip realizing Tara knew nothing about that. So I said, "That's a surprise."

"Why is it a surprise? He was seventy-eight, and had a heart attack. Happens all the time."

"Yeah, but I mean, he looked so…so… healthy. Guess you never know what's going on inside your body."

Tara looked at me kind of funny, but fortunately the newscaster went on to the next story and she turned back to the TV. *What the hell happened to him, I wondered.*

Spider and I, as you can imagine, had many discussions about Haywood's death, and ten days later, when word of the death of Associate Justice of the Supreme Court Vincent Maggiore hit the morning papers, we had a lot more discussions. "Fell down the stairs?" Spider said. "I don't fucking think so."

"Why not? He was seventy-nine."

"Yeah, but we know he had the physical body of a guy thirty years younger. What the hell's going on here, Danny?"

"Beats me. Let's make sure we read at least two papers everyday. Let's see if anything else develops."

We alternately read the *New York Post* and the *Long Island Chronicle,* and not two weeks later, we spotted the wire service story in both papers. It was only three paragraphs long and buried many pages after the main stories of the day. It seems Duncan Sanford had died mysteriously under suspicious circumstances, the suspicion being created by two facts – he had been healthy and vigorous for a seventy-five year old and looked as if he were only forty-five, and a neighbor who attempted to render assistance to the stricken man had been quoted as saying, "My God, poor Duncan looked to be ninety years old. What the hell happened to him?"

"Uh, oh," I said because we knew Duncan Sanford was one of the eleven embezzlers who Spider had re-interviewed. And all involved in that investigation – Vince Genova, Mike Havlek, Tara, and – most troubling – Allison Havlek, knew all those names.

"Uh, oh, indeed," Spider said. "I'm surprised Allison hasn't called already."

"With any luck she hasn't seen the article, and may never will."

"Dream on, Danny Boy."

Not two minutes later – at the *most* – Manny Perez shouted out, "Lois Lane on line three for you, Danny."

"Told you so," Spider said grinning and pointing at the phone. "You handle the famous, intense, ace investigative reporter."

I thought fast and punched the button. "Hey, Allison, how are things going? Kids okay? Mike...?"

She cut right in and said, "Did you see the article in today's paper about Duncan Sanford's death?"

"No," I lied. "Who's Duncan Sanford?"

"Don't bullshit me, Daniel Boyland. You know damn well who he was. He was one of the eleven embezzlers in that Summerlin Institute case. How could you forget any of those names....?"

"It's been a long time, but he does sound a bit familiar. I'll have to check my case file, though. Can I get back to you?"

"Make it quick, and read the story. The important part is what he looked like when he died."

"What did he look like?"

"Go read the damn story."

"Yes, ma'am," I said. "It was nice talking with you. So nice of you to inquire about my family's well-being, and Spider's family..."

"Okay, stop. I'm sorry. You know how I get when I'm focused on a hot story. How is everyone up there?"

"Everyone is peachy, but please enlighten me —what hot story are you talking about again?"

"Are you kidding? The Summerlin case, of course! What aren't you getting?"

"What am I not getting? Allison, the Summerlin Institute case is *closed* – and has been for many years, remember?"

"Well, I'm re-opening it. Please fax me any and all information from your case file as soon as you can."

And then she hung up.

Uh, oh. Uh-fucking-oh.

"What are you going to do? Spider asked.

"Shouldn't that be what are *we* going to do, *partner?*"

"Don't get your tighty-whitey's in a snit," he said grinning at me. "What are *we* going to do was, of course, what I meant."

"Stall her as long as we can, I guess."

"That won't be for long – or easy."

"We gotta think, Spider. We gotta think."

* * *

So we thought it out, and I called Allison back from the speakerphone a couple of hours later. I said, "I'm going to fax over my case files that I had to search long and hard for on the computer."

"If they're on the computer, just email them to me."

"No can do. Not permitted by the rules and regulations of the NYMPD. I printed them out, so I can fax them to you." Now I knew what was in these official files was stuff Allison probably had, so she wouldn't be satisfied when she got them. I also knew what was coming next.

"How about your notes and reports which are *not* in your official case file?"

"What do you mean?" I asked, glancing at Spider who, arms folded across his chest, wasn't helping me with his stoic silence.

She sighed and said, "Danny, I know how you operate. You keep *everything* on your cases, and you keep it at home."

Shit!

"I'll certainly dig through my stuff tonight, and whatever I find, I'll get over to you tomorrow morning."

I hoped that would satisfy her for now, while I had a chance to think some more. Then I hit her with an idea Spider had come up with. "Allison, Mike has more on this than any of us. Have you reviewed his material?"

"I couldn't. The case is closed, and Mike can't access the files anymore."

"Why not? It was his case."

"His access is blocked, and he's wary about questioning his higher-ups."

Here was my chance. "Shouldn't that tell you something? This case has hair all over it. Prying it open could be dangerous – to you, to Mike, to all of us."

"So are you saying I should back off and leave this alone? Back off what could be the biggest story of my career?"

"Yes, most emphatically."

"Well, I won't. You disappoint me, Danny. What happened to your courage? What happened to your *balls?*"

I looked over at Spider who raised his hands in a *don't look at me* gesture, but he was grinning at me as he did it. I put my head in my hands and said, "Okay, Lois Lane, I'll get whatever I have and send it over to you. Go for it, you stubborn psycho broad."

"That's better, Danny Boy. Send it all over first thing in the morning."

"I hope you didn't mean that," Spider said after Allison hung up.

"Mean what?"

"*Go for it.* She could end up dead."

"I didn't know what else to say, and you were no fucking help either sitting here like a stone sphinx."

"How about we call Mike, and maybe the three of us can figure something out."

"Good idea. Let's do it."

* * *

After we related our conversations with Allison Mike said, "Yeah, she used that *no balls* line on me, too."

"So, there is no way to stop her from running after this story?"

"None that I can think of. Guys, I pushed hard, and I don't want to jeopardize our marriage, and our family."

"Mike," I said, "do you really think she'd walk out on you if you threatened her with an ultimatum?"

"You mean like, 'Hey honey, it's me or the story?'"

"Yeah."

"I'm afraid to do that, because I'm afraid of the possible consequences."

"Is she that bull headed?" Spider asked.

"Yeah, more like a pit bull when she gets her teeth into something. She's gonna run with this, and I'm hoping she runs into a dead end."

"Keep us in the loop, okay?" I said.

"Sure, guys. Talk to you soon."

I looked at Spider and said, "Can you guess what I'm thinking about doing now? As a last resort?"

"Yeah, going down there and giving her the scoop on our kidnapping. But that still might not stop her – might only add fuel to the fire."

"You're right. What I'll do is go through my stuff at home like I promised her, and fax her lot of unimportant stuff. That should keep her busy awhile."

"And then what?"

"I don't know. I guess we'll have to play it by ear."

* * *

We left the squad at a few minutes after five and were walking the block to our parking lot when a big dude, dressed in black, stepped out of the shadows and blocked our path. "Hi, guys," he said with a grin on his ugly face.

I immediately recognized him as one of the goons who kidnapped me and Spider five years ago. "Hi, yourself," I said. "Where are your three buddies?"

"Not needed. No strong arm stuff necessary this time. Mr. Phil wants to speak with you. He's in the limo around the corner. I'll follow you there."

We got in the back seat, the door being opened for us by the goon, who then got into the driver's seat, and we took off. "Hello guys," Phil said from his perch at the far end of the limo, right behind the driver.

We both responded warily with a, "Hello, Phil."

He scooted down the side row of leather seats until he was right next to us. The five years that had passed had not treated him well. Instead of seventy-seven, he looked eighty-seven. He said, "Have you any idea why this meeting is necessary?"

Spider glanced at me and I nodded. Spider said, "The Senate Majority Leader, the Supreme Court Justice, and the late Mr. Duncan Sanford, who appeared to be old beyond his years, when he suddenly and mysteriously died."

"I continue to enjoy, and respect, dealing with intelligent people."

"What's going on, Phil?"

"You are approaching fifty, Danny. Did you think I asked you here to give you a long drink of eternal life?"

"No, I never believed you would do that for me and Spider. We sure don't fit the profile."

"No, you don't, but I couldn't, and *wouldn't,* give it to you now. You see, it seems the elixir of life has morphed into the liquid of death."

"What?"

"Those three are not the only deaths. We managed to cover up the first seven, but eventually the deaths of high profile people, like Senator Haywood and Justice Maggiore, are difficult to put a lid on. And Duncan Sanford was an unlucky break."

"As Danny asked before," Spider said. "What's going on?"

"It seems after about twenty years the infusions lose their potency, and turn deadly, reversing their positive effects. All the deaths so far have been original members, the ones who have been on the program the longest."

"Maybe it's not nice to fool around with Mother Nature," I said.

"Or with God," Spider said.

Phil shook his head and said, "Maybe one, or both of you, is correct, but now we have a big problem."

"*We?*"

"Yes, you two as well, but I'll get to that in a minute. My problem – the *group's* problem – is desperate. We have to find out what's going on, and fast, before the next batch of people die. And they die a horrible death, like in the old vampire movies."

"You mean like when the sunlight hits them and they turn to dust?" I asked.

"Not quite as drastic, but yes. They go from their present-looking age – say forty-five – to their current age – say seventy-eight – *in a matter of days.* But then they continue to age well beyond their years, and die a few days later."

"Of old age?"

"Yes, the last disease we set out to conquer."

"Your scientists must be in a panic," Spider said.

"That's putting it mildly. Now for your part in this. We will continue to keep this covered up as best we can, but we can't afford to let anything about Summerlin leak out. You two have proven your ability to keep your mouths shut, and your inquisitive detective personas suppressed. I appreciate that, but not everyone involved in the original case has your strengths."

"Not everyone involved in this case has been kidnapped and threatened with death either." I said.

"Correct, but at that time it wasn't necessary to threaten everyone. Now I'm extremely concerned about one person from back then who could readily upset the apple cart…"

"She already called," Spider said. "And she's ramping up and ready to go. We tried to put her off, but we might as well have tried to stop a burning building with a water pistol."

"Goddamn her! Allison Havlek must be stopped!"

"Don't you have any more super informants to throw her way to keep her occupied?"

"You guys figured that out? Again, I respect your talents. Now, keeping in mind the group will stop at nothing to protect its secrecy, identity and purpose, what are you two going to do to shut her up?"

"There's only one way, Phil," I said. "Get *our* little group together and fly down to D.C. right away. Tell her not only will she be killed, but her husband and two children will be killed, and maybe all of us will be killed as well. That should make an impression on her thick skull."

"Maybe, but you're going to have to back up those words with some facts. She won't bow easily to mere threats, I'm certain."

"We'll tell her about our kidnapping and transfers, and about our meetings with Vicki – I still have my written notes from our conversation."

"That might do it. It had *better* do it, because if she puts *anything* in the paper…"

"Speaking of Vicki," Spider said, "how is the lovely Miss Bennett doing?"

"She's doing fine. Still a valuable employee at one of our main regional facilities."

"How long does she have before she goes Dracula?" I asked.

"About five years, assuming we don't find a solution."

A vision of the lovely Victoria Bennett flashed through my mind, and I shuddered at the fate that might await her. "Okay, Phil. We'll do our best to get Allison to back off."

"You better get her to back off," he said, giving us his menacing stare for the first time. Then his shoulders sagged a bit and he said, "Please, convince her."

"Phil," Spider said. "Can we assure Allison the goals of Summerlin are still benevolent? There's a better word I'm searching for..."

"Altruistic?"

"That's it."

"The group seems split right down the middle on that. Half wants to market the product to everyone – that is, before this turn of events happened – and the other half wants to keep it for themselves and rule the world for their own power and pleasure."

"Which faction do you think is winning?" I asked.

"At this moment, neither side."

"But if the problem gets solved, which side do you think will prevail?"

"Your guess is as good as mine. I think we're done here. Thanks for listening to me. Now go do what I asked."

A few minutes later the limo stopped where we had been picked up and we got out. No good byes, no handshakes, and we left a somber looking Phil for what I assumed was the last time. As we walked to our cars in the parking lot, Spider and I made some tentative plans. We would lay it all out to our wives tonight. Then I would ask Tara to call Vince Genova to get him on board and join us for a visit, ASAP, down to the Havlek's, where we would give Allison our best shot.

Chapter 32

After dinner that evening, I poured two additional glasses of wine and said, "Tara, let's go sit in the den and leave the TV off. I have something to tell you, and it's a long story."

"You're not leaving me are you?"

"Why in the world would you say that? Of course not."

"Well, you look so serious; I mean you got me scared here."

"Did you think I fell under the spell of another Dragon Lady like Niki Wells?"

"Uh...I..."

"It has nothing to do with our relationship. It has to do with the Summerlin Institute. Spider and I have been holding out on you and Marla, and everyone else involved in the investigation, for over five years. It's now time to 'fess up...'"

"Summerlin? But..."

"It would be best to take a long sip of wine, lean back and listen to the entire unbelievable story. Then I'll answer your questions, okay?"

"Okay," she said, with obvious skepticism in her eyes. "Fire away."

Twenty non-stop minutes later, I paused and took a sip of wine. Tara seemed too stunned to move, too stunned to say a word. After what seemed like five minutes she reached for her glass of wine and took a big swallow. "Unbelievable story, you said? You were certainly right about that."

"And have I sufficiently explained why Spider and I kept all this to ourselves?"

"As you said, if these guys have the nerve to kidnap two New York detectives…"

"They could kill us all."

"I get it."

"You'll go with me and Spider to D.C.?"

"Of course, and I'll go see Vince Genova tomorrow and lay it all out to him. I'm sure he'll join us, although I heard he's retiring soon."

"He is? I didn't know that. We're losing a lot of good guys who are going to be tough to replace."

"We all get old, Danny."

"Not everyone – not if the group solves its problem."

"You did get the license plate number of Phil's limo, didn't you?"

"Are me and Spider ace investigators?"

"And?"

"It was a Jersey plate stolen from a car parked in a driveway in Mahwah. Guaranteed it's no longer on the limo."

"No doubt," she said.

With all on board, I called Mike Havlek and imposed ourselves for a visit this coming Saturday, two days away. "Mike," I said, "Tara and I are doing some hiking again in the mountains and thought we'd shoot over for a quick visit to see you guys and the kids. We won't stay long."

"Hey, old friend, we have nothing major going this weekend, so visit as long as you want."

"See you then," I said, neglecting to mention Tara and I would not be coming alone. Although this was a dead serious mission, it would be good to see Mike and Allison and the kids. Christopher, now four yeas old, had been joined by a new sister, Mary Ellen, who was now almost two. The kids were our ace-in-the-hole to convince Allison to leave this story alone. We all hoped her motherly instincts would triumph over her lust for another big prize.

* * *

When Allison opened the door to their new home in suburban Virginia and saw the five of us standing there she said, "All of you? This is not an ordinary visit, is it?"

"Far from it," Vince Genova said.

"And it's got to do with Summerlin, doesn't it?"

"Yes," Tara said as Mike joined his wife at the front door.

"Honey, aren't you going to ask them in?"

"I'm not sure. What's going on?"

"Let's say hello to the kids first, and then we all have to talk," Spider said.

"Sure," Mike said. "Come on in, and I'll make us a drink. The kids are playing in the backyard."

If Mike was worried, he sure wasn't showing it. Realizing, in the heat of the situation, we forgot to bring a gift for Christopher and Mary Ellen, Marla nudged Spider and me and whispered, "Get your wallets out and give them something."

Vince followed suit and we gave them $20 each for their piggybanks. Mike and Allison brought our drinks out back and we sat around the patio table. After a while the kids left us and went over to the play gym on the other side of the yard. Getting right to the point Allison said, "Okay, let's hear it."

Spider did the speech this time, the same speech I had given to Tara a few days before. When he had finished, Mike and Allison looked at each other for a couple of minutes. Mike spoke first, "So, in essence, if Allison doesn't back off, we're all in serious jeopardy of our lives."

"Correct," I said, and though I wasn't sure the group would kill the children as well, I lied and said, "Phil told us they'd kill the kids first, and if that didn't work, Mike would be next…"

"Why not just kill me?" Allison asked.

"Because they are sadistic, power hungry bastards who want to rule the world and will stop at nothing to achieve that goal," Spider said, exactly as we had rehearsed.

"Here's what I suggest, Allison – what we all suggest. Keep following the story as things progress, and maintain a file on all events possibly related to Summerlin, but do not do any proactive investigation at all. By the way, I also brought *all* my notes and case files for you, all the stuff I previously withheld. And when the Summerlin group blows up, and they all die of old age, you can be first with the scoop. You should be safe if they are all kaput."

"And what if they don't all go *kaput*? What if they solve their problem, regroup, and move to conquer the world?"

"I think, my dear, we will cross that bridge when we come to it," Mike said.

"I can't believe my Superman is giving up so easily. And you two so-called ace investigators are crawling away like cowardly snakes. Disgusting."

I figured this was Allison's last parting shot in the face of obvious defeat. I said, "Superman has been shut down by people way over his pay grade. Walt Kobak has been shut down. Commissioner Charlie Carson has been shut down. This is way over all our heads. When are you going to face the goddamn facts and come to the same conclusion we all have?"

A tear rolled down her cheek, "I feel so goddamn helpless…I…"

She broke down and Mike rushed to console her. We all felt terrible, but we had achieved our objective. Allison would live to write more great stories – just not this one. At least for now.

At least until the group crashed and burned, and turned to piles of dust.

Or rejuvenated their magic potion.

* * *

So Vince Genova retired and we all went to his party. None of us, by some shared subliminal message, said a word about Summerlin, and we didn't have to force ourselves to have a good time. With all our attention focused on shutting down Allison, I must admit it was as difficult for Spider and me to shut ourselves down from pursuing this case. After all, we were hunters, and were frustrated we had to give up the chase while the quarry, though not yet in our sights, was still out there – somewhere.

So we did the only thing we could – we plunged right back into our case work and put the group, and Phil, and Summerlin – or at least tried to – on the far back burner of our minds, under a tiny flame.

And we watched the TV news. And diligently read the papers. And we waited.

* * *

We did not have to wait long. Six more unusual deaths were reported in various local newspapers scattered throughout the country, and we knew this because Allison let us know by faxing the news clipping over to the squad as soon as she found it on her computer, which had been programmed to screen for such stories. The faxes came without comment, but we figured she must be going crazy that she couldn't blast the whole thing wide open.

Two weeks later, when a young, enterprising journalist from the Midwest apparently connected these six deaths with the three previous others, his Kansas City newspaper boomed out the headline, NINE DEATHS ATTRIBUTED TO MYSTERIOUS RAPID AGING across its front page. The story inside, with Harold T. Smith's byline, was speculative at best and weak on details, but Allison reacted immediately – and explosively – calling us that afternoon, right after she faxed us the story. Without as much as a hello she said, "You two…two…*cowards* allowed me to be scooped by some Midwest yokel…"

I cut her off before her language and castigation of me and Spider got any worse saying, "Good to hear from you, Allison. And Spider and I are happy to note you are still alive and kicking."

"Screw you, Danny Boy. The biggest story of my life and this…this… hick…"

"I believe his name is Harold Smith," Spider said.

"Well, whoever the hell he is he figured it out, and I'm left out of the picture. I hope you two are happy that you ruined…"

"Allison! He's figured nothing out," I said. "Calm down, and go have a drink or two. Let it play out."

"Easy for you to say as this Smith guy gets my story – and my Pulitzer."

"Or gets himself dead," Spider said quietly.

"Come on Allison," I said. "I'm sure you've already had this discussion with Mike, and he feels the same as us."

"You mean my super hero? Superman, Batman, Robin – what a joke!"

"How are the kids?" I asked, hoping to inject a dose of reality into her rage.

"Don't start that crap with me. No one is in any danger. It's all bullshit."

"You are wrong about that, you pig-headed fool. Now shut up, and stay the hell shut up."

With that I disconnected the speakerphone, looked at Spider and said, "You think she'll back off, at least for a little while?"

"I hope so, but I wouldn't bet any money on it."

"Poor Mike, he must be getting ragged on unmercifully. I hope he can calm her down and make her listen to reason. "

"Wouldn't bet any money on that, either."

* * *

The follow-up story by Harold T. Smith in the next day's edition of the *Midwestern Examiner* had little additional hard news, but he promised to reveal incredible, factual material over the next few days concerning a failed experiment by a group of elite people in their search to achieve immortality.

Harold's promised revelations never made it into print. That evening, the thirty-three year old reporter crashed his car into an abutment on the interstate at a high speed killing him instantly. His blood-alcohol level of 0.24% was three times over the legal limit, which was unusual, as Harold was never known to consume more than two beers at one sitting. Spider said, "Looks like Phil, or the group, found themselves another Richard Mangan to stage one more *accidental* death."

Allison had not called after the news of Smith's death broke over the wires, and we chose not to call her. We figured it would not be wise to give her an "I told you so."

She was smart enough to figure it out without our pompous comments. With Harold's passing, no more stories appeared in the *Midwestern Examiner* – he obviously had not passed his information or notes on to his editor before his untimely demise – or anywhere else for that matter. The story faded away, replaced by the next ones of mayhem, murder, drug deals and political corruption.

As the weeks and months slipped by, Spider and I rarely spoke of the Summerlin case. But one day in the coffee room, with no one else around I said, "You think the group solved its problem?"

"What in the world are you talking about, partner?"

I knew he was tweaking me, giving me his innocent Denzel grin when he said that. "You fucking know well what I'm talking about, *partner*."

"Yeah, I think they did, all right. No more Dracula deaths for a long time now. Yeah, they solved it."

"So what do you think will happen now? Which side of the group will win their internal battle – the good guys or the bad guys?"

"I don't know, and maybe I don't care. It's all beyond our control. Know what I mean?"

"Yeah, and who the hell wants to live to be 150 years old? Not me."

Our musings on the future of mankind were abruptly interrupted by the loud voice of Father Finn's replacement, Sergeant Bob Ripp, formerly of Brooklyn North Homicide, and now our squad's second-in-command. He strode his six-foot, three-inch lanky frame into the coffee room and said, "We got a hot one! Get ready to roll." His blue eyes sparkled, and he grinned knowing this was what we wanted to hear.

I could feel Spider's adrenaline shoot up, and I could see it in his eyes and his taut muscles. And I felt, and I knew, I looked the same way as we awaited Ripp's next words. "Up in Sound View Point. Rich old lady. Dead. The gardener. Dead. The delivery man from the florist. Dead. The German shepherd. Dead. No suspects, no nothing. Get going, my two ace investigators."

We jumped up and I grabbed the keys to the squeal car. Spider said, "Sounds a bit more than the usual barking dog complaint up in the kingdom of gold, huh partner?"

"Oh yeah, this sounds like we got ourselves a real mystery, for sure. Step on it."

"Or maybe it was merely a barking dog after all," Spider said glancing at me as he gunned the sedan out of the lot, tires squealing.

"What the hell are you talking about?"

"The delivery man from the florist pulls up and the shepherd barks his head off at him. He shoots the dog. The gardener grabs the gun and shoots the delivery man. The rich old lady runs out and thinks the gardener shot her beloved dog. She grabs the gun and shoots the gardener. Makes sense, right?"

"And who shoots the rich old lady, Sherlock?"

He gave me the Denzel grin and said, "Nobody. She shot *herself*. Suicide, after she realized what she had done. She had no reason to keep on living without her beloved dog. Case closed, Danny Boy. I might as well slow down."

"Slow down, my ass. You must be smoking a lotta weed. And you tell *me* I read too many crime books and watch too much TV?"

"We'll know soon. About ten minutes away."

Life, death, immortality, infusions, the Methuselah gene, Phil, the group, the Summerlin Institute. Right now, I didn't care about any of it. Right now, I was on my way to a major whodunit with my partner and best friend, Spider Webb.

And right now, that was all that mattered.

ACKNOWLEDGMENTS

Once again many thanks to all my readers, especially those of you who kindly took the time and effort to post a positive review of my previous works on Amazon or Goodreads. Reviews are important to assist potential readers to evaluate my books and encourage them to hit the "buy now" button, and yours have helped them to do so.

This manuscript was typed on the computer by two industrious people – my wife, Lorraine, and my neighbor, Anne Cram, who both deserve high praise for correctly interpreting my longhand scribbles. Since I edit the work once more, any errors you may find are not theirs – they are all mine. And Lorraine, as always, provided much needed input on the story itself, especially to prevent me from meandering into irrelevant areas.

If you enjoyed *Forever Young* a visit to my website, www.henryhack.com, will acquaint you with the three Danny Boyland novels that preceded it, as well as my other books. I hope you enjoy them all.

AUTHOR'S NOTE

Novels featuring Harry Cassidy and Danny Boyland are set a few years in the future primarily in and around the City of New York. The New York Metropolitan Police Department (NYMPD) was formed by the NYPD's take-over of police services for the City of Yonkers and the County of Nassau, and all precincts were re-numbered with #91 - #99 assigned to Patrol Boro Nassau.

CPSIA information can be obtained
at www.ICGtesting.com
Printed in the USA
BVOW06s1150310817
493658BV00005B/19/P

9 781548 652746